Ryan took the opening to learn more about her. "So, no traveling? Didn't do a year after college backpacking across Europe?"

"That sounds terrible, and no." Mia grimaced. "I've always been happy here in Charlotte. No reason to roam."

"I don't think I can imagine a life without traveling. I've done it since I was a teen," Ryan commented.

He watched her mouth firm into a thin line. It gave her a stern look. "To each his own." Mia's atttitude must have shifted. Now she smiled.

Ryan drank in the beauty, wondering what happened in her life to turn her off the adventure of traveling. It wasn't something he could ask her right after checking in as a guest in her home. But oh, how he wanted to.

Dear Reader,

The story of *A Home for the Doctor* featuring Ballad Inn is built around the first house I fell in love with in Charlotte. In 2005, I moved here to marry my husband, who had just returned from deployment. One evening after dinner with the sunset behind it, we saw this beautiful yellow house graced with honeysuckle and bathed in color as the sun fell behind the horizon. From there, the inn lived in my head and in pictures on my cell, waiting for characters to take up residence.

I'm happy to say the Ballad sisters made that house a home and now it will be filled with love from each of their stories. It starts with Mia and Ryan's journey to a love that will last a lifetime and a cornucopia of interesting characters that makes the Sardis neighborhood what it is. I hope you enjoy our little slice of heaven in Charlotte, where the honeysuckle grows wild and family is everything.

Hugs and cheesecake!

Kellie

HEARTWARMING

A Home for the Doctor

Kellie A. King

HARLEQUIN®
HEARTWARMING™

ISBN-13: 978-1-335-47567-1

A Home for the Doctor

Copyright © 2024 by Kelly Ann Pearson

Recycling programs for this product may not exist in your area.

For questions and comments about the quality of this book, please contact us at CustomerService@Harlequin.com.

Harlequin Enterprises ULC
22 Adelaide St. West, 41st Floor
Toronto, Ontario M5H 4E3, Canada
www.Harlequin.com

Printed in U.S.A.

Kellie A. King is the *USA TODAY* bestselling author with a hint of Caribbean spice. Born and raised in Barbados, she now lives in Charlotte, NC, with her large family. Kellie is married to her longtime love—her "Sarge" is always with her for every adventure. As an author of color, Kellie features strong heroines with a proud cultural heritage. Writing is her passion, and she hopes to inspire your imagination within the pages of her books.

Books by Kellie A. King

A Home for the Doctor

is Kellie A. King's debut title for Harlequin Heartwarming.

Look out for more books from Kellie A. King coming soon.

Visit the Author Profile page at Harlequin.com.

To Ione King and Rachel Pearson.

Two women I love dearly for
very different reasons.

PROLOGUE

THEY COULDN'T EVEN wait until morning to leave. That thought filtered through Mia Ballad as she watched her parents move their luggage from the upstairs of the house to the front door. Brian and Rosie Ballad talked to each other and laughed, and all the while she stood there rubbing the soles of her Converse against the hardwood floor. They didn't even notice her until they were pulling on their coats. Enid stood waiting to hand Mia's mother her purse. It was then her mother looked over to see her standing close to the banister and approached with a smile.

"Mia, shouldn't you be in bed?" she asked gently.

"I'm fourteen. My bedtime is eleven now. You'd know that if you stayed home more," Mia answered sullenly. "You're leaving without even telling Margo or Micki good-bye."

Her father came over. "You'll do that for us, won't you, because you're our big girl."

"Maybe I don't wanna be your big girl," Mia muttered, and her lips trembled. She pressed the heels of her palms against her eyes, which prickled hot with tears. "Why can't you just stay home this time, please."

Her parents glanced at each other. "Sweetheart, we travel so our girls will know there is a whole wide world out there for them to explore. We'll be back in eight weeks, with gifts for Micki's birthday and great notebooks for you...even new pens."

"I don't want any of it." Mia swiped at more hot tears. "And when I grow up, I'm never leaving where I live and the people I love, not like the two of you."

She rushed past them up the stairs and into her room. From the door she could hear her parents talking.

"She's old enough, maybe we should tell her." Her mother's voice was low but filled with worry.

"A child shouldn't be burdened with that," Enid said pointedly. "She'll be fine, and the girls will be okay. You go do what needs to be done."

"Mia…"

A tiny hand tugged on the leg of her blue pajama pants, and she looked down to see her little sister Michelle, or Micki as they called her. Their bedrooms were all on the third floor, with a door between each room so the sisters could either leave them open or close them for privacy. Micki's was in the middle, cocooned by her older sisters on each side.

"Hey, Cricket, you should be asleep." Mia lifted her five-year-old sister in her arms.

Margo arrived, rubbing her eyes. "They left again, didn't they?"

Mia nodded while Micki laid her head on her shoulder. "They just left."

"What about my birthday?" Micki asked.

"It will be the best birthday ever, I promise. Mom and Dad said they'd be back in time," Mia reported. "I hear you may have gotten the exact thing you wanted as a present."

"Really?" Micki smiled up at her.

"You betcha." Mia would tell Enid the next day that Micki wanted a skateboard, and they would make sure she was careful using it.

"Can we stay with you tonight?" Margo asked.

"Yeah, come on."

Mia sighed, knowing the routine when their parents left on each trip. Luckily her bed could hold all three of them easily, and she put Micki in the middle as usual while nine-year-old Margo climbed under the covers on the other side. Mia turned on the twinkle lights strung along the ceiling of her bedroom, and both girls giggled.

"Now, go to sleep, you two," Mia ordered with a smile.

The three sisters snuggled close, and Mia vowed again to never leave the people she loved. Fourteen or not, she knew how it felt when people walked out the door and how much it hurt. She wouldn't do that to anyone. She was quite happy living in her slice of the world.

CHAPTER ONE

Twenty Years Later

THE SOUND OF hammering came through the open window on what could only be called a perfect spring day in Charlotte. The Carolina blue skies were vivid when Mia looked outside before heading downstairs with a smile on her face. She loved her neighborhood of Sardis Woods. They usually kept the windows and doors open so the scent of the honeysuckle that grew everywhere swept into the house. This was one of the main reasons they had turned the family house into the Ballad Inn. The size of the house was perfect for a bed-and-breakfast and how she chose to live her life. The comfort of the Ballad home always made her feel better when she stepped through the door.

The house also smelled like fresh sweet rolls and hot coffee courtesy of her sister

Margo. She ran the kitchen and prepared the meals for the bed-and-breakfast outside her regular job. The hammering and the low sound of an electric saw would be Micki, who had turned her tomboyish nature into being their handyman. Mia shined in the office, where she tracked the accounts, reservations, income and expenditures for the business. Having a solid foundation meant a secure business plan.

After her morning to-do list was done, Mia planned to head out to inspect the landscaper's progress. He'd started the process of updating the garden around the gazebo and adding the koi-pond waterfall feature they'd agreed upon. The barn out back was going to be a second part of their business, a wedding venue. The quaint country-wedding look within the grounds would only serve to enhance the property—and their profit. The Ballad Inn was beautiful all year round.

Mia saved her spreadsheet and left the office. Margo came out of the kitchen holding a small bowl and a spoon.

"Here, taste this," her sister demanded.

Margo was at least three inches shorter than Mia and had a headful of long braids.

They all had the same light brown skin and full, thick curls of black hair. Mia kept hers in a shoulder-length cut, Margo liked her braids, and Micki had a short, flirty cut that suited her round face.

Mia sniffed suspiciously. "What is it?"

"My new roasted sweet corn salsa to go with my fresh pita bread chips," Margo replied. "Enid thinks it's too spicy because I added an extra half jalapeño to the food processor."

"You know Enid dislikes any type of heat to her recipes." Mia took the mouthful and chewed. "It's super delicious."

"As per Enid, flavor comes from good spices, not heat." Margo smiled and winked.

"It's the Caribbean way." They both repeated the words of the housekeeper who was more like a mother to them than anything else.

Sometimes the only mother. The thought flashed through her mind, and she quickly pushed it aside.

"Well, I like it." Mia smiled. "I have to head outside to see how Hunter is faring. I don't want him ripping up any of our honeysuckle or the azalea bushes."

"I'm telling Enid you said it's perfect," Margo called to her retreating form.

"Great, because then she won't give me her side-eye looks all night over dinner," Mia answered with a laugh. Enid tended to use these passive-aggressive looks instead of words to let her unhappiness be known.

Outside, the large truck blocked the view of the gazebo. Mia knew that Hunter would be at the side of the house with his two-person crew. That was why she had hired him. His small company, Hunter's Land, was known for its excellent service and unique work. It also helped that she knew Hunter and his wife from high school.

"Mia! Mia Ballad!"

Her name being called made her grit her teeth, and she forced herself to smile. Their neighbor Mr. Webber had poked his head over the top of the white fence that separated their properties.

"Good morning, Mr. Webber. How are you today?" Mia inquired politely.

"Fine, fine." He waved his hand impatiently. "Have you seen Doodle?"

He was referencing his orange tomcat that always seemed to be on their property—

mostly because the animal had some kind of vendetta against Margo's bearded dragon, Monty. The cat often found a way to get out of his owner's clutches and into the inn. It was like one of the Saturday morning cartoons she and her sisters had watched growing up, with all the high jinks that ensued. Except that if Doodle ever caught Monty, Margo would be devastated.

"I have not seen your cat," Mia replied.

"Why is he always in your yard? I swear that lizard your sister has either teases or coerces him into your house," Mr. Webber grumbled.

"Coerces?" Mia said skeptically.

"Yes!" Mr. Webber said. "I think he prances at the windows, and Doodle can't stand it. Have you seen him walking back and forth on the branches?"

"He's a lizard, so that's what he's supposed to do," she pointed out.

"If you keep the blinds closed—" he began.

Mia interrupted. "He needs sunlight and warmth, for one, and we are not going to pull every shade in our home because your cat has boundary issues. How does he get out of your house, anyway? Doodle is an inside cat."

Mr. Webber began to stammer, and his face turned red. "Well, now, he is a cat after all, and I can't follow him every minute of the day."

She sighed. "If I see Doodle, I will deposit him back over the fence so you can give him a stern talking-to."

"Thank you very much," Mr. Webber said. "You are a sweet lady. You'll find someone special. I don't see why everyone calls you a spinster."

"Wait, what? Who calls me that?" Mia hollered to the man, but he was already bustling toward his back door. "I'm not a spinster. I just have higher standards," she muttered to herself as she turned away and went back to the original task of finding Hunter.

He always kept the beautiful honeysuckle that grew around the property magnificent, manicured even, since it could take off like a weed. She found him and his crew moving the bushes. They took care to protect the roots and a hefty amount of soil from around the edges to shift part of it closer to the barn. The rock feature and koi pond would be going in by the small bridge over the creek that ran through the acreage.

They would add large stones, and the bushes would be replaced. When it was time to fix the gazebo, she hoped there was a way to save the honeysuckle plants. If push came to shove, they could replant from the many vines that ran up the trellises on the side of the house. Mia was so deep in her musing, she didn't even see Hunter walk up to her.

"Hey there, Mia," he said with an easy smile.

She startled with a laugh. "Was I in my own head again?"

"Typical Mia Ballad move." Hunter grinned and pulled his dreadlocks back. "Come to check up on me and my team?"

"I know you all are amazing at what you do, but yeah." Mia returned the smile. "You know me and my schedule."

"Only girl in high school who had a daily planner and personal digital assistant." Hunter chuckled. "The bushes will be safe and sound for forty-eight hours until we get the water feature finished. We brought planters so they'll be nice and hydrated and not stressed."

"That's why you're my favorite, Hunter. You talk about plants like they're at a spa," she said. "By the way, how did your wife's spa weekend go?"

"She came home talking about some heated bed they used to give her a prenatal massage. It was memory foam and cocooned her. Now she wants one for the house." He rolled his eyes.

"That sounds lovely, and I'm not even about to give birth." Mia looked at her watch. "Okay, I have to get back to work. As per Enid, if she sees any of you eating fast food for lunch, she will come out here and ask if your taste buds have addled. I suggest eating what's provided in the kitchen."

Hunter nodded. "And this is why I love having you as a client. I eat, they eat, Audrey gets treats. It's a win-win all around."

Mia laughed. "I'm glad you enjoy your work so much."

She couldn't help but wonder if she would ever be the one who had a husband, let alone a child. She was thirty-four, and apparently the neighborhood thought she was a spinster. To be fair, compared to her sisters, she always had acted like the adult. Mia couldn't even recall if she'd had a favorite doll. Her favorite books had been read at night when her sisters were in bed and the house was quiet, and that was after homework. Was being practical the thing that kept love from her life?

By the time she opened her computer again to work on the financial accounts for her clients, there was a frown on her face. Being a certified accountant blended well with her running the bed-and-breakfast. It may not have been the most amazing or exciting job combo, but it suited her just fine.

A knock came on the frame of the open door. "Hey, sister unit."

Micki stood there in a Carolina Panthers jersey, a pair of scruffy jeans and her well-worn boots. A blue bandanna tied her curls back, and there was a soft sheen of sweat on her face.

"Michelle," Mia drawled, using her sister's actual name.

Micki narrowed her gaze. "I am carrying a hammer."

She folded her hands on her desk. "What can I do for you, Cricket?"

"Don't use that one, either. The gazebo, I

wanna rebuild it," Micki said bluntly. "Since we're redoing the barn for weddings, I could expand it and make it big enough for a large wedding party."

"Shouldn't we get through the barn build first?" Mia asked.

"We should," Micki said slowly, "but I have these plans I've been working on. I can show you."

"Okay, show me," Mia said just as Margo passed by the office door. "Hey, Marg, Doodle is on the hunt again. Beware of the orange fur of doom."

"That fur ball." Margo stopped. "I leave for my shift at the rest home at four. Can y'all make sure he doesn't hurt Monty?"

"Sure thing." Micki unrolled the plans.

"What are y'all looking at?" Margo asked, stepping inside the office.

"Micki wants to extend the gazebo," Mia answered. "Come see her designs."

"Now, see, I can make the roof more gabled, and we can go with a stained wooden floor. I want to match the wood lattice to the stain color," Micki explained. "I'm thinking the soft caramel shade we are using for the barn is good for the trim."

"This is really amazing, Micki. Why don't you go back to school and finish up your degree?" Mia said. "I mean, look at this. It rivals any of the architects uptown, and you did all the plans yourself for the barn."

Micki looked uncomfortable. "I did this for our home, Mia. It doesn't mean I want to do it for the rest of my life."

"Micki, you're twenty-five…" Mia tried to cajole her sister.

"And I like myself and my life the way it is," Micki answered firmly. "I'm not you guys. Let me be me."

"Mia just doesn't want you wandering the earth like the parents," Margo said dryly.

Mia wasn't sure where they were currently, either on a cruise or in Casablanca. She and her sisters usually didn't know their location unless there was a card from some random place.

"Mom and Dad's life isn't so bad. They've seen the world," Micki retorted. "How many people could really say their lives were filled with culture and experiences?"

"Eh, and some people just like being in one place," Mia murmured.

"So do we have the budget for the gazebo, or do we need to have some wedding bookings under our belt first?" Micki asked, deftly changing the subject.

"I think this is worth the extra cost," Mia answered. "We could have the full cost recouped with what we earn from at least three bookings. It doesn't have to be just weddings, but photo shoots, who knows? They're filming more in Charlotte. Let's go for it."

"Yeah!" Micki did a little hip shimmy. "I'll get a rough estimate of expenses for you. I know how much you like to add numbers to your spreadsheets."

Mia rolled her eyes. "Ha ha, very funny."

"But is she lying?" Margo teased. "I have to get ready for work. We have chicken for dinner in the kitchen. You two make sure to eat together, no hiding away because I'm not around. Family dinner."

Micki saluted. "Ma'am, yes, ma'am."

"I will be dutifully at the table," Mia promised. "Have a great evening at work."

"Don't work too hard, sisters of mine." Margo blew them a kiss as she left the office.

Micki left soon after with her gazebo designs rolled under her arm. There would be two new guests coming in and another late booking, so Mia got the guest book ready and made sure the fresh biscotti were out in the sitting room along with the hot coffee and tea carafes. That was until, out of the corner of her eye, she saw an orange streak go by—and then heard a loud shriek from upstairs.

"Doodle, you little fink, leave Monty alone!" Margo yelled.

And so the game begins. He's infiltrated the house again, Mia thought, rushing out of the room in time to see Margo chasing the huge orange cat down the stairs, Enid arriving from the kitchen with a broom and Micki on the other side of the stairs coming from the mudroom. Doodle was cornered, and the only place to go was the front door that stood wide open. Mia knew this was her chance to catch the cat and deposit him back in his own yard. Doodle glanced at her like he knew, and they both moved toward the door in a dead run. She was able to just touch his fur before he slipped out in triumph and she tripped. Mia couldn't stop the forward momentum.

"Ballad girl going down!" Mia cried out to her sisters and heard them racing toward her.

"Oh shoot! Take Monty, Enid," Margo called.

"I'm not touching that thing," Enid said firmly. "Give it to Micki."

While they argued, the floor of their wraparound patio came up to greet her… until two strong arms caught hold of her and kept her from hitting the hard wooden surface. Mia stared up as startling blue eyes looked at her in amusement. The man who had saved her took two steps to the side, moving them out of the way of the rest of her family, who barreled into each other as they and Enid skidded to a stop.

"Ballad girl safe," he murmured.

"Nice to meet you," Micki said, passing by them. "I'm going to get the orange menace."

"I didn't even tell her my name," he commented with a smile, still focused on Mia. "Hello there."

Mia straightened her blouse and skirt. "I am so very sorry. It's not usually like this. We are always in a battle to keep that cat out of our house and away from our lizard."

"You have a lizard?" he asked.

Margo held up Monty like a winner's trophy. "He's family."

"To you, maybe." Enid wrinkled her nose on a face you could barely tell was over sixty.

"I got him!" Micki came around holding the offending cat. "I will personally deliver our nemesis Doodle to Mr. Webber and figure out how this cat is getting out of his house."

"Thanks, Micki." Mia smoothed her hands over her skirt, very self-conscious about her clothes all of a sudden. "And you are our last-minute booking, correct?"

"Yes." He held out his hand to her. "Dr. Ryan Cassidy."

Mia shook his hand. "Mia Ballad. My sisters and I run the bed-and-breakfast. Micki is the one with the cat, and Margo is the one with Monty, our lizard. Enid is our housekeeper, and if you need anything, you can let any of us know."

"Sounds good. This has already been very entertaining." Ryan grinned, and Mia felt her heart rate pick up just a bit.

"Let me get you checked in so you can

find your room, Dr. Cassidy." She ushered him inside. "Again, we're sorry for this little incident. It's usually more serene at Ballad Inn."

"Please don't apologize. I can see it will be my kind of place," he said. "And call me Ryan."

Mia walked behind the desk and pulled out the guest book. They tried to keep the experience as vintage as possible, and signing the guest book was just part of it. In the back, everything was computerized so they could take credit-card payments for rooms and services. She took the time to glance at Dr. Ryan Cassidy as they went through the policies of the B and B and a thick brochure of everything the house and Charlotte had to offer.

Ryan stood around six feet tall or so, and he had a head full of sandy-blond curls that weren't tight spirals but more like waves. His eyes drew her in, like deep blue pools reminding her of the Caribbean Sea she'd seen in postcards from her parents. She wouldn't have thought him a doctor given the way he was dressed in a blue T-shirt with a superhero's shield on the front and faded blue jeans. He looked more like a surfer than anything else. The delectable mouth on his angular face curved in a slow smile when he caught her looking at him. She straightened her back and focused on her task.

"You are in the Cigar Room, last door in the hall on the third floor." She handed him a key. "We don't do card locks here because we don't want to change the authentic look of the house. If you are a person who tends to lose keys, we can make a copy."

"Do I share a bathroom? I know some bed-and-breakfasts do stuff like that," Ryan said.

"Luckily you have one of the rooms with its own bathroom." Mia smiled. "You listed that you will be here for an extended stay, so we wanted you to be as comfortable as possible."

"I very much appreciate that." He folded the key into his palm.

"Dinner is at seven each night. As a doctor, you probably work long hours, which we understand. There will be a plate warming for you in the kitchen. That includes dessert." Mia smiled again. "We ensure our guests are well-fed."

"Good to know." Ryan beat a little tune on the desk in front of him. "Thank you very much. I am going to go crash for a few hours. Very nice welcome, Ballad girl. I think my decision to come here was the right one."

"You're welcome... I guess," Mia answered doubtfully. "Do you mean the house or Charlotte in general?"

"A little of both," he answered and flashed her a smile.

Mia watched him head up the stairs and noted that her family were scattered in nearby places pretending to do something but were basically snooping. Micki was grinning and giving her a thumbs-up from outside one of the windows that faced the veranda.

"All of you are so weird." Mia said the words loud enough for them to hear and turned to go back into the office.

Ryan Cassidy had definitely caused a stir—even within her—and Mia didn't know if that was a good or a bad thing. *It's neither*, she told herself firmly. He was a guest, nothing more, nothing less, and she tried to put their new resident completely out of her mind.

IT HAD CERTAINLY been a culture shock leaving the busy schedule and skyline of Minneapolis to drive to Charlotte. Many of Ryan's friends at the hospital thought he was foolish to make the drive instead of taking a flight. But why shouldn't he? His stuff was packed up in a pod, waiting to be shipped to Charlotte or wherever, depending on what he decided to do. And with the drive he could take his time and watch the scenery change.

At that point he wasn't sure if he was staying in Charlotte or not. The job was a trial run to see if he and the hospital meshed. There was also his work with Medicine Across the World. On the one hand he wanted to give it up: he was possibly burned out; on the other, he felt as committed as ever. So many different things were going on inside him, the turmoil of the past would play a large part in his future, he knew. It was very clear to Ryan the next few months would be the deciding factor.

Driving through Charlotte, toward the inn, he'd noticed the tall buildings of city streets and several neighborhoods. But once he was on the property of Ballad Inn, his attention was quickly on the blooms and the lush foliage that grew in this charming spot right outside Uptown.

The Sardis Woods neighborhood was like a little step back in time with tree-lined streets and white picket fences. But it was the Ballad Inn that had really caught his interest. The property had vines running everywhere. When he'd taken a deep breath, the sweet smell of honeysuckle had filled his senses and cleansed his lungs. Then he'd met the owners in the most unique way. Ryan smiled as he unlocked the door to the Cigar Room and thought about catching Mia Ballad in his arms. *Definitely not a bad start to my maybe-new life*, he thought.

She was a breath of fresh air with bright eyes and wild curls, which she fixed back into a bun once he had set her on her feet and she'd regained her composure. Her glasses were still slightly askew, though it only added to her appeal. Mia wore a fishbone skirt and a blue top tucked in. Also of note were the cute heels she had on.

As she spoke, he could tell she was good at her business because she was concise and to the point. But her soft brown eyes with bronze flecks were warm and friendly and revealed another side to her. He also kept wondering how it would be to kiss her until both their heads swam and her straitlaced persona fell away. And that was just from their first meeting. How would the rest of his time at the inn go?

He realized he shouldn't even be thinking like that—the loneliness sometimes swamped him—and his track record with relationships was two to zero, and not in his favor. He liked the feel of the home: it was much better than the housing option given to him by the hospital.

Ryan wanted no more high-rise apartments or living out of a suitcase most of the time. If this job afforded him the opportunity to be in one place permanently, he just might take it. So while he worked and stayed at Ballad Inn, he might think about house-hunting as well. It was all very much in the air at that point, it made no sense worrying it to death, especially when he was dog-tired.

The Cigar Room had nothing to do with cigars but definitely had a manly theme to the decor. The rich sienna overstuffed recliner was a pleasant touch of relaxation. French doors led to the third-story balcony, and a window was open to the wonderful fresh air of Sardis. On the bed was a thick down comforter that matched the rich browns and beiges of the room. It felt homey and comfortable, much better than the single-man bachelor pads slash doctor housing or sterile apartments that felt cold, boring and usually only looked out at other tall, anonymous buildings.

Ryan put down his luggage and sat on the bed with a heavy sigh. He had the rest of his things in the trunk of the car. Going back downstairs meant he would see Mia again, and a grin crossed his face. With renewed energy, he left the room and bounded down the stairs. He felt a little disappointed when he didn't see her at the front desk.

Back outside, he took a moment and sat on one of the white rocking chairs on the wide veranda. A patio that went all the way around a house was something special, not often usual in a lot of neighborhoods. In all actuality, Ryan had only seen houses like this in books or magazines. The beauty of the property astounded him, the bright colors of the flowers set against a sky so blue he felt like he could swim in it. The whole area seemed quaint. Across the street, two men sat opposite each other playing chess at a small table. Ryan raised his hand in a greeting, and they both waved back.

"Is the room to your liking?"

Mia's voice made him turn, and Ryan saw her approach from the far end of the house to where he sat. She'd changed into cotton slacks with suspenders over a formfitting white top. She'd taken off the hair band completely, which had been knocked free with her foray with the orange cat. Now she let her loose curls frame her face. Ryan noted that he took his time assessing her features and everything about her.

"It's perfect, feels like home," he answered. "Something I don't have much of."

"How so?" Mia took a seat on the rocker next to Ryan. She raised her hand in a wave to the men across the street. "Mr. Marley, Mr. Bolton, wonderful weather we're having."

"Gonna rain soon. My bones hurt," one of the men called back. "My gout is acting up."

"We'll make you some soup and bring it over this week," she said and turned her attention back to him. "That's Mr. Bolton.

He's kind of crotchety, but he and Mr. Marley play chess on that patio daily. Mr. Webber next door is even more grumpy. He's the one with the assassin cat you saw earlier."

"I take it it's a frequent thing you deal with when it comes to…Doodle, is it?" Ryan asked.

"He's got some kind of fixation on Margo's lizard." She shrugged. "I mean, he's an inside cat, and no one can fathom how he escapes Mr. Webber's house."

"Ever think he lets the cat out so chaos can ensue?"

Mia's eyes widened. "That's dastardly and could more than likely be true. He is not a friendly sort."

Ryan rocked the chair idly with his foot. "Or he's lonely, and this way he can interact with the three sisters in the house next door."

"We have lived here all our lives, and Mr. Webber has had the very same disposition since we were kids," she told him with a laugh.

Ryan took the opening to learn more about her. "So no traveling? Didn't do a year after college backpacking across Europe?"

"That sounds terrible, and no." Mia grimaced. "I've always been happy here, no reason to roam."

"I don't think I can imagine a life without traveling. I've done it since I was a teenager," Ryan commented.

He watched her mouth grow firm. It gave her a stern look. "To each his own," she said with a nod.

Ryan drank in her beauty, wondering what had happened in her life to turn her off the adventure of traveling. It wasn't the type of thing he could ask her right after he signed in to be a guest at her home.

"This is completely different to any place I've ever been. I drove here from Minneapolis."

"It's always felt one of a kind. Lots of historic areas nearby as well." Mia brushed a fleck of dust off her pants.

"I lived in the city, close to the hospital, in an apartment not worth what I had to pay for it," Ryan told her. "The Armstrong children's hospital is considering me for the head attending here so we are feeling each other out. There are certain terms I need to have their assurance on before I say yes. If it's offered to me."

"So you work exclusively with children?" Mia asked.

"Yes, but in Minneapolis I was in the ER with more trauma cases than long-term kids' health." Instantly, he felt the same tiredness that settled over him anytime he thought of the last ten years. "I want to heal kids, see them smile. After a while, dealing with so much else, you forget how to breathe and only anticipate the next hard situation. Here...I know it will be hard, especially with really sick kids, but it will be different. I can put my heart into it and not have to try to numb myself to it."

Mia was staring at him, and a moment of silence stretched between them, making him feel uncomfortable.

He shrugged in embarrassment. "I might have said too much, being raised in the Midwest might have made me a talker. Most folks there tend to be super friendly."

"What you said, or how much...it's not a problem." Mia hesitated before she continued. "The fact that it still affects you says you have empathy and that you're probably an amazing doctor. You maybe need to add some self-care into your routine so you have an outlet."

"I do." Ryan grinned and reached behind her ear and pulled out a quarter. "Laughter is the best medicine."

Mia smiled. "Ah, so you're a magician, too. Did you smuggle a rabbit in a hat into your room?"

"I may dabble… Why? Is my furry friend not welcome?" Ryan said teasingly.

She laughed. "No, I'm just worried about him being kidnapped by my sister Margo. She has a thing for animals."

"Well, then, my bunny is in safe hands," he said and grinned. "What do you do for fun around this place?"

"Check the brochure, Dr. Cassidy." Mia stood and gave him a wide smile. "Part of your new adventure is to find the little nooks and crannies of Charlotte that make it feel like home, if you decide to stay."

"I accept that challenge." Ryan continued to sway the rocker with the heel of his shoe. "But I was hoping you'd play tour guide."

"Not part of my job title," she said gently. "Don't forget, dinner tonight. We have another couple who are here on their honeymoon."

"What's for dessert?" he asked.

"Peach cobbler and homemade vanilla bean ice cream," Mia told him. "Bye for now."

"See ya," he called after her.

I was hoping talking to you all night would be the treat. Ryan whistled softly as the surprise thought filtered through his head. What happened to him staying aloof until he figured his own life out? *Settle yourself down, dude.* He rocked slowly and mused as his mind jumped from one thing to the next. The breeze that came to him again was filled with the smell of the sweet namesake of the beautiful yellow Queen Anne–style house. It calmed Ryan's soul. For once, his own bad memories seemed far away.

He finally stood to go get the rest of his things from the car, and as his mind wandered back to the very stunning Mia, his instincts warned him to stay away. With Mia, he could tell slow and easy would be the right path to a relationship, but he had no interest in this path. He wasn't even sure what he wanted, and she hated travel and that was definitely one big barrier between them already. Attraction didn't mean a thing when the logistics didn't work. He'd learned that the hard way one too many times on the job.

CHAPTER TWO

RYAN BOUNDED DOWN the stairs after a decent
nap. He'd expected one, maybe two hours
of sleep, but with the windows open and a
spring breeze blowing, the sweet scent of
honeysuckle combined with the birdcalls,
he was out like a light. It was absolutely refreshing, and then a shower just seemed to
give him a boost of energy.

His stomach rumbled hungrily at the aroma
of dinner that filled the house. It would be
another interesting experience to sit around
a table in a traditional family-like setting.
He hadn't had that growing up, and with
his work schedule back in Minneapolis, he
grabbed dinner either on the way home after
a long shift or from the hospital cafeteria.

It was an absolutely charming scene when
he walked into the formal dining room and
saw the table set and a beautiful warm meal
laid out for the family and the inn's guests to

enjoy. A couple sat in the corner talking intimately while sipping from glasses of wine, and outside the French doors, the solar lights down the path to the gazebo gave the mood a magical aura. He made a note to sit outdoors with his dessert later and just enjoy the relaxation that eased the tense ache in his shoulders.

"Hey," a soft voice came from behind him.

Ryan turned around and smiled. "If I remember correctly, you are Margo."

"Right on the first try. It seems I am so committed to work I went in on my day off. They looked at me like I was a space alien who'd crash-landed," she said with a laugh and placed the dish she held onto the table. "Would you like some wine or a beer? Charlotte has a bunch of new breweries now with a lot of great flavors. We stock a few different kinds."

"Surprise me," he answered. "It's all an adventure at this point."

Margo smiled. "Sounds good to me. I'll be back."

"Okay."

Ryan watched her leave, the long braids in her hair swishing merrily with her jaunty steps. You could tell the Ballads were sisters. They all held a hint of the same features, apart from their height. Mia was the tallest, while Margo was a few inches shorter, and Micki was the pixie of the three. They were all pretty, of course, but already he had eyes just for the oldest sister, who hadn't made an entrance into the room as yet. Margo came back with his beer in a tall frosted glass, and Ryan accepted it, taking a long sip.

"Hmm, not bad. Is that a hint of citrus in there?" he asked.

"You'd have to ask Micki. A beer drinker I am not." Margo wrinkled her nose. "I'm more of a fruity cocktail girl."

"And Mia?" Ryan asked conversationally.

Margo grinned. "She doesn't like most adult beverages, but she's an aperitif buff, or vintage cocktails. There are a couple of speakeasy-style bars and restaurants that she's been to here in Charlotte."

"Good to know."

"I think so," Margo said. "In case someone feels the inclination to ask her out."

Ryan let that comment slide on by. "So who came up with the family-style dinners for the B and B?"

"That would be me. I just like the homey feel," she answered. "I better get the last few dishes out before Enid catches me chit-chatting."

Ryan chuckled as she turned and left the room again. He casually hung out by the fireplace, drinking his beer and getting a feel for the house. Finally, the meal was ready, and Micki came in wearing jeans and a T-shirt with a huge yellow smiling emoji on the front.

"What's up, Doc?" she teased.

Ryan laughed. "Hey, Micki."

Mia rushed in next and gave an audible sigh. "Great, I'm not late."

"Would there be a problem if you were?" Ryan asked as he walked over to greet her.

"Only Margo and Enid giving me the side-eye over the table," Mia replied.

She wore the same clothes from the afternoon, but he could tell she had added a little makeup and a light coral gloss to her lips, making them more kissable. Ryan looked away quickly because he felt that oomph of boy meets girl, boy likes girl kick in. *You're acting like some silly teen who's never seen a girl.*

"Everyone, dinner is ready!" Margo called, coming in with a huge pie and bowl of ice cream that she set in ice on the buffet bar that graced the left side of the room.

"Ryan, this is Heather and John, our newlyweds," Mia said by way of introduction. "Guys, this is Ryan, and he will be staying at Ballad Inn as well."

Ryan shook hands with Heather and John. "Nice to meet you both, and congratulations."

"Thank you." John smiled warmly at Heather. "Best wife ever."

"Only wife ever," she said with a laugh and pressed a kiss on his lips.

Public displays of affection didn't faze him in the least, but as dinner progressed, Ryan had to look away from the goo-goo eyes that the couple made at each other. They were in their own happy bubble, understandably, so he focused on the food and the sisters. He took another bite of the roasted chicken. The rest of the meal was creamy mashed potatoes, green beans sautéed to perfection, buttery rolls and a fresh leafy salad.

"Amazing dinner. My compliments to the chef and or chefs," Ryan said.

"Chefs," Mia answered. "Enid is just the best cook ever, and Margo got certified as a culinarian before she became a nurse."

"At Armstrong Medical?" he asked, hoping there would be a friendly face there Monday morning.

Margo shook her head. "That hospital's way too high-pressure for me. I work at one of the newest assisted-living communities in Matthews. It's pretty close by, and I prefer working with seniors."

"Commendable. Not many people sign on to care for our elderly." Ryan frowned as memories filtered in. "Too many times, older folks get dropped off at the ER by facilities that don't want to take care of them anymore, and then it's often difficult to track down their family members. I lost count of how many seniors I had to sign over to government facilities because no one came."

"That's terrible!" Micki cried out.

Margo sighed. "Unfortunately, it does happen, but I'm one of the head nurses and it certainly won't under my watch."

"I've seen worse in scarier situations outside the country," Ryan said. The dark thoughts made his chest tighten.

"I thought you worked with children?" Mia asked.

He smiled sadly. "It is my primary field. I'm a pediatric surgeon that deals with heart defects in children as young as a few days old. But in challenging situations, no matter what your specialty is, everyone becomes a general practitioner when help is needed."

"That has to be tough," Mia said. "What was your most difficult surgery?"

Ryan offered a small smile. "I repaired the heart defect of a baby girl in utero. We fixed her tiny heart and left the rest up to Mom. She was born two months later, and now she's around six and thriving."

"That's beautiful," Mia breathed out.

"In my line of work, we try to focus on the good moments." Ryan frowned, thinking about the past. "But sometimes there's not a thing even I can do. Those times tend to stick in your memory forever."

"You do your level best, and that's all anyone can ask for," Mia said, and he heard the comfort in her voice.

He shrugged, a stiff movement to ease the ache in his tense shoulders. "We try to tell ourselves that, but as doctors we want to do more, heal them all."

"And that's very commendable and what defines a doctor." Mia smiled.

"So tell me about you, Mia," Ryan said, suddenly redirecting the conversation.

His words made her choke, and she had to take a fast sip of iced tea while Micki thumped her on the back. Mia fanned her eyes, which had begun to water, and cleared her throat before she spoke.

"Me… You want to know about me?"

Ryan nodded. "Yes. What else do you do?"

"I'm a certified accountant," she said. "I have my own business that I manage from home, and I take care of the everyday running of Ballad Inn."

"Wanna do my taxes?" he teased.

"It will cost you," Mia replied.

"I'm willing to put it all on the table."

"Are you sure? My fees may be too much."

"For you, I'll take the risk."

Micki, Margo and Enid watched the verbal volley as if it were a game of tennis, and when Mia noted their smiles and knowing grins, she looked away and went back to her meal. She shifted in her seat. Ryan grinned broadly because he knew he'd gotten under her skin just a little bit.

John finally came out of the intimate conversation with his wife. "Dr. Ryan Cassidy? Why do I know your name? Your face looks familiar. Have I seen you on TV?"

It was Ryan's turn to be uncomfortable. "Probably not. I just got here from Minnesota."

"It's easy enough to find out," Micki said, whipping out her phone.

"Micki, no phones at the table," Enid warned.

"Come on, it will be quick," she said, her fingers flying.

"I'd rather you didn't," said Ryan.

"Holy—" Micki gasped out loud.

"Language!" Enid didn't let her finish the sentence.

"Sorry." Micki apologized and looked over at him. "You have a whole wing of the hospital you used to be at named after you? Why did you ever leave?"

"It wasn't a place where I wanted to work anymore," he replied stiffly.

Micki read from her cell. "'Dr. Ryan Cassidy at the Phoenix Charity Gala. The handsome doctor attended the event alone, where the Cassidy Pediatric Wing was named in his honor. Dr. Cassidy performed lifesaving surgery on Isaac, the one-year-old son of Julia and Michael Gallagher, and this was their thanks to the hospital. With the cutting of the ribbon and his warm smile, the donations poured in.'"

Everyone was looking at him, and he wanted to melt into the floor. He had hoped it would be longer before people found out about him, and he could just settle in. He already had the board at the new hospital tripping over themselves to please him.

"They gave you a grant, didn't they?" Margo asked. "Is that why Armstrong Medical wants you so badly, to pour it into their programs?"

"I don't think that's anyone's business." Ryan heard the bite in his tone and softened it. "I'm just a regular doctor."

"A regular doctor with a real wing named after him," Micki enthused. "Mia, it looks like he could afford your fees after all."

"I'm sure," she murmured.

"Trust me, I can't." Ryan hated being put on the spot.

"It's nothing to do with us, and you're a

guest here. You don't have to explain anything to anyone," she pointed out. "Please
let the man alone."

"Yet, the look in your eyes went from
warm to ice the second your sister read that
article."

"Again, Dr. Cassidy, it is your life, nothing needs to be elaborated on."

Mia glanced at him and back to her food
without another word, but Ryan could tell
the air between them had changed. Most
people were either too interested in his story
or shied away from him. It seemed Mia was
like the latter because the relaxed teasing
between them had fizzled as quickly as it
had begun.

"Great dinner." He wiped his mouth. "I'll
head up to my room now…and, yeah, work
or something."

"Ryan, don't go," Margo called, but he
was already moving quickly toward the door.

"Dr. Cassidy, staying at the same spot
where we are honeymooning! The man is
a legend in the medical world. Wait until I
tell my friends we met him," Heather gushed
while he listened from the hallway.

"He seems to want that aspect left alone,"

Margo commented knowingly. "Actually, *he* wants to be left alone and to just practice medicine."

"But can he do that with all that prestige he has? There is no normal there, right?" John countered.

"He is no different than the man who checked in this afternoon. He's a guest," Mia said briskly. "Let's finish dinner."

Guest. One word that set him firmly in his place. Ryan turned and went up the stairs to his room, not wanting to hear the rest of the conversation. Once again, that element of his life had become more important than himself, his work and what he wanted to accomplish.

Thirty minutes later, there was a knock on his door. His half-packed bag sat open on the bed. Instead of finishing his packing, he'd been staring out the window, inhaling the flowery perfume of night-blooming plants. Answering the door, he found Margo standing in the hallway with a large bowl and spoon in her hands.

"I brought you dessert. May I come in?"

He couldn't resist the gentleness in her

voice, so he nodded and stepped back while she entered the room.

Margo spied the bag on the bed. "Oh, Ryan, don't leave."

He shrugged and sat down heavily. "Kinda seems that who I am throws a big wet blanket on my staying here."

"We were just shocked, that's all." She put the bowl on the small table next to the recliner. "Like, why would someone like you stay here? You could stay anywhere, or buy a home straight-out in the Ballantyne area, where a lot of the doctors live."

"It's not the house that makes a home," Ryan said and ran his hands through his hair in frustration. "I'm here to see if Armstrong Medical and I will work out. I sometimes have to travel at a moment's notice… Maybe I don't want that anymore. There are a lot of reasons, Margo, but this place, from the time I stepped inside, comforted me, as if all the demons I battle each day seemed to go to sleep. You have something unique here, filled with warmth and love. Ballad Inn is truly special."

He looked at her, hoping she would understand. "I'm not into people going overboard to please me or to show me up when it should be about the work, about saving lives. So they named a wing after me—big deal. I left because the board was ignoring what was important and saw me as a cash cow to bring them large donations."

"You want them to take the patients' lives into consideration over money," Margo said quietly.

"Exactly."

"I get that, being a nurse. For me and my sisters, this is home, and it's very important to us, Mia especially," Margo said. "Stay and enjoy it."

He shrugged. "The way Mia looked at me, I don't think she wants me around."

"Mia has her own baggage to deal with," she explained. "Maybe she'll tell you about it one day…if you stay. Don't pretend you aren't interested in her. Everyone can see it's the opposite."

"And it hasn't even been a full day. It's one of those instant things that I always laughed at in the movies." Ryan smiled sadly. "I wasn't going to deny it, but it might not be good for either of us."

"Hmm, time will tell. Mia needs a shake-

up, and from the looks of it, you do as well."
Margo smiled. "We Ballad sisters are feisty
and hard to catch."

He smiled back. "Understood...if I stay."

"Oh, I think you already made that decision," Margo said knowingly as she walked
over to the open door. "Eat your dessert before it's all mush."

He watched her retreating with a genuine smile on his face and felt reassurance
blend with the doubt. He had six months to
decide where he wanted his life to go. Folks
didn't realize that the path he walked could
make him the loneliest person on earth. He
never really knew where he would be next,
given his cases and assignments, and always
wondered what the ulterior motive was behind every action. His sort of life bothered
Mia. Maybe that could be considered a good
thing. Save them both in the end from getting hurt.

Looking out the window, Ryan put a big
scoop of ice cream with peach cobbler in his
mouth, and the flavors burst forth, making
him close his eyes at the deliciousness. He
grinned around the second bite, knowing
that if he did stay and become the doctor

he wanted to be, there might be a future for him in this space.

Where Mia fit in…now, that was the big question.

CHAPTER THREE

SATURDAY AND SUNDAY passed quietly, which was one of Mia's favorite types of weekends. Nothing broke or went wrong, and she didn't get a call to come pick Micki up after a concert or party, or from some warehouse rave thing. She worried about her little sister. From the time Micki was born, Mia protected her fiercely, and even as an adult, nothing had changed. Micki was intelligent, more than people often realized, and while Mia felt she should hone those skills, Micki was on her own journey.

Her younger sister was a Renaissance type of woman with a new adventure or idea each week. Mia envied her in some ways— her ability to embrace life and to be so daring. Just the thought filled her with anxiety. It always felt like things would fall apart if she took a vacation or something would happen if she were not there to take charge.

"Wow, I really need to work on myself," Mia muttered under her breath.

An image of Ryan filtered through her mind. He had kept to himself mostly since the first dinner, and a full week had passed since his arrival. Every night at the table, he kept the mood light and laughed with everyone. There were no secret smiles for her, no teasing or the spark of interest he'd shown. Disappointment filled her, and Mia tried to push it away. She claimed she wanted him not to be interested, so why did she feel a sense of loss with their polite but formal interaction?

"If those lines between your eyebrows get any bigger, your face is gonna freeze like that," Margo said, coming up to the desk.

"You'll look like some evil cartoon villain, and I don't want to explain it to the neighbors." Micki leaned on the main reception desk. "It's Sunday. Why are you behind there, anyway?"

"Finishing up some work before I go upstairs," Mia answered. It was a big ol' lie, one her sisters saw right through.

"Oh please, you have everything tied up neatly by Friday evening so your weekends can be free," Micki snorted. "Plus, we don't have any new guests for a few weeks, that's why we're doing all of this landscaping and renovating now."

Margo smiled. "Maybe she's waiting to see Ryan. Today was his first day as attending, and he was gone before she woke up. Don't worry, I made sure he had coffee and breakfast before he left."

Micki clasped her hands to her chest. "She's waiting for her li'l boo to come home and ask him how his day was."

"I certainly am not." Mia felt her face warm. "Y'all, stop that."

"Her twang always comes out more when she is flustered. Look, she's blushing," Margo said teasingly.

"I am not," Mia retorted. "The man is some kind of surgical hero and probably has the ego to boot."

"He does magic tricks for sick kids at the hospital. I saw him leave with a magician's hat," Micki told them the little tidbit.

"Well, that's just adorable," Margo gushed.

"Are y'all done singing his praises?" Mia asked.

Micki tweaked her nose. "Don't be a sour-puss, sis."

"Mr. Webber said people call me a spin-ster," Mia said suddenly. "Is that true?"

"It certainly is not," Micki said hotly. "And now I'm like two seconds away from knocking on his door and giving him a piece of my mind."

"Don't be giving him any of your atten-tion," Margo warned and then sighed. "Mia, you know he was only trying to get under your skin. He's just mean."

Mia fiddled with the papers on the desk, not willing to look up at her sisters. They would surely see the insecurity and hurt on her face. She put a lot aside to take care of them and the house and to make sure they had the stability not found with their travel-ing parents. Romantic love was the victim of all that focus.

"I guess I could see why people might say it," she murmured.

"No, you don't see a thing. You are warm, vibrant and smart," Margo insisted. "You are the strongest person I know, and if peo-ple can't handle that, well, they can go…go jump in the ocean."

"Jump in the ocean?" Micki's lips twitched. "That's the best insult you have?"

"I'll tell you where you can go in a few seconds." Margo glared at her sister.

Mia laughed. "Okay, don't fight, you monsters."

That was another pet name she had for them when Margo and Micki decided to fight. One provoked the other, and then it turned into a verbal scrimmage that amused Mia immensely.

"Look what you caused, Mia." Margo's smile was wide. "You like him, there is such a thing as instant chemistry."

"That's not what's happening here," Mia said in a firm voice.

"But he reads books outside at night on the patio and is an old-movie buff like you," Margo countered.

"How would you know that?" she asked incredulously.

"I cook and see things," Margo answered with pride. "Just admit you like the man."

"I will do no such thing." She folded her arms.

Enid came out of the kitchen, wiping her hands. "What's going on? I can hear y'all from in there while I'm making the short-cake for dinner."

"Mia likes Ryan and won't admit it," Margo teased.

"Micki and Margo came out here to pick on me needlessly," Mia piped in, wanting her side to be known.

Enid rolled her eyes. "Oh, for goodness' sake, girls... We all know they are circling each other like bees to honeysuckle."

"Hey!"

"Yes!"

"Booyah!"

Mia shook her head. "You all are incorrigible, and I don't like—"

The front door opened, and one of the major players in their conversation walked through it. It didn't help that he looked devastatingly handsome in his graphic T-shirt and faded jeans with the worn-out knees. He also wore the kind of shoes skaters wore, and a beat-up type of duffel was in his hands. While people at his job might think he purposely dressed like that to make the children more comfortable, it was actually his personality. Mia claimed to like more sophistication in men, but Ryan was downright endearing. His stethoscope was still around his neck, and she could only assume he'd forgotten that it was there.

"Hey, Ryan." Mia cleared her throat. "How was work?"

"Good, finally met everyone, saw my patients, took residents through what to expect on a pediatric rotation," he replied. "Amazed it's been a week already. You?"

Mia shrugged. "Same ol' here, Sunday at the inn…"

"Well, let's make it interesting." Ryan moved his hands with a flourish and dipped into his bag. He came out with a bouquet of fake flowers and presented it to her.

"You know that's not magic, those flowers were in there all the time," she said dryly, taking the offered colorful bouquet.

"Hmm." He pulled out a magician's hat and put it on his head. "Oh, wait, I think I hear a leprechaun and he is looking for…" Ryan reached behind her ear and produced a gold coin. "His gold."

Mia's lips twitched with a smile.

"Ooh, there's another and another." Ryan pretended to pluck more coins from each ear. "Hey, how many coins do you have back there?"

A laugh escaped her. "Okay. That's pretty cool."

"Thank you." He bowed, and his hat fell off his head into his hands. "Oh, what do we have here?"

This time Ryan pulled out a real rabbit and Margo squealed in delight.

"It's a bunny!" she said, rushing forward and taking it from Ryan. "Did that mean man put you in a smelly hat?"

"My hats don't smell, dude," Ryan said to no one because Margo was already leaving with the bunny.

"Margo, you can't keep—"

"Mine!"

"But you can't have—"

"Let's get you some lettuce, find a place for you to stay. I have a great spot for you out in the shed." Margo cuddled the all-white little hopper and was gone in seconds.

"The bunny," Mia finished her sentence but let the words trail off as she put her hands on her hips and faced Ryan. "Look what you did."

He grinned. "I know. Wasn't it great?"

"You are incorrigible." Mia waggled a finger at him. "Dinner will be ready soon. I know you're exhausted, so if you want a plate brought up so you can crash, it's okay."

Ryan moved closer to the front desk. "No, I'd like to come down and interact with everyone. It's kinda a good way to relax."

Mia noted how Micki and Enid said nothing but still watched their interaction with very rapt interest. Darn it, how did a stethoscope make him cuter?

"So I'll see you…"

"I wanted to ask…"

They both spoke simultaneously and then gave a small laugh.

"You go first," Mia said. "What is it you want?"

"You."

Mia gulped. "M-me?"

A slow smile spread across his face. "I can't stop myself. I know it's spur-of-the-moment, but I wanted to ask you out on a date with me."

"Oh… Oh!" she gasped as realization of what he was asking hit her.

Ryan reached behind her ear, pulled out

yet another gold coin and handed it to her. "What do you say?"

"Yes, I'd love to go out with you," she answered. "To see the town and all that. There's tons of places we can go."

"Great. I'll pick you up Saturday night around seven?"

She laughed. "We live under the same roof."

"Still, seven okay?" Ryan asked.

She nodded. "It is. I'll see you then."

"Well, you'll see me at dinner and all the times in between until then," he said playfully.

"Very true."

Mia smiled, and he winked before heading up the stairs, taking them two at a time. The silence reigned for only a moment before Micki and Enid both started talking excitedly.

"This is so wonderful. My Mia is being courted." Enid clapped her hands. "I need to get back to this cake… So wonderful."

"*Courted?* It's like a romance novel lives in her head," Micki murmured. "Okay, Mia, you need to wear something super gorgeous and knock his socks off. I have this little black dress that never fails to get me into a club."

Mia looked at her aghast. "No. Thank. You. And is that how you have, like, seven VIP cards in your wallet?"

"Those who get VIP access and free champagne sit behind the gold ropes. Those who don't, stay at the bar." Micki lifted her chin. "I'll bring it for you to try on anyway."

She walked off, and Margo came back in holding a piece of lettuce that the bunny was chewing. Together they watched Micki go.

"Where's she off to?" Margo asked.

Mia shook her head. "Ryan asked me out and she wants me to wear a dress she has."

"I guess she doesn't realize you are taller than her and her dress would fit you like a tank top." Margo arched a brow.

That set both of them to laughing, and a ball of paper came flying at them.

"I hear all and know all," Micki called from around the corner.

The sisters smiled before Margo deposited the bunny, now named Smores, in Mia's hands. "Here, hold him while I find a cage or basket or something."

"You are in a house full of unique and

eccentric people, Smores," Mia whispered to the animal. "Apparently, I am, too, since I'm talking to a bunny."

The realization then hit her that she would be going out on a first date, something she hadn't done in a very long time. *Okay, I'm attracted to him*, she admitted to herself, but he was everything else that she claimed not to want. Ryan could go anywhere and do whatever he wanted, no ties or conditions, and that part scared her. Mia was always happy and contented being home. Fancy trips only gave her hives.

It's one date, she told herself firmly.

LATER ON, DINNER WAS another pleasant affair, with everyone talking across the table and laughter coming quickly and easily. When Mia glanced at Ryan, there was always a look in his eyes as he met her gaze, one that made her flush and feel a warmth envelop her. Maybe the impromptu invitation for a date made him feel more relaxed. The standoffish barrier between them was gone and had been replaced with the sweet ache of new possibilities of romance.

After dessert, everyone headed off in different directions, the newlyweds to sit in the gazebo and her sisters to do whatever they pleased. Enid went to bed right after dinner to watch her shows. Mia wandered outside after her evening ritual of having a great lavender-based nonalcoholic drink that came from a distillery in Tennessee. As she followed along the path, she realized the air was getting warmer each day. A whistle caught her attention, making Mia look around.

"Look up," Ryan's voice called. She did so, and saw that he was sitting in the crook of a large branch of one of their red maple trees.

"What are you doing up there?" she asked with a laugh.

"Enjoying the night. Come on up," he said encouragingly.

"I don't think so. I haven't climbed a tree since I was fourteen."

"You never forget how to climb a tree, and since you grew up here, these should be easy-peasy." Ryan grinned. "Unless you're scared…"

"Not of any trees on this property." Mia kicked off her shoes.

"Barefoot, look at you," he said laughing.

"Lucky I had jeans on tonight," Mia murmured to herself.

In a matter of seconds, she was perched in the wide branches, close to Ryan, and she looked down at the place where she grew up.

"I forgot how beautiful Sardis Woods is from up here," Mia said and sighed.

"Did you climb trees a lot growing up?" he said.

She nodded. "It was a good way to escape from annoying sisters and read." Mia hesitated before she spoke. "Why did you ask me out? For the past few days, you were overly polite but distant."

"I was. But being around you has made me see things differently," Ryan admitted. "Honestly, the fact that my life seemed to bother you made me step back a bit. And then I thought, yes, my work is important, but it isn't all that I am, Mia. Although, I should've probably not asked you out."

Her heart dropped, and she asked in a soft voice, "Why?"

"Because relationships seem to be my kryptonite," Ryan admitted. "I'm a simple guy, but I've spent the last ten years working or traveling for work. Relationships seemed to be good one minute but usually ended up with me being hurt or me hurting someone I cared about."

"It looks like we are in the same boat. I think dating imploded for me years ago," she said, "but I'm sorry for equating you with someone who just traverses the world for fun."

"Would you believe I never climbed a tree until I got to college?" Ryan swung his legs casually off the branch.

She looked at him in surprise. "How does one go that long without being in a tree?"

"My parents were kind of sticklers about me not falling or being hurt, no trees, no bike riding, no skateboarding, no anything they thought was inherently dangerous."

Curiosity got the best of her. "Why?"

"My older brother died. He was playing in the park and fell off the monkey bars. Fractured his skull badly enough that it caused brain swelling and a subdural hematoma he couldn't recover from," Ryan explained. "I was a baby, so I never knew him, but my parents were traumatized enough that they would have wrapped me in Bubble Wrap if they could have."

He scooted closer as he spoke. "I don't get why because I rarely saw them. I ate dinner alone most nights in a hollow house that felt cold and void of happiness. It was like they never stopped mourning, and while they wanted to protect me, they kinda checked out. I tried to get them help, but they couldn't face it. I used college, then med school, to break free of that grip and finally begin living."

"Where are they now?" Mia asked gently.

"They've passed on. Dad had a heart attack, Mom a stroke soon after, sadly." Ryan stared at the ground. "I've always wished that they found peace. The kind they couldn't find in life after Mark died. I hope they are together somewhere, happy and laughing."

"I'm so sorry, Ryan." She reached out to squeeze his hand.

"What about your parents? Why are three sisters running a bed-and-breakfast?"

"My parents sold it to us when I was twenty-five for a fraction of what it's worth." Mia gave a sarcastic chuckle. "They have spent their lives going on a series of adventures. They had no trouble forgetting they had three daughters always waiting at home.

Oh, they'd show up with gifts from India or Japan, but it was never for long. They would get the itch, that look on their faces, and go."

"That had to be tough for you, especially with your sisters being younger," Ryan said with tenderness.

"I was a certified accountant by then, and I got a loan to buy the house." Mia ran her hand along the coarse bark. "I'd rather us have it than my parents selling it off and us all living in apartments or places away from each other. The bed-and-breakfast pays the mortgage and Enid's salary quite nicely, and our regular jobs sustain us and the house."

Ryan's voice was soft when he spoke. "I mean, growing up with parents always being gone."

Mia shrugged. "I managed, and I made sure my sisters never missed a birthday celebration or important school event. Even now, our parents are somewhere in the world, and I literally have no clue where exactly."

"I love the closeness you share with your sibs," he admitted. "Kinda jealous, really."

Mia laughed. "You are not."

"Okay, *jealous* may be the wrong word. Maybe *envy* works better."

A comfortable silence settled between them for a few minutes, until Ryan spoke again.

"What are you thinking right now?"

Mia glanced at him. "Nothing. Just enjoying the night... You?"

"About kissing the woman I am sitting next to in a tree," he confessed. "But in my defense, I've been thinking about kissing you from the first day I caught you in my arms."

"Oh."

His rich laughter rang out. "Just an *oh*?"

"What else can I say?" Mia's heartbeat began to race.

"Say, 'Yes, Ryan, I would love you to kiss me.'" His voice became this low, sultry timbre that made Mia tremble as he moved closer.

"I would like you to kiss me," she whispered.

Without hesitation, Ryan pressed his lips to hers, and Mia's eyes fluttered closed. It was a kiss that built from a simmer. She felt the smooth caress and the sweet friction of their connection.

Ryan pulled away slowly, and when she opened her eyes, he was staring at her, the periwinkle blue of his irises beautiful in the low light.

"That was nice," she said.

"I fear I might not ever get enough of kissing you," Ryan told her. "But slow and easy was the way to go."

She didn't have time to wonder what he meant because the first spray of cold water hit her before the exact same thing happened to Ryan. Below, Micki stood with a garden hose and a wide grin.

"Mia and Ryan sitting in a tree," her sister sang out.

"Micki, you rotten little—" Mia cried out. "I will get you back for this."

"You'll never catch me." Micki merrily made loud smooching noises as she walked quickly away.

Ryan's rich laughter rang loud into the night. Mia couldn't help it. She smiled wide, too. It seemed she couldn't be mad at Micki when Ryan found the entire thing so entertaining.

She and Ryan made it down the tree, and Mia picked up her waterlogged glass, all thanks to her sister, before they strolled together back to the Ballad house. With another soft kiss, he wished her good-night, and Mia watched him go up the stairs.

"I'm in trouble, so much trouble," she muttered as she locked up for the evening. Her heart would be on the line if her feelings for Ryan grew, and the thought of it breaking terrified her. Mia made her way up the stairs, knowing she couldn't run from how Ryan made her feel. This was the biggest plunge into the unknown she would ever take, and there was no safety net to catch her.

CHAPTER FOUR

THERE WAS SOMETHING different in the air for Mia, a light flutter in her chest, a smile on her lips and how the house felt when she woke up.

Not having much experience with men was part of the price she had paid for doing what she thought was right—taking care of her sisters while her parents were gone. Mia had given up prom—not that she'd had a date in any case—and other social activities. She went to college at the University of North Carolina, Charlotte campus, so she could drive home every night to be with them. She could count the number of serious boyfriends she'd had using only one finger.

The guy she'd thought was right for her… well, he planned to capitalize on her plans for the inn. He believed he could live there rent-free, run the business and put the profit in his pocket without her knowing. That made her even more hesitant about men, and now she was kissing a guy in a tree and feeling the warmth of romance wind itself around her heart.

Ryan in the Ballad house was interesting to say the least. So far there was a huge puzzle they had started in the solarium, and on Wednesday night he'd taken over Enid and Margo's kitchen to make one-pot spaghetti for everyone, including the newlyweds. Mia thought Enid would faint, while Margo kept peeking through the door. But his meal was good, and though the garlic bread was store-bought, everyone ate the big family-style meal with plenty of wine, teasing and conversation.

As usual, noise outside her office piqued her curiosity. She got up from her desk and spotted Micki just coming through the inn's front door.

"What do you sound like? A team of horses?" Mia demanded.

Micki rolled her eyes. "These are called work boots, and I was sent to get you."

Mia's brow furrowed. "By whom?"

"Your boo thang," her sister drawled.

"He's out in Crawford's Field behind the house."

She instantly worried. "Is he hurt or something? I told that man that even though this is kind of like the city, we have rural spots in Sardis. I bet he tripped in one of those rabbit holes and twisted his ankle."

"Chillax, chick. He's flying a kite." Micki looked at her, waiting. "Man, that escalated to the dark side quickly."

"He's flying a kite," Mia said slowly. "Like a *kite* kite."

"He wants you to come out there and fly the actual thing with him and maybe share an apple or something weird like that."

A smile spread across her face. "He has fruit?"

Her sister threw up her hands in exasperation. "Stop quizzing me and go find out for yourself. I would suggest changing those cute yellow pumps for sneakers before one of the rascally rabbit holes gets you."

"Good idea." She kissed Micki's head as she passed. "Thanks, sis."

Mia ran up the steps with a pep in her step, then abruptly stopped for a moment because she wasn't the bouncy, perky type.

She shook her head, embracing the fact that she felt lighter and happier. She also had self-doubt and pessimism poking at the outer edges of her subconscious, waiting for the other shoe to drop and ruin whatever this was. Still, while she changed from her blouse and neat slacks to jeans and a T-shirt with her sneakers, and headed back down to the main foyer of the house, Mia chose to ignore the practical and embrace the whirlwind that was Dr. Ryan Cassidy.

To get into Crawford's Field the quickest, it meant going to the back of the house and climbing over the white-painted fence that led from their landscaped property to the grassy field on the other side. Mr. Crawford had long ago died, and his son had yet to figure out if he would sell the acres of land. Mia kept her fingers crossed that he would because it'd be perfect to buy to extend their little slice of heaven in Sardis.

It was easy to spot Ryan in the low grass of the wide-open field, but Mia didn't expect to also see the newlyweds, a distance away with their own kite, enjoying the sunshine.

"You have our honeymooners out here,

too?" she commented casually, coming up behind him.

While he affixed the string to a blue-and-yellow kite, Ryan's sunglasses were pushed back into his hair, and he glanced at her with a smile. The blue of his eyes made her jaw drop. The intimate thought of their kiss last night made her look away for a moment with a warm, flushed face.

"They were all for it when they saw me pull out the box from the back of my Rover," Ryan answered. "I had a second one, and red was the lady's favorite color, so they went for it."

"And you sent Micki to invite me to fly a kite." Mia grinned. She teased, "Should I be insulted?"

"Never," he said huskily. "Consider this me wanting to see you outside your natural element of the office. You look cute all dressed down."

"Micki had to remind me to change. I'd have struggled trying to hop a fence in my pumps." She kicked at the soft grass with the toe of her old sneaker.

"But you'd be awesome trying." Ryan cleared his throat.

Again that sweet warmth twined its way around her heart, and this time he held her gaze. The spark between them was as clear as the Carolina blue skies. She knew there wasn't a chance in the world she could say no to this type of feeling. It made Mia think about the future they might have together. *No, girl. Fix your face before it looks like you want him to get down on one knee and propose*, Mia told herself firmly.

"So, who's going to be running and getting this up in the air?" she asked, noting her tone was a tad breathless.

Ryan offered her the kite. "It's up to you."

"I thought I was here to hold it or whatever?"

A slow grin spread across his face. "I don't think that's how the aerodynamics of this works."

She held up her hand. "Fine, fine, but sweating in the heat doesn't look good on me."

"You're killing me here," Ryan said and laughed. "I heard you were this big tomboy growing up and now you're worried about sweating?"

"I was a kid then, deodorant was optional." Mia smiled. "After a few times of Enid saying—and I quote—'you smell like outside,' I got the drift."

"How about I just run with the kite?" he suggested, clearly amused.

"Nope. I'm committed now." Mia held out her hand. "Give it to me."

Ryan passed it to her. "Remember, give it a little slack. The wind is coming from the east, so run that way. When you feel the wind tugging it from your hand, let the string slide through your fingers slowly until it starts to fly."

"Okay, got it," Mia said firmly.

Ryan caught her face in his hand and kissed her quickly. "You're so darn cute. Have fun, Mia. It's not a job or a task. It's a day in the sun, flying a kite."

"Okay."

Who would've thought that she would be out in Crawford's old field, running around with a kite in her hand at thirty-four years old? Yet, here she was, racing through the uneven grass with the wind in her face. The breeze pulled the kite from her fingertips. Following Ryan's advice, her breath coming out in short pants, she let the string slip gradually from her grasp and felt the toy take flight and drift toward the sky.

"Go, Mia, go!"

She turned to see he was running as well, a huge grin on his face, and a laugh of exhilaration escaped her as the bird-shaped kite took to the skies and the string spiraled off the loop. Finally, Mia stopped, breathing hard from the run. Under the shade of the huge magnolia tree on the far side of the pasture, Ryan finally caught up with her and she couldn't help it. She giggled in delight.

"I did it," Mia announced with pride.

"Look at you go," Ryan said, panting. "Did you run track?"

"Used to in high school for a little while," she said. "Last year Micki convinced me and Margo to do the Zombie Run for charity, so we trained all summer."

"Exactly what is the Zombie Run?" Ryan took the string and made sure the kite was steady in the sky before they sat down in the grass with the tree shading them from too much sun.

"It happens in the fall, October obviously. It's a charity run for a group of women's shelters in Charlotte," she explained. "You sign up and you run the course with mud traps, obstacles and zombies—well, people dressed up like the living dead. Your goal is to reach the end without a flag on your back to show you've been caught. The first was so successful, they opted to have a second event in the summer."

"Sounds fun. Sign me up." He leaned back and pulled his sunglasses down. "And you did this?"

"There's a different sort of run coming up, same premise except no zombies. By the end, you're covered with powder chalk of every color imaginable."

"Uh, sounds…dirty?"

She turned to face him. "Why, Mr. Cassidy, are you afraid of getting dirty?"

"My parents are probably screaming in the afterlife." His tone was dry. "I'm game."

"Micki trained us like we were expecting the actual apocalypse, and Margo tackled a zombie to save me." She followed his relaxed posture and stared up at their kite. *Their kite.* The words made her smile.

"Good on Margo," Ryan said and chuckled. "She looks like a scrapper."

"Oh, she is." Mia recalled their childhood

with a laugh. "The boys were scared of her, for sure. Neighbors, they'd all say, 'Uh-oh, here come those Ballad sisters.' Our parents were mostly gone, so people thought we were feral."

"You, feral? Never."

"I was a little terror myself," Mia boasted. "I was good at roller-skating and skateboarding and could climb the tallest trees the boys didn't dare go up. I had to be rescued by the fire department once. I went up and couldn't find my way back down."

"What happened between then and now?" Ryan questioned carefully. "You seem to think a lot about every step you take."

"I had to in order to make sure me and my sisters were taken care of," she said simply. "Enid couldn't do everything or be everywhere, so I took over paying bills and being responsible for the general upkeep of the house. Bringing another person into the household would upset Enid, and it didn't seem necessary. That's how I came up with the idea of a small, cozy bed-and-breakfast. I had to put away childish things and be the grown-up for us to survive."

"Your parents didn't help at all?" he asked, sounding curious.

Mia shrugged. "They tried, and honestly, they still do, but we lived without them for so long. I mean, at first, we saw them like every eight to twelve weeks, but as we got older, the time away got longer. One time they didn't come home for six months, and when they were here, it was like they were another set of guests."

"Whereas my parents would've hired a professor to teach me at home," Ryan shared. "If they were alive, my being with Medicine Across the World would've upset them, but being stifled my entire life, I've needed to explore, to inhale the air of different places."

"We seem to be opposite sides of a coin." She nudged him with her shoulder in a teasing gesture. "My family feels like we're in the middle of a catch-22. Maybe my parents had every intention of staying home more, but when they saw us actually thriving without them, they started to live for themselves. I just wish we'd had more of a childhood with them and I could've—"

"Been more of a kid," Ryan finished her sentence in a soft voice.

"Or been less reserved," she admitted. "I have a tendency to shy away from new adventures."

"But here you are with me, flying a kite." Ryan looked up into the sky and bounced to his feet. "That seems to be taking a nose-dive!"

Mia rose beside him and watched as he reeled in the string, trying to keep the kite in the sky.

"We gotta run," Ryan yelled and took off.

Mia was on his heels, and that was how she spent her afternoon, running across a field with a kite in the air, and laughing with a man who embraced life to its fullest. His laugh echoed in the wind, and it drew hers out as well. When it was her turn with the kite, Mia was going at a good clip as she tripped on a clump of dirt.

"It's— Ack!"

She fell into the grass, and the spool of string slipped from her hands. She rolled over to see the kite floating away, untethered, into the neighborhood.

"Oh no, Mia!"

She lifted her head to spot Ryan running toward her.

"Watch out! There's a mole...hill."

Ryan hit the same pitfall, and she watched him fall in her direction and roll away. They both ended up in the grass, facing upward and laughing into the sky.

"How do I always end up swept off my feet when you're around?" Mia closed her eyes, feeling lighter than she had in a very long time.

"Maybe it's fate telling us something," Ryan said, chuckling.

He laced his fingers with hers. "I always say one should never tempt fate, just go where it leads."

Mia intended to voice her doubt, but then she felt his lips brushing hers and it seemed like time stood still, the connection between them palpable. The sweetness of the kiss humbled her, and a soft sigh escaped her.

"Ryan, we're in a field," she whispered when he pressed a kiss at her temple.

"So that's why your lips taste like the sun." He smiled and it slowly fell away. "I don't know why you affect me the way you do. I came here to focus on the hospital and found something more from the very moment you fell into my arms. And the kiss in the tree only sealed it for me."

"There's a lot to consider in all this, your career and more. I'm not the exploring, taking-risks type." Mia sat up. "I need to take things slower. It's not my nature to jump in with both feet."

"I know." Ryan sat up beside her and then a small beep went off and he took his cell from his pocket. He checked the screen. "I have to go. We have a young patient being brought in."

"Oh, okay. Right. Don't worry, I can find the kite, you should get going. There's a child that needs you."

"Let someone else find it and have some fun." Ryan helped her to her feet.

With a charming grin, he plucked pieces of grass out of her hair before they jogged back and climbed over the fence. Ryan ran to the house while she took her time walking across Ballad Inn property. When she finally went up the steps, he was driving away with a honk of the SUV horn.

On the main driveway there was a truck with the supplies to renovate the gazebo. The materials had arrived early, which pleased

Mia. Mr. Marley and Mr. Bolton were in their usual spot, and they looked over casually, noting her disheveled appearance.

"Rolling in the grass again, Mia?" Mr. Marley commented.

"Excuse me?" Mia stopped.

"Like when you guys were kids, always coming home messy from that field," Mr. Marley elaborated.

Mia laughed. "I was flying a kite."

"It's not unusual for one of y'all Ballad sisters to be out there. Good for you, reliving your childhood. Although, that is why Mr. Crawford put up that fence," Mr. Bolton commented. "There used to be cows, too, remember when you tried to rodeo a milking cow?"

Mia winced at the memory. "Bye-bye, now!" She waved and steered toward the house.

Inside, Margo took stock of her rumpled, sweaty look with only a curious glance. Of course, her appearance would be brought up later, at the perfect moment, when it could be used to tease Mia unmercifully.

In her room, Mia showered and got dressed with a smile on her face. Spending the afternoon flying a kite and being kissed in an empty field had not been on her to-do list for the day, but she wasn't unhappy either thing had happened. Ryan was different, new and alive.

"Some kind of wonderful," Mia said as she left the bedroom and went back to work more excited for their first date than she was before.

RYAN ADMIRED ARMSTRONG MEDICAL, one of the best hospitals specializing in child health care in the country. The glass-and-chrome design let sunlight in, and the large amount of foliage gave it a breath of life, making the open common space inviting. Even so, stepping through those doors had to be one of the scariest moments for children and their worried parents.

Ryan was proud to be one of the doctors who would do everything to ensure as many children as possible went home healthy. As he walked through the main corridor, someone played melodic tunes on a white baby grand piano that could be heard throughout the hospital.

Being the new, albeit temporary, attending pediatric doctor here, Ryan had seven new doctors who would be completing their residencies while he was here. He had completed his own specialty fellowship in cardiothoracic surgery in the pediatric field some time ago despite his relatively young age. Admittedly it was a tough job, and sometimes it affected him deeply. But still, there was no other place he would rather be.

When a child left the hospital with a chance at a full, long life, it outweighed anything else he might feel. He pushed away the dark thoughts of one patient that he could never forget, the pain it caused…

No. Don't think of that now.

After dropping his satchel in his office and pulling on his white coat, Ryan went to see his patients and find out how they'd fared overnight. Three of his residents were waiting by the nurses' station for him to arrive, like baby ducks lined up to follow their mama.

"Dr. Cassidy, here are your patient charts updated with last night's vitals, medication, and whether there were any issues." Dr. Carol Major handed him a stack of charts.

She was tenacious. Ryan worried her exuberance might lead to oversights when it came to patient care. All of the residents were young and new, keen to apply what they had learned in medical school. His troupe, as he called them, consisted of seven doctors with varying personalities he was still getting accustomed to.

"Thank you, Dr. Major." Ryan flipped the pages of the first chart. "Who was on last night?" He already knew but wanted them to be able to answer questions about each patient as they went through rounds.

"Dr. Sorenson, Dr. Major and Dr. Seale," Dr. Adams, another resident, spoke up. "Oh, and Dr. Yao."

Ryan frowned. "Dr. Major was supposed to be off. Dr. Finch had the night."

"I didn't mind," Dr. Major said quickly. "I wanted the extra hours to give me a chance to do more research and also work on patient care."

Ryan was disappointed. "Dr. Finch, could you have done the shift? You weren't tired or feeling ill, were you?"

"Sure, I could have done it," Dr. Finch replied.

"I set your schedule so that each of you

can get an adequate amount of sleep," Ryan explained. "I don't want tired residents dealing with patients and potentially hurting them in the process. If any of you switch around the schedule again without permission, I'm throwing you off my rotation. Is that understood?"

"Yes, Doctor," they all answered quickly.

"Dr. Major, please go home and sleep. You'll be on night rotation from now on."

"But, Dr. Cassidy, I'm fine. I had a nap in the break room and coffee—"

"This isn't a matter for discussion, Dr. Major. And since I will be down by one resident, Dr. Finch will handle your load today, and I want all charts finished before he leaves for the night. Understood?"

He pinned Dr. Finch with a steely gaze.

Dr. Finch nodded and kept silent.

"Good. Let's get going. Our patients are waiting," Ryan said.

Those words had the two remaining residents scrambling behind him as he went to the first room. He was promised leeway on how he managed the staff, so at one of their first meetings, he'd implemented the policy that all doctors give their residents adequate sleep and set up a schedule to suit this mandate. He also spoke to the residents and asked them to let him know if the new rules were not being followed.

It was late afternoon before Ryan sat down behind his desk to eat a sandwich from the cafeteria, while looking over test results on his computer.

Dr. Jackson, one of the other doctors at the hospital, poked his head around the door. "Got a minute?"

Ryan nodded. "What's up?"

He and Matthew Jackson had formed a fast friendship based on mutual respect and a similar determination to always do the absolute best. If there was a pair of hands he could trust on a delicate surgery, it was Dr. Jackson's. Ryan could see his natural talent at once. Matt was also a transplant, from Chicago, you could tell by the way he pronounced some of his words. He was tall, well over six feet, and joked that because of his height and skin color, which was akin to burnt umber, in his old neighborhood many assumed that Matt would play basketball and help the community financially. He loved the game, but it wasn't in his heart. He chose another way to give back, going into medicine. His career was his dream, and now he worked not only to pay off his student loans but to make sure a lot of his former friends and neighbors got good health care. When he wasn't at the hospital, he spent time at the community clinic he'd helped set up.

"I have this patient, six months old, heart murmur. Of course, their first doctor told them the opening would close on its own, but the baby isn't feeding well, and the breathing is labored." Matt came in and sat down. "He was brought here, and the echo shows a septal defect between the upper and lower chambers. It's a surgery, but the old doctor told them open-heart surgery would be too difficult for their son, and now they won't consider cardiac catheterization. The kid needs this to survive, but it's a no-go without consent."

"Show them the video of how straightforward it is. No big scar or open-heart op, and the baby can go home in a day or two after observation if everything goes according to plan."

"Sounds good, almost-new boss." Matt grinned, levering himself up out of the chair.

"You know there's a perfectly good buffet across the street that delivers." He pointed at Ryan's sandwich wrapper.

"Too much hassle. Besides, I go home to some scrumptious meals when I'm not working nights," Ryan answered. "Wait, since you've been here awhile, where's a good place for a first date?"

"Look at you, being all social in a matter of—what?—a week or so of being here?" Matt said jokingly.

"Might not be my best idea, but we'll see where it goes," Ryan said.

Matt frowned. "Why would dating in Charlotte be a bad thing?"

"Because I may not be staying. She has a thing about traveling, and I have my own baggage, literally and metaphorically," Ryan explained.

Matt looked at him. "So what you're saying is you like being Mr. Serious-and-All-Angsty-Doctor."

"What are you talking about?"

"Dr. Cassidy, you came into Armstrong all dark and broody." Matt lowered his voice and imitated Ryan. "Hi, all... I don't, uh, have much to say except glad to be here, and, um, looking forward to working with you."

Ryan glowered at him. "I do not sound like that."

"Oh yeah, you do, and I swear I saw five nurses in the unit make a note to heal your broken soul." Matt laughed. "So, who's the lucky one to get a first date?"

"That's not a thing, is it? About those nurses?" Ryan was skeptical but a little worried. "And none of them are my date, she's a certified accountant."

Matt didn't answer, he just grinned.

Ryan glanced at his screen and typed something quickly before redirecting the conversation.

"Do you have any real input on where I should take her to dinner, or are you here to just make me worry about the nurses in this hospital?"

"My man...take her to Heat Wave. It's a restaurant on top of this swanky hotel, roof-access elevators with bouncers to keep the riffraff out," Matt told him. "Nice beat, good food, and it's overlooking Charlotte."

"It's not all clubby, is it? Like you can't

talk over the music and people are dancing by our table?" Ryan asked with a frown.

Matt shook his head. "Nope, and they have this nice balcony with blue firelight and you can sip after-dinner drinks out there. When are you going?"

"Saturday."

"Let me hook you up. Around eight, I presume?"

"Exactly."

Matt gave him a thumbs-up. "I'm on it. I'll even get you a nice spot in the covered seating on the balcony, super intimate."

"Thanks," Ryan said gratefully. "I'll look it up online."

"So you can be assured it's not a club?" Matt teased.

"Yep."

"Where's the trust, my friend?"

Ryan laughed. "You can have it all after this date if it goes well and there's no thumping music and a packed crowd."

Matt smiled. "You'll see."

The door closed, and Ryan went back to his lunch and making notes on each of his patients. He also went through some new research to see if it could help his patients in any way. There would be a pediatric convention next year in Sweden to talk about advancements in his field. Ryan planned to go and wondered if Mia would go with him. *Would it be such a big step? Would they even be in touch then?* He hoped so. Though knowing her aversion to travel, was a simple trip like that even possible? They both had the means but would she feel as if it would change her life?

With that thought in mind, Ryan finished his lunch and returned to the patient floor. All the while, excitement and doubt surrounding Mia filled him, but he had to push that aside and do his job.

Yet each minute until the first date ticked by all too slowly, and he looked forward to it more than he realized. Loneliness was a cold enemy, and he had been steeped in its grasp for far too long.

CHAPTER FIVE

LATER, WHILE SITTING at his desk at the hospital, Ryan noticed some of the tension ease in his shoulders. That feeling of having to work twice as hard to prove he was a good doctor and not merely playing at it disappeared a little. None of the staff cared what his name was or what he'd achieved in the past so long as he could do the job in Charlotte. The hospital CEO was downright thrilled that he was able to procure a surgeon of Ryan's acclaim and add him to the roster of doctors.

While the chief of staff seemed impressed, the nurses still kept him on his toes if his instructions weren't crystal clear or his handwriting was illegible. It was fantastic just being able to work without the hospital bigwigs coming to him to be a spokesman to bring in large donations. Ryan had no problems with philanthropic endeavors, but in

Minneapolis he'd felt more like a cash cow than a physician.

Ryan listened to a research conference about pediatric valve replacement. This was what he'd signed up for, to care for people, and he relished even the routine tasks that came along with it.

The cell on his desk vibrated and danced across the wood. Ryan picked up the phone to see the image of the wild, windswept hair of his easily recognizable friend and long-time colleague. Mackenzie "Mac" Cromwell the third, was one of the most dynamic doctors that Ryan had ever met. Sometimes he was also called "Crumbs" because if there was the smallest donation, he could always make it stretch to do the most good for the most patients. He was also the vice president of Medicine Across the World and coordinated all the boots on the ground.

If Mac was calling, then something important was needed, but he could just as easily have sent a text knowing that Ryan would always reply.

"What's up, Mac?" Ryan asked in lieu of hello.

"Bro, not even a *good morning, afternoon*?

Nothing?" Mac's smooth Southern twang came through loud and clear. "How ya doing, Ryan?"

"Pretty good, trying to get a foothold here in the new job," Ryan answered.

"You planning on taking it?" Mac asked. "I never thought you'd leave MAW, man."

"I haven't taken anything yet, but even if I do, the stipulation will be in there for me to travel when needed." Ryan changed tack. "Now we've done with the pleasantries, what do you want?"

"Fine," Mac grumbled good-naturedly. "I need you to meet me in Turkey. We have a little girl with a pretty serious heart defect."

"Mac, I just got here, so this might be a tricky time for me to leave."

"I know, and I wouldn't call you if I didn't really *need* need you. You know how it is."

Ryan was torn. "Okay, send me the details, patient file, I mean everything, even blood work, so I can look it over on the flight."

"No problem. I knew you wouldn't say no," Mac said, sounding part grateful and part relieved.

"One of these days, I will," Ryan warned. "Oh…I forgot. I have a date this weekend."

"That's interesting. You're leaving the deep, dark, serious hideout to date?" Mac whistled. "It's the angry, somber doctor thing, isn't it?"

"Why does everyone think that?" Ryan asked in exasperation.

"Bro, you're like one of those chick flicks with the broken-but-brilliant hero." Mac chuckled but got serious quickly. "About the assignment, are you going to be okay with everything? We're at the same compound, close to Dena."

Ryan tasted the bitterness on his tongue. "Dena hates me for what happened, so I doubt I will be running into her."

"That wasn't anything you could control, Ryan," Mac said in his gruff yet gentle way. A beat or two passed before he spoke again. "So, tell me, who's the fine woman who has got you all shook up?"

"She's a full-time accountant and runs the B and B where I'm staying." Ryan brought the image of Mia to mind, and a smile slipped across his face. "She's very cute, doesn't give a hoot about the articles and write-ups about me. But the part of the no-madic life with Medicine Across the World bothers her."

"It's been important to you for a long time," Mac said. "Are you willing to give that up?"

"I don't know." Ryan ran his fingers through his hair. "This life, running on adrenaline like how we do when we're in dangerous parts of the world… How long can I do it, you know, before it's too much and I'm maybe burned out?"

"Well, that's the big question, isn't it, along with what it is you truly want?" Mac replied, his sweet, slow tone of voice making everything sound like it would be all right.

Ryan frowned. "Yeah, I guess so."

"You have a lot to think about. But in the meantime, when should I expect you?"

"It's Thursday. If I can get someone to cover for me until Monday morning, I can leave tonight," Ryan said. "But I need to be back ASAP, so no detours to other danger zones."

"Uh-huh. I'll send the linkup details."

"See you soon."

Ryan didn't trust Mac's innocent reply.

His colleague knew and relied on the fact that he would never leave a child's health in jeopardy if he could do something about it. Fair enough. His mind drifted back to what had happened the last time he'd visited a makeshift hospital to treat refugees and asylum seekers in Turkey.

You promised! You promised he would be okay, my little boy! I will never forgive you, not as long as there is breath in my body.

Those words echoed in his head and his lunch turned sour in his stomach.

Ryan stood, taking his white coat, and on his way out the door pulled it on. He went to see his boss. Thankfully, the chief of staff was willing to work with him to facilitate him taking the weekend for this humanitarian call. It was easy enough, since Friday and Saturday were his days off, and with Matt saying he would step in for him on Sunday, Ryan was clear to leave that night. The only thing left was to change plans with Mia when he got home. Ryan certainly wasn't looking forward to telling her they'd need to reschedule their first date.

That night when he walked into Ballad Inn, the scent of freshly baked pound cake caught his attention. Ryan's stomach rumbled. He still needed to grab a backpack and shove some clothes and travel documents into it before heading to the airport…

"Hey, Ryan, something wrong?"

Margo's voice brought him from his reverie.

"Uh, no, yes… I got caught up thinking about something," Ryan said in embarrassment. "Have you seen Mia?"

"In the kitchen, cutting strawberries for her slice of pound cake."

Ryan noted that she was wearing her scrubs and the colorful shoes that nurses usually wore that made hours on their feet as comfortable as possible.

"Heading to work?" Ryan asked.

"Yep, I have an eight to eight tonight," she replied.

Ryan stepped forward as she moved to grab her purse. "Okay, quick question. I have to reschedule the first date I planned with Mia. How will she take it?"

"Reason?"

"Gotta leave the country to help a baby with a major heart defect."

"Returning?"

"Monday, and we can go on our date the Friday after that." Ryan succinctly answered the questions fired at him.

Margo frowned. "Is this going to keep happening?"

"I don't know, and that's the honest truth," Ryan said. "It's not in my nature to put my personal needs above the responsibility for a child's life."

Margo looked over at him. "Of course not. Though, honestly, she's not going to be pleased. But explain about the tiny humans, and she'll cave. There isn't a baby that Mia hasn't tried to hold or snuggle with."

Ryan breathed out a sigh of relief. "Thanks for the input."

"Hey, Ryan," Margo said with her hand on the doorknob. "If you do find this is going to be happening all the time, let Mia know so she can make an informed choice. She has a thing about people bouncing in and out of her life. Don't start something that you can't finish."

"I feel like I want to finish any and everything with Mia but…" Ryan, worried, looked at Mia's sister. "That part of my life isn't something that can be put on the back burner, I'd expect Mia would just understand that."

"I get you but Mia has been put on the back burner all her life…for all of us." Margo sighed. "And here I'm torn because I see the change in her due to you and I have hope. But I don't want to see her heart broken, either."

"That's not my intent," Ryan said firmly. "Maybe this weekend away is a time for me to think things through."

"Maybe it is. Night, Ryan."

She said the words with a slight wave before she headed off. Ryan looked at the watch on his wrist, noting that his flight would be leaving at midnight. He made a beeline for the kitchen. Mia sat at the large island with a plate that held a large thick slice of cake, strawberries and whipped topping. He drank in everything about her while he stood at the door.

Mia wore an oversize lilac knit top over white leggings, and her feet were bare. He spotted the hot-pink toenail polish that belied the pale nude color on her fingernails. All that glorious thick hair was piled high on her head with a scrunchie, and she still wore her glasses. She was cute—*beautiful*, Ryan amended mentally. But right now, the no-makeup fresh face did it for him, stirring his attraction for her.

"That dessert looks almost as good as you," Ryan commented.

Mia turned to grin at him and took a large bite before speaking. "I could say the same thing about you."

"I would need actual proof of my own dessert to confirm the hypothesis." Ryan heard huskiness in his tone, that always seemed to happen when he was around her.

She cut a piece of her cake and held it out for him. Ryan took the forkful in his mouth, and his eyes never left her as he did.

"That's one," Mia said softly.

Ryan chewed and swallowed, then cupped his hand around the back of her neck and drew her to him. "Sufficiently proven to be yummy, now let's see how the two compare."

He kissed her, tasting the hint of strawberry and fresh whipped cream on her lips. The gentle sigh that escaped endeared Mia to him all the more. Ryan could see himself staying, taking the job at the hospital, making Charlotte his home and all just to be with her. That also terrified him, and he pulled away reluctantly.

He cleared his throat. "I can't pick which is sweeter."

"I'll take that as a compliment," Mia said, sounding encouraged. "Do you want dinner? Enid left some warming for you."

"In a minute. Mia… I have to reschedule our date." Ryan pulled the Band-Aid off with one clean swipe.

"Why, work?" Mia asked.

"Yes, but not at the hospital. I have to leave tonight for Turkey. There's a baby who needs my help," Ryan explained and then added quickly, "I'll be back Monday, and then we can have our date that Friday after?"

"Ah. The long distance rears its ugly head already," she murmured.

"Mia, this is something that's a part of who I am," Ryan said gently.

"And part of who I am is to not wait for anyone like I did for my parents for most of my life," Mia said coolly. "I just thought you had mentioned not traveling anymore."

"I said not as much as I used to," he pointed out. "This is an urgent case, and

I've done more of these surgeries than most doctors." Ryan touched her cheek. "This is me telling you that I'll be back sooner rather than later, and then we'll be on track again."

"Ryan, I don't want to get involved with you if you are always coming and going in and out of Charlotte at random moments." Mia spoke honestly, he knew. "I can't be someone who waits for their partner to come home. I've seen military spouses do it—some of them are my clients—and it's hard, too hard for me. I can't be the one trying to keep stability at home until the itch to travel hits, then watch you leave again."

"Mia, I am going to hopefully save a life, not heading off to party, and neither are those folks facing deployment," Ryan said, a bit irritated. "I'm not your parents."

"Did I say you were?" she snapped back at him, and stuck a spoonful of cream into her mouth. "But it's the adrenaline that you, that they, crave. I understand that you said it's a child, and you by all means must go help them. But I am also telling you my truth that I cannot be that person who just sits tight at home or hangs around waiting. While you're gone, maybe we should rethink this whole thing. You've only been here for a couple weeks and this moved so quickly..."

"Mia, part of building a relationship is traversing the bumps along the way."

"This is a really big bump," Mia countered. "Let's think on it and see where we are when you get back."

Ryan nodded. "I understand, but this spark that's growing between us won't be easily quelled. I don't know where we're going, but *I think* I'd like to find out."

Mia smiled sadly. "I guess you need to get on a flight, so maybe something to eat before you go?"

Ryan leaned in and pressed his forehead against hers. "I'll be back."

"You've got to do what you need to do," Mia said. "I am in awe of how you are willing to cross the world to save lives."

"Everyone deserves a chance at a healthy life," Ryan replied and watched her move around the spacious kitchen. "At the end of the day, if I can make one family smile, then I know I've done the right thing."

"I wish more people had that mindset, the world would be a better place." She set a plate of chicken and dumplings with the steam curling up gently in front of him. "Now eat, and when you get back, we'll know where we both stand."

Ryan hoped she was right and agreed. "Yeah... I guess so."

He left Ballad Inn later that night, a quick shower and a kiss goodbye to Mia that felt almost like an ending. He thought of their conversation as he headed for the airport. Was he lying by saying these types of occurrences would be few and far between?

Patients, especially children, were essential to Ryan. Using his skills and knowledge however and whenever gave him purpose. But he was tired, emotionally and physically, and even now, he felt the weight of the previous years when his own life had also been on the line settle heavily on his shoulders.

Maybe it was time for a change.

"THAT WAS THE tiniest little heart." Ryan leaned back in his chair in Mac's makeshift office with a satisfied smile on his face. "You wouldn't have believed it, Mac, and after the surgery, the blood was going exactly where it needed to. It was beating like a champ. Her pulse ox is already up past eighty percent and rising."

"How long before she'll need another surgery?" Mac asked, sitting across from him. His unruly hair was pulled back into a short ponytail of dark blond curls. The same color highlighted his beard.

"When she's two, likely, and again when she's five and so forth," Ryan answered. "Until I can take a patch of graphing vein from her leg to fix the defect permanently. What's her living situation looking like?"

"The father was killed, so it's just her and her mother. We've got the lawyers working on asylum papers to get her into the US," Mac explained. "Her husband was working with American troops and was killed for it. Right now, she has a small house on our compound, but when I leave, they'll be coming with me."

Ryan almost choked on his beer. "Wait, what? You always keep your work separate from the people you help. You said it was survival, remember?"

"She reminds me of my little sister," Mac said. "My mom is already attached to both of them, they've spoken so much over video link. So, we're going to be their sponsor family."

Ryan went over to him and clapped him on the shoulder. "That's good, man. Imagine you, having a heart three sizes too big."

"That's called an enlarged heart, and it will eventually kill me," Mac retorted.

Ryan laughed. "You have a strange sense of humor."

"Me?"

The doctors, nurses and tech specialists were in a protected compound within a small village in Turkey, located close to the border with Syria. This was where the compact but critical hospital was established out of necessity. Of course, Turkey had its own infrastructure, but the medical compound dealt with many wounded refugees that came across the border hoping to find aid and relief.

Relatively speaking this was safe territory, but nowhere was without its dangers, so there was a security team on-site made up of veterans who'd signed on to work with the doctors' organization. Medics and other staff could also carry weapons to defend themselves if necessary. Ryan hated it but understood it.

He grabbed his backpack from the chair. "I need to go outside the compound for a little while."

"Bro, I know you can blend in with the tourists and all, but if bad guys catch wind of your credentials, you are a big ol' target," Mac said worriedly.

"I get it." Ryan nodded. "Leaving my stuff here, taking my passport, nothing more."

Mac reached into his own bag and pulled out what looked like a walkie-talkie. "Take a sat phone. Don't leave anything to chance."

"If I'm not back in two hours, you can send out the search party," he told him.

Mac leaned back. "To where exactly?"

"I got a line on where Dena lives and it's close by. I want to go see her and try to apologize again."

"Listen, Ryan, you couldn't fix it. I don't care how good of a surgeon you are," Mac said, a hint of frustration in his words. "That heart was too weak and couldn't even hold a graph."

"Let me do this, okay?" he pleaded. "For my peace of mind and to close the book on the past." Ryan took out his phone and texted Mac a link. "That's where I'll be."

Mac pointed at him. "Two hours max, or I send the guys to get you."

With a mock salute, Ryan left the cramped office and exited the compound through the central gates. The disapproving looks of the security guys followed him until he rounded the corner. Even at night the small market nearby was filled with life. The smell of searing meat and spices filled the air while merchants tried to offer him everything from textiles to fresh vegetables.

Buying four silk scarves for the ladies at Ballad Inn and some fruit and skewers of meat for the group of little boys sitting on the corner made him smile for a second.

The apartment he was looking for was over a food store three streets from where he'd started. The gate to the apartment was at the side of the building. There was a small bell and he pushed it, his heart pounding. He braced himself for the hate that would come from a mourning mother. Dena opened the door, her dark hair long and flowing down her back and her skin a darker olive than he remembered. In her arms was a baby girl.

Dena's eyes widened when she saw who stood at her door.

"Dena," Ryan said gently, "how are you?"

"Dr. Cassidy... Ryan, why are you here?" Dena asked, her voice monotone, holding no emotion.

He tried to smile. "It's been three years. I, um, came in to see a patient and hoped we could talk."

"Talk," she said, making no move to let him inside.

"I'm so sorry about Amir." Ryan's voice broke as he said the words. "I was trying to save him—"

"And instead, you took the last few months of his life from me," Dena finished for him.

"That was not my intent."

"Go back to where you came from, Ryan. You'll find no forgiveness here."

"I understand."

Ryan gave a stiff nod, and his eyes turned to the little girl with big dark irises staring at him. He saw some of the symptoms of Dena's first child, like low weight, a sickly pallor and listlessness as she lay her head on her mother's shoulder.

"She has the same defect as Amir, doesn't

she?" Ryan looked at Dena. "You should take her to the clinic—"

"For what? So that I may never see her again?" Dena asked angrily. "I will never go where you are, Ryan, never again."

He grabbed the gate between them and pleaded, "Dena, take her to the clinic. I won't be there, I swear. I'm leaving tonight. Please let someone look at her."

Dena shook her head adamantly. "I will do no such thing. I will not lose a second child to some other doctor full of pride and swagger."

With that she closed the door forcefully and left him standing on the street. He wanted to knock again and argue more, but he knew Dena wouldn't listen. Losing a child had to be too much to bear. All he could hope was that she'd admit her daughter needed medical intervention and would get treatment for her.

Ryan got back to the compound and went directly to Mac's quarters. Ryan rarely drank, but he needed a second beer at that point. Mac was there, and Ryan sat down with him to tell him about Dena's daughter and to keep an eye out in case Dena changed her mind about seeking care for her child.

Knowing that the flight back would be hard and he'd be dealing with serious jet lag because of the quick turnaround, Ryan finished his drink and opted to find a bed for a few hours' sleep.

"Okay, I'm going to crash, leaving my small patient in your fine care. I'm heading home in a few hours." Ryan put his hands on the table and stood up.

"Oh no." Mac got out a bottle of tequila and placed it on the table. "This is our goodbye night. Who knows when I will see you again."

Ryan shook his head. "Didn't we do this when I left Colombia?"

"But this is our *goodbye* goodbye." Mac poured two shots.

"Sure, until you call me again."

Mac covered his heart. "Would I do that?"

"Sure, you do it all the time, and this conversation is exactly like the other *goodbyes*," Ryan said accusingly and made air quotes.

"Just enjoy." Mac slid the glass over. "What could one shot hurt?"

"This is déjà vu."

"No, this is the good tequila."

One shot—that was all he had—but still he ended up being at that table longer with Mac. They laughed and talked, with Ryan telling him how excellent Charlotte and Mia were.

The mood changed instantly when someone knocked lightly on the door and entered. Ryan saw his friend's smile fade, and he turned to see who had joined them. Paula came forward. Their eyes connected. Brunette hair, still thick but cut at the shoulders now, and, as always, dressed as part doctor, part Indiana Jones. Looking at her, Ryan felt nothing, wondered how he had ever thought she could love him when there was nothing but cold darkness in her eyes.

"When did she get here?" Ryan asked Mac.

"She wasn't supposed to come in until well after you were gone," Mac said. "We needed another pair of safe hands and she volunteered."

"Ryan, it's good to see you." Paula's greeting was warm but then, of course, she goaded him. "I thought you'd retired from this type of work and settled for a country practice or something smaller?"

"Mac needed the best for a hard case, so he called me," Ryan answered, not rising to the bait but seeing his response hit the mark.

"That means we can catch up." She put her hand on his shoulder, and Ryan moved away. "You know how much fun we always had reliving old times."

"Um, no, I don't, and we won't," he replied. "On that note, Mac, I'm going to get some sleep before I head home to Charlotte."

"Charlotte?" Paula's smile was more of a sneer. "So you've moved on and got yourself a pretty little domestic setup?"

Ryan laughed, not bothering to correct Paula. He'd let her believe what she wanted. "Paula, you just wouldn't understand genuine goodness and beauty that shines from within."

Mac smothered a guffaw somewhat unsuccessfully.

Ryan was about to leave when his cell buzzed in his pocket. A FaceTime call from Mia! He forgot Paula was even there when he eagerly connected with the amazing innkeeper.

"Hey, Mia!" Ryan waved.

"Hi. I thought you'd still be up since it's

about two here. How did the surgery go?" She furrowed her brows. "It sounds so loud. Are you on the street?"

"I'm in the doctors' compound. It's close to a busy town. The surgery went well. I'm heading to the airport in a few hours, hitching a ride on an evac flight, then when I get to the airport, a regular flight home."

"Oh, that's good. I was worried about you." Mia smiled shyly. "Kind of missing you around here."

"See, I'm growing on you." Ryan smiled wide.

"Hi, Mia! We're just here, hanging out, having a few rounds of tequila!" Paula popped up behind him, putting her chin on his shoulder and smiling into the camera.

Ryan shifted away, scowling at Paula before turning back to the video call. Of course, he saw the change in Mia's face, a combination of hurt and anger.

"Who was that?" Mia's tone was crisp.

"That was Paula… She's a colleague, who's making a nuisance of herself," Ryan said firmly and added quickly, "Mac is here, too."

He turned the phone, and Mac waved. "Hey, Mia, nice to meet you."

That didn't make Mia look any happier.

"I see. Well, I'll let you get back to your… friends," Mia said stiffly. "So happy the surgery went well that you could go out and celebrate."

"It's not like that, Mia." His tone was low while his irritation at Paula rose.

"You don't have to explain to me, remember? We're in the process of evaluating things," she replied.

"This isn't even an issue. Paula is a—"

Mia disconnected the call, and Ryan pocketed the phone.

"Oh no, did I cause trouble?" Paula asked sweetly.

"I don't understand you," Ryan said in frustration. "But the thing is, I can go home and talk to Mia to fix this while you, Paula, you will always be you, unless you can do something about that."

"I hate you, Ryan." Paula said the words, but her lips barely moved.

He turned away, deftly ignoring her. "See you around, Mac."

"I'll walk with you. The company in here isn't to my liking." Mac stood. "You can finish the tequila, Paula."

"Sorry about that, man," Mac said when they were outside. "She is a good doctor but not the coolest person."

"That's being nice about it," Ryan murmured. He embraced Mac. "I'm going to grab my stuff and head over to the evac site. Love you, bro. Hopefully no more emergencies for a good, long while, and definitely none if she's involved."

"Love you, too, Ry. Get home safe and let me know if you fixed things with Mia."

"Plan on it," Ryan called over his shoulder as he walked away.

Ryan knew he would have to explain to Mia about Paula and hoped she hadn't chucked his stuff out on the front lawn. They hadn't even got to a first date before a nasty ex threw a wrench into something very new. Ryan trusted that he could get Mia to see Paula for who she really was.

He headed off to Charlotte with only Mia on his mind.

CHAPTER SIX

MIA SPENT THE NIGHT, then most of the following day, silently steaming about that disaster of a video call with Ryan. It seemed her perception of him being a playboy doctor might have been correct, or at least the fact that his life choices were an adrenaline high for him. Either way, attraction or not, Mia didn't want to be on the receiving end of that chaos. She'd lived it and been hurt by it before.

There was a knock on her office door, and Ryan stuck his head into the room. "Hey, can we talk?"

"Sure. Something wrong with your room?" Mia kept her voice light even as her heart beat faster. How could she be a woman with practical common sense and have reactions like these to a man like that?

"Come on, you know that's not it." Ryan

came in and closed the door. "It's about us, Mia."

She put her pen down and remained seated behind her desk. "Ryan, why do you want this? We're so different. You like to travel, and I'm happy in Charlotte. I'm not going to suddenly be okay with your jumping into danger whenever you need to."

"Mia, that's not going to happen," he said.

She gave him a look. "It literally just did, Ryan. I tried to change myself for people more than once, to make them happy, and then I wasn't. I'm not doing it anymore."

Ryan looked confused. "So you're willing to give up on something that could be great because of uncertainty?"

"No, I'm not willing to cry or deal with heartbreak," Mia said firmly. "I like you, Ryan, I really do, but not at the expense of my happiness or yours. I wouldn't want you to change for me, either."

Ryan turned to leave and stopped with his hand on the doorknob. "Mia, this could be something real forming between us."

"Paula might not be too happy about that." Mia couldn't help herself. She was hurting from that video call.

"Paula is…" Ryan paused and grinned. "You know what, if you want to know about Paula, say yes to our date."

"That's not how it works, Ryan."

"But you're curious, so say yes." He gave her a quick smile and left.

"Curiosity killed the cat!" she called after his retreating form.

"Tell that to Doodle!"

"He's right, that cat's a survivor," she muttered.

Micki appeared next. "Just go on the date. You want to know and so do I."

"Were you snooping?" Mia demanded.

Micki made a face. "Of course, like, you know me, duh."

AFTER TWO DAYS of beating around the bush, Mia did say yes to the date but first she got more insight into his life and Paula. They were never a couple: Paula may have wanted it, but Mia could tell by his words and body language he hadn't been interested.

What really made him more endearing was the story of Dena and the loss of her child. She could still see that it affected him, not because of how the mother blamed him but the guilt he felt for losing a child in his care.

"So when you went to see her, she wouldn't accept an apology," Mia summarized as they talked.

It was late evening in the Sardis neighborhood, and the fireflies had finally started to grace the darkness with their tiny glow. At night the smell of the flowers and honeysuckle filled the air, with just a hint of chill. It was beautiful, quiet, peaceful and one of the things she loved the most about where the family house stood. Barely any traffic came through their streets at night; occasionally there was a couple taking an evening walk with pets, and the older residents used this time for an after-dinner stroll.

She and Ryan sat on the swing that faced the landscaped backyard of Ballad Inn. He moved the rocker lazily with his feet as they shared.

"Yes, but with her daughter, you can see the same symptoms easily." Ryan looked frustrated. "Now she won't even consider taking the baby to the clinic in the compound. The girl has to be a little over one, and her body would handle the surgery much better than Amir, who was a little over two months old and so very weak already."

Mia gentled her voice. "I hear you listing all the medical logic, but you still blame yourself for something you couldn't control."

Ryan smiled sadly. "That's true of every doctor, those losses stick with you, and it was worse because I cared for Dena and Amir like family. Now she looks at me with disgust."

She took his hand and squeezed it. "Ryan, she is hurting, and I know you understand that, but you are, too, and it's clear that you did your best for Amir."

"Maybe one day I'll let myself believe that." She felt Ryan run his thumb across the soft skin of her knuckle. "But you know what would make me feel better?"

"What?"

"Going on the date we had planned," Ryan proclaimed.

Mia felt her lips twitch with a smile. "Oh, that's playing dirty, sir."

He kissed the tip of her nose. "I know."

That was what led to her getting ready for her first date with a man who made the butterflies take flight in her stomach with one look. Mia stared at herself in the mirror, aghast at what she saw. Why had she tried on Micki's super-revealing "dress," which was more like handkerchiefs and duct tape? A knock came at her door, and Margo opened it without waiting for Mia to answer.

"Wow! What are you wearing?" she cried out and closed the door quickly.

"It's Micki's dress." Mia couldn't stop staring at herself. "I—I think we should burn it."

"Put it in the dustbin and I'll get the match!" Margo exclaimed. "Unless it's what you want. Then you do you, baby girl."

Mia hurriedly took the dress off. "I'd like to not give the neighborhood a reason to call me a nearly naked spinster. We need to go through our dear sister's closet."

"Good point. I'm in," Margo said jokingly. "Did you forgive him after the whole thing with his ex popping up on the FaceTime call?"

"There was nothing to forgive," Mia said. "It's not like Ryan and I were a hot and heavy couple, and he came back and we had a good talk. He explained that she was just being a jerk."

"You wanted to tell her off, didn't you?" Margo teased.

Mia flashed a devilish grin at her sister. "Oh yes, I did. She had that sexy adventurer look with a sheen of sweat and dark hair that she probably braids and holds a blade in while she does kung fu."

"Well, you have that regal, classic gorgeousness going on," Margo complimented her. "She has nothing on you, that's why Ryan looks agog whenever you pass by."

"He kissed me in a tree a few days ago and then in Crawford's Field." Mia pressed her hand against her chest. "I think my heart melted."

"Then they are some fine kisses." Her sister sat on the bed. "Until Micki set the hose on you two."

"I still owe her for that." Mia analyzed the contents of her closet, hanger by hanger. "What should I wear that says *I like you, but I still have my doubts*?"

Margo pointed. "The soft yellow one, with the black belt and the yellow heels."

"Hair?"

"Leave it down. It looks fun and carefree," her sister answered.

"As opposed to my usual uptight self?" Mia felt a bit offended.

Margo stood and hugged her. "As opposed to all the stuff you take on here. You deserve a night out. Get dressed. Your date will be here soon."

"Here? He already stays here."

Margo's only answer was a light laugh when she left the room. Mia soon knew what she meant when she went downstairs and the doorbell chimed merrily. When she opened the door, Ryan stood there with a charming smile, holding a bouquet of real flowers. This time he wore gray slacks with a light blue shirt and a tie. It was a completely different look to his usual T-shirt-and-jeans motif.

"Hi," he said with a warm grin. "May I come in?"

Mia chuckled. "Hello, and yes, you may."

When he stepped inside, Enid temporarily blinded them with a flash from a camera.

"What the— Where did you get that thing? Don't you have a phone?" Mia asked, blinking, trying to clear her eyes of the bright light.

"Those things are complicated. My camera will be just fine," Enid said. "Now pose, Mia. You didn't go to prom in the end, and I have been waiting forever for a nice pic of you with a gentleman caller at your side."

"Gentleman caller?" Mia blinked at Enid.

"How about we go with it?" Ryan shrugged. "I never went to prom, either."

He stood behind her and wrapped his arms around her waist, and Enid took more pictures. All the while Mia was very aware of the man who held her. Then Enid pulled out a second roll of film.

"Okay, Enid, it's time for us to go. Bye-bye." Mia had to stop the impromptu photo shoot because they'd never leave otherwise.

"I didn't even know they still made regular film for cameras," Ryan said as he opened the door.

"Right! But it's Enid. She refuses to go quietly into the modern age." Mia stepped out onto the veranda.

Ryan laughed, and Mia found she loved the rich, deep sound.

"May I add you look drop-dead gorgeous?"

"It's the dress," Mia said quickly.

He bent his head to her ear while opening the car door. "It's the woman wearing it."

His breath was so close to her ear it made her shiver pleasantly. Mia started to relax as she settled herself into the comfortable leather seat of his Land Rover and put on her seat belt. Ryan got in beside her and sent another warm smile her way before starting the vehicle and maneuvering it down the long drive of Ballad Inn.

"So tell me about Charlotte," Ryan said conversationally. "Growing up here had to be fun."

Mia looked out the window as he drove down the I-77 heading toward Uptown Charlotte.

"It's changed a lot. Uptown has gone from this little area where people could go on Saturday nights to being called Little New York," she explained. "The skyline is beautiful."

"I've seen it on my drive on the John Belk Freeway. You almost want to stop and just marvel," he said. "But that wouldn't be good driving, now, would it?" He laughed. "Have you seen how some folks drive when it rains? Like, what's that about?" he said.

"There is always a boost in accidents when it rains."

She chortled. "Wait until it snows, or at least our version of it, which is like three snowflakes and an ice cube. People go into the stores and buy all the bread, milk and meat. It's like they're stocking up for the apocalypse."

He nodded. "I look forward to the experience."

Ryan deftly maneuvered the Land Rover around the exit that would take them uptown. Finally they hit McDowell Street and stopped outside the swanky hotel known for its rooftop restaurant. Ryan helped Mia out of the car before passing the keys to the valet.

With his hand on the small of her back, he escorted her inside, where two very large men watched over the elevators that would take them up to the fancy restaurant.

"Is your name on the guest list?" one of the pair asked Ryan, looking at the tablet in his hand.

"It should be. Dr. Ryan Cassidy, reservation for two," Ryan answered. "Or I hope it's there... Someone made the reservation for me."

The stern face of the bouncer turned upward into a smile, and he hit the button to open the elevator. "You were right on the top. Welcome. They are waiting for you upstairs."

"Thank you." Ryan smiled as he and Mia stepped inside.

The bouncer grabbed the door before it could close. "Hold it."

His action made Mia jump, and a small squeak escaped her lips.

"Your VIP card." The bouncer handed him a sleek matte black card with gold lettering and flames. "Use it anytime you're coming in. No reservation, no waiting."

Ryan took it. "Thanks, man. I appreciate it."

The elevator door closed before Mia asked, "Who do you know that got you instant VIP status?"

"A doctor at the hospital. Apparently he has his fingers on the pulse of Charlotte." Ryan pulled out his wallet and slipped the card inside. "I now owe him and think we're best friends."

Mia's laughter was soft and clear, and Ryan took her hand as the elevator opened up to reveal the restaurant. Her mouth dropped open: it was more extravagant than she could've possibly imagined. The black and gold on the card seemed to be the decor of choice. Each table had a gold candle holder on a black tablecloth. Even the plates and utensils carried the contemporary look. The view took her breath away, the Bank of America building lit up in soft pink for Couple Appreciation Month. Beyond that was a new apartment high-rise, and its lights danced.

"Dr. Cassidy, welcome to Heat Wave," one of the hostesses said, and yes, she was dressed in black and gold. "Follow me to your table."

"See that building to the left?" Mia pointed it out to Ryan.

"Mmm-hmm, the one with the dancing lights?"

She nodded. "Yep, that one. The lights are in bars. So when you touch any of them, they play a different tune you can hear, and the lights on the building move to the music."

"That's pretty cool," Ryan said as they trailed the hostess.

Their table was right at the window so they could enjoy the view, and after they were seated, the hostess handed them drink menus.

"I don't drink alcohol so... Oooh, they have Ghia aperitif," Mia said approvingly. "I think I'll have that with a dash of extra bitters and tonic water."

Ryan gave her a curious look. "How are you the only woman I know that appreciates Ghia?"

"So this is a true story. I was dating this guy—"

"Already hate this story."

Mia snorted. "Are you going to listen or not?"

"Fine, but he better not be more handsome than me," Ryan retorted.

"Trust me, he was not." She was amused. "Anyway, he decided he was going to take me to a cigar bar in Matthews where they serve exclusive drinks. He wanted to impress me, and it went horribly wrong. He couldn't take a sip of Ghia without grimacing, and I found I had a taste for it. He ended up leaving because he couldn't handle it. Sad, really."

"That's how they serve it in the Mediterranean and Middle Eastern countries," Ryan said matter-of-factly.

"Exactly!" Mia exclaimed. "That's what the hostess said. I showed him up. I ended up talking to the hostess all night and trying some of the best nonalcoholic beverages in the world. She'd just moved here from the south of France."

"Ah, fragile masculinity at its best," Ryan murmured.

"Good evening. I'll be your server for tonight. May I take your drink order?" a young man asked.

"Yes, two Ghias over ice with tonic water, a dash of extra bitters, please," Ryan replied.

"Very unusual, but good choice, sir," the server said and left them.

"Look at us, setting trends." Ryan grinned.

"So does that mean your man vibes are not intimidated by the fact that I won't be ordering a mojito or a pinot noir?" Mia smiled.

Ryan took her hand and kissed it. "Absolutely not. It makes you more intriguing."

Their drinks arrived, and Mia rolled the deep, fruity taste across her tongue. Her breath caught just when she caught Ryan staring at her with a sparkle in his eyes. *You've got to stop doing that.* She shifted slightly as a warmth spread through her from his gaze.

"Mia... Earth to Mia," Ryan said with a smile, bringing her back to their conversation. "I lost you there for a minute. Was I boring you?"

"Not at all. My mind wandered to other things." Mia took a quick sip of her drink.

Ryan's eyes met hers. "Good things, I hope."

She smiled. "Depends if this leads to a second date or not."

"I look forward to making any of those thoughts a reality." His tone was sweet, implying the start of a special type of romance.

"So, Paula..." Mia brought the subject up again. She didn't know the whole story but couldn't help being intrigued.

Ryan answered easily, "She likes the adventure, pushing the envelope, and the patients always take second place. At first, it was exciting, but then I got to know her, and when she figured out that I wasn't the type to fall under her charm and sign my fealty over to her, she really showed her true colors. It became her mission to undermine me and hurt me professionally."

"Did she?" Mia questioned.

"Not in the least. People know my credentials and the type of person I am," Ryan replied. "I let it roll off my back and did the job I was there to do. Paula saw I wasn't fazed and tried to be 'friends' again with apologies and a lot of fake tears. I was done and grateful to her for finally being so honest about herself and the truth."

Mia looked at him aghast. "This is some deep dive into soap-opera drama stuff."

"You're telling me." Ryan had a sip of his drink. "This is nice, being here with you, but I have my phone notifications on, so I'll just be having this and ordering a water if that's okay."

"That's just fine with me," Mia replied. "I was thinking of a cranberry punch for a hint of tart with dinner."

"Another thing we have in common. Good heads on our shoulders." Ryan raised his drink in a toast.

Mia lifted her glass. "Here's to first dates and so far this is one of the best I've had."

"Me, too." Ryan clinked his tumbler with hers. "Cheers."

For an appetizer, the grilled oysters with Parmesan pesto was divine. Mia would never tell Margo how delicious they were because her sister would then go on an obsessive tear to re-create them. She and Ryan decided to share a special bone-in rib eye with caramelized bacon, brussels sprouts and Thai lobster fried rice. Mia found out that besides liking the same foods and beverages, he also loved books, and that they shared some of the same favorite authors and classic movies.

"Confession time," Ryan said, spearing another brussels sprout with his fork. "I love old B movies, or the horror ones, like *Attack of the Killer Tomatoes.*"

"Or *The Blob!*" Mia said excitedly. "Oh, I have the entire collection of them."

"What's your favorite Hitchcock?"

"The Birds!" they said simultaneously and laughed.

"Favorite noir mystery?" Mia countered.

"The Maltese Falcon," Ryan answered automatically. "You?"

"The very same." She smiled at him. "I think we have a classic-movie night coming up for us."

Ryan grinned. "Does that mean there's a second date? Have I charmed you with my personality?"

"Maybe. But yes, there will be a second, and maybe even a third date." Mia hesitated before asking, "Why Charlotte, the move, the new job, if there is a wing literally named after you at the hospital you were at before?"

Ryan took a drink and then paused. "I left because yes, the wing was named after me, but I was becoming too jaded at my job. All I was seeing was sadness and tragic loss in the ER, and when I traveled with Medicine Across the World, it only showed the disparities in care even more."

"Is that burnout? I hear it can be bad, especially for doctors who travel extensively doing volunteer work." This time, Mia took his hand. She couldn't help but be worried about him almost instantly.

"Kind of. No matter what anyone did

where I was on assignment, there was always an ongoing crisis for health care and supplies," Ryan told her. "I can say that at least I helped set up one hospital that's run well where people can get the treatment they need without having to worry about paying. Good doctors are there and some positive change is going on."

"That's a good thing." Mia caressed the skin over his knuckles, trying to offer a little comfort.

"It is." Ryan smiled sadly. "But then coming home, after seeing such despair, and dealing with the trauma of people hurting each other, overdoses, accidents or just reckless behavior, and I couldn't do it anymore. I needed a change of air, to breathe. And from the first scent of Charlotte air and the honeysuckle of Ballad Inn, I kinda felt like I was home."

"Are you planning on traveling again?" Mia asked bluntly. "I mean for Medicine Across the World."

"In all honesty, I want to try not to. It's like you said, burnout. Maybe it's partially PTSD that stems from all I've seen and had to live through." He smiled, and she loved the little wrinkles around his eyes when he did. "Between you and me, I'm seriously considering the job here if it's offered to me on a permanent basis."

"I'm glad you're staying put," she said firmly.

"Would you worry?"

"Very much so."

"Then, I hope that I'm staying close to home as well."

They shared a secret smile before Ryan paid the bill. Their leftovers were bagged up for them to take home. He carried the package while they strolled outside to the balcony that overlooked the Charlotte skyline. Two after-dinner coffees were brought to them, and they sat together in a wide wicker cabana with white cushions. His body was close enough she could feel the warmth of him, and Mia had to admit she wanted to get closer to Ryan.

It was funny: she went from being happy not dating to wanting to explore the feelings he elicited. But she was still hesitant since she could get involved so quickly. And if she put her heart on the line, it might get broken. He wasn't her version of safe or rooted like she was. He could just leave at a moment's notice, take off for a new life anywhere.

"This is nice." Ryan laced their fingers together. "Thank you for coming out with me."

"I'm enjoying your company." Mia smiled at him and saw a flicker of something in his eyes, something that made promises she hoped he could keep.

"Oh, don't do that," he groaned. "That gentle look in your eyes made me think of kissing you."

"You don't hear me saying no," Mia answered in a voice low and soft. Ryan kissed her and Mia longed to give in to the sensation of love trying to pull her under its sweet waves. Was she being whimsical, believing in Prince Charming and those fairy tales she used to tell her sisters at night? Would reality enter and break her heart like it always did? Mia needed to hold on to her wits and be practical…didn't she?

She'd been jaded about the magic of falling in love. The main reason being all those not-so-happy endings she saw in her life. But his kiss drew her into thinking of the possibility again. Ryan could be the one that made her forget the past and follow him into the future without hesitation. There were still barriers, but maybe they could overcome them. Mia began to hope in earnest, something she hadn't done in a very long time.

Ryan broke the kiss and pressed his forehead against hers. "Mia, the things you make me feel… Why does my heart soar when you're around?"

"I know," she whispered. "I haven't felt anything like this, and it's terrifying."

"What do we do, Mia?" His eyes implored her for answers. "We both have aspects of our lives that are important to us and clash. At some point something has got to give."

"That's why we are taking it slow," she replied.

Ryan cupped her cheeks. "*Slow* doesn't mean the way I feel will ever go away. I find myself wanting to know everything about you and that's an anchor in itself."

"Th-that keeps you someplace you don't want to be?" Mia asked, unsure. "Would you resent what you feel for me, if you stayed?"

He shook his head slowly. "No, I could never feel like that, but the consequences

are the unknown factor. Remember relationship kryptonite."

Mia sighed. "One step forward, two steps
back."

"Come 'ere. We should take a picture together." Ryan pulled out his phone.

"Selfies?" Mia chuckled. "We go from a
serious talk to taking photos in the blink of
an eye. Enid is rubbing off on you."

"I want to memorialize our first date," he
replied.

With a quick snap, the moment was frozen
in time, and Mia felt her phone vibrate in her
purse and knew he'd sent her the picture.

They continued to enjoy the ambience and
being on top of the world, at least, from this
spot in the city, talking about a bit of everything before the bubble burst and they
resumed their regular lives. It was almost
midnight when they finally stood outside
the door of Ballad Inn.

"Should I kiss you good-night at the door
or at the stairs?" Ryan teased.

"If you kiss me at the stairs, we'll have an
audience," she answered.

"Very true. Enid and that camera might
be lurking around."

"I sure don't need her showing everyone in the neighborhood a picture of us kissing." Mia laughed.

"Good point." Ryan drew her close. "A kiss at the door it is."

He pressed his lips to hers and held Mia in his arms where she felt safe and secure—something that she'd mostly had to create for herself ever since she was young. He made her feel special, wanted, and in such a short time. It seemed as if he had always been in her life. They held hands, walking up the stairs, until he had to stop at the third floor, and she would go on up to her room. As he moved away, their hands slowly parted until only their fingertips touched, and then the intimate connection was broken.

Mia watched him go into his room, and hesitated on the step, realizing she was staring at the closed door. Passing the mirror, she looked at herself: hair wild and free, lips curved in a soft smile, there was a gleam in her eyes she'd never seen before. In any book she'd read where the hero and heroine connected within days or hours, Mia always had a sense of skepticism because it happened all too quickly. But now, as she gazed

at her own reflection and touched her lips,
she wondered… Could it be she was falling
in love? Would it be her downfall?

CHAPTER SEVEN

"OKAY, SO WHAT'S Sardis Woods Alive again?" Ryan asked, as Mia parked her car. Two weeks after their night out, he and Mia were forming a bond that Ryan relished watching grow between them.

He felt a bit folded or squashed into her car, but he wouldn't want to be anywhere else. It was easy to see the streets blocked off by blue barriers, hear the music from large speakers, the tents and food trucks, plus kids' games. But knowing exactly why and what it was all about was another thing.

"It's our summer festival, where the town helps promote artists and small businesses in the area," Mia explained. She kicked off her sandals before grabbing socks and sneakers from the back seat and slipping them on quickly.

"Am I missing something? Do I need better footwear?" Curiosity made him wonder as he studied her.

"No, this is just me. I'm meeting my sisters later for a thing," Mia answered. "Anyway, the breweries have outside seating. Then there are games and a mini carnival for the kids. Artist Alley, where people can showcase their crafts. It's a lot of fun, and it gets bigger every year."

Ryan noticed that she pulled two pairs of roller skates out of the small trunk of the car and held them up.

"They built an old-style rink for the die-hard retro skaters like me."

"Now, that's another thing I didn't know about you."

Mia winked. "I can't tell you everything all at once. It's nice to be surprised."

Ryan pulled his sunglasses down to shade the bright Sunday afternoon. He understood now why they called it Carolina blue. The sky had zero clouds and was simply dazzling.

"Okay, is there funnel cake?" Ryan asked, rubbing his hands together, eager for a sweet treat.

"There is the best ever, and it's served with

Georgia peach compote and powdered sugar," she replied.

"It's official. I love this town," he said with affection and then asked, "Quick question, how are you okay to be roller-skating in a dress? I mean, it looks like you'll be hot in a matter of minutes. Not that you're not cute as all get-out in it."

"Great catch," she said dryly. "But wait, there's more."

Mia was wearing a simple white denim wrap dress, and he looked at her intently when she worked at the tie at the waist. The material parted to showcase a yellow retro Roller Derby shirt and shorts with white trim to match. It went with her socks and white sneakers, and with her thick pigtails. Now Mia went beyond cute to drop-dead gorgeous.

"Have mercy," he managed to say.

She did a twirl. "Classic Roller Derby style."

"On one hand, I want to buy you this outfit in various colors." Ryan took the skates. "On the other, I want to put on a T-shirt with *Security* across the front and tackle everyone that notices you."

"Sounds like a conundrum," Mia teased.

"Don't worry, big guy. I only have eyes for you."

"So now my ego is all puffed up," he said with a hint of pride.

"Silly."

Ryan was sure this was what he had been missing. The small-town feel of community that came with living in Sardis and being a part of Charlotte. It certainly was enhanced by having Mia at his side and enjoying the very first street fair of his life. Of course, state fairs were all around Minneapolis, and everywhere in the United States, but no woman he had previously dated would ever go to one or be dressed like Mia.

It was as if being a top-notch doctor made people forget their childhood or take the small things for granted. His brother didn't have a chance to live any of it, and Ryan's parents then denied him the very same.

He had found out more about Mia in this one outing alone than all of those other previous dates. And when she led him directly to what she considered the best funnel cakes in North Carolina, he was more than just a little in love. Strolling along Artist Alley, he bought art and little trinkets and suncatchers that would brighten up his patients' rooms. They rode rides and screamed just as loud as teens when they went too fast or high. He won her the largest orange-and-pink flamingo, which they had to take to the car with the rest of his purchases before they could continue their fun.

Ryan thoroughly enjoyed the day. The sun went down too quickly in his opinion. When the lights came on over at the roller rink, Ryan got to see why Mia and her sisters were dressed alike.

The dance routine was to the song "Shake Your Groove Thing," and it was with six other women. He cheered along with the rest of the crowd, seeing Mia laugh and dance and open up just a little bit more. She was comfortable here, happy in her skin around these people, and he envied her for this freedom he never seemed to have.

Mia came over to him and leaned on the wooden railing. "Get your skates on and join me."

Ryan dumped the empty cup from his lemonade Frosty into the trash and sat on the bench to put on the skates she'd brought for him. Moving gingerly to the rink, he finally breathed a sigh of relief when the wheels hit the polished floor.

Ryan rolled slowly up beside her and held on to the railing to stop. "Be gentle with me. I barely learned how to use these things ages ago, and you look like this is your main mode of transportation."

She turned and placed his hands on her hips. "Stick with me, kid. I'll show you the ropes."

"As long as we aren't trying the *Dirty Dancing* lift, I'm good."

"The fact that you made that reference has definitely gained you brownie points."

With the music pulsing around them, Mia pushed off, and soon his feet matched her own while they went around the rink. The warm air filled with the scent of everything from barbecue ribs to cotton candy, while people had a fine time dancing and enjoying samples from the breweries or food and drink from a variety of concession stands. He caught sight of Enid, Margo and Micki, plus more of the faces he now knew from around the Sardis community.

But when an open spot on the wooden floor opened up, he moved closer to Mia, and with his hands still on her waist, he lifted her off her feet. She screamed and laughed while they rolled across the smooth floor, and Ryan knew the sound was just for him. The ache of falling in love was there, throbbing along with the music, pulsing in his veins.

The next song started and Mia turned in his arms to twine her own around his neck for the couples' dance. Together he and Mia moved in unison to the music, and he smiled at her before kissing her nose.

"I'm so happy to have you here with me, Ryan." Mia's eyes danced in merriment. "I think I have a condition, Doc."

"And what is that?"

"Heart pangs, right here." Mia put her hand over her chest.

Ryan couldn't help the laughter that escaped him. "Wow, that was so corny."

"But yet you laugh."

He heard Mia cry out in surprise. One minute they were talking, and the next his arms were empty.

"Come dance with your old school beau." Billy Hollingsworth tried to grasp her hand but she deftly scooted out of his reach.

"What's wrong with you?" Mia snapped. "Where's your wife?"

"Lauren left me, so I'm a free agent. Let's rekindle—"

"Move on." Ryan had stepped up beside Mia.

"Get lost, man." Billy staggered toward Mia, who sidestepped away.

"You're drunk." Mia was clearly disgusted.

Ryan leaned into Billy so the guy could hear him above the music. "Now, while it looks to everyone like we are simply having a word, I want you to know that no matter what's going on with you, that doesn't give you the right to scare, hurt or annoy anyone else, let alone Mia, is that understood? You should go home and start to sober up. Now, apologize to Mia, and leave. Am I clear?"

Billy gave a stiff nod. Ryan said, "There's a good program at Armstrong Medical that does outreach in the community with AA meetings. Come to the hospital and ask for me, we'll get you sorted out, if you want the help."

"I—I think I want the help," Billy stammered.

Ryan nodded. "Monday, ask for Dr. Cassidy. Ask your wife to come. There may be services to help her, too."

They watched Billy leave. "You didn't have to do that. Why did you?" Mia asked. "Most guys wouldn't have been so nice or show that kind of concern."

Ryan shrugged. "Everyone needs a little bit of kindness now and again. Maybe he hasn't seen much of that in his life."

"You're a good man, Dr. Cassidy."

"I try to be." Ryan focused on Mia. "Are you okay?"

She smiled. "I'm good, and thank you for taking care of it so it didn't turn into an even worse spectacle."

His lips twitched. "I aim to please."

She stood on her tiptoes to kiss him on the cheek. "Exactly. Besides, it was kinda nice watching you defend my honor."

"Well, call him back. I'll defend it as many times as you need me to." Ryan puffed out his chest jokingly.

"Maybe we can find something else to do…" Mia winked.

"What?"

She skated away. "Figure it out, big guy."

"Hey, come back here!"

Mia's laughter filled the warm night air and Ryan chased after her. He found out that her version of *something else to do* was riding the pirate ship ride without throwing up. But he did get a kiss while they were sitting on the grass behind Ballad Inn, counting fireflies. Ryan didn't understand why simple moments like the one they were sharing now made him feel like he was again on top of the world.

Later still, as he lay in bed, he stared at the shadows that played across the ceiling thanks to the breeze blowing the lacy curtains at the window. Mia was so close and yet so far. Ryan longed to make her promises but knew, until he figured out what he wanted his path in life to be, he wouldn't be able to keep them. It would be so easy to say the words she wanted to hear, words that he wanted to say. But something inside Ryan wouldn't allow him to voice what he already knew was happening. He was falling in love.

RYAN FIXED HIS TIE. The suit stifled him as he sat in front of the hospital hiring committee. These people would vote on whether or not the job was his and so far things were looking good. Ryan didn't know if he liked that or not. There were questions about how he could commit to an attending job. Those questions were fired at him hard and fast now.

"Doesn't Medicine Across the World divide your time?"

"I think it enhances my ability to treat my patients here," Ryan replied. "We see the worst cases and we cure more than we lose. Coming back to Charlotte with that experience can only give me a broader insight into my hospital patients and their care."

"I have an issue with the complex some doctors have, the going-rogue persona. What do we do if you get bored and decide to leave on one of your excursions?"

"These are not excursions," Ryan said coolly and met each of their gazes with his own. "This is service to lives that hang in the balance, and we are not playing at being action heroes. We want to see that everyone gets a chance at proper health care and a better future. If I take this job, my dedication to my patients will never waver."

"I'd like to add that his work with MAW

is good press for Armstrong Medical," the chief of staff said. "A great way for our financial donors and the press to see we are well-rounded and have philanthropic endeavors outside the country. We could even fund one or two of these trips to aid our new attending."

"I don't want to be a figurehead or see my face on anything," Ryan pointed out. "I really just want to do the work and interact with and focus on the patients."

"Oh yes, we know," the chief of staff said, waving off his concerns.

That action irritated Ryan. It was as if his words were being dismissed. He had to remember that Dr. Garrison was looking out for the interests of the hospital and was a good man with a heart dedicated to the patients. Not much older than Ryan, Dr. Garrison had a stocky build and an unlimited amount of energy. Ryan smiled to himself. Dr. Garrison ran on some type of high-octane personality fuel that Ryan couldn't match.

"But donations always help, am I right?" Dr. Garrison asked with a wide grin.

"Yes, they do," Ryan said slowly.

"How many times a year do you think

you'll be traveling, five, ten or more?" another committee member asked.

"I can't be sure. Sometimes I leave for eight weeks at a time, sometimes I'm called for an emergency case that only lasts for a few days," Ryan admitted. "I guess the real question is would you be comfortable with me taking sabbaticals for volunteer work overseas?"

Glances were exchanged among the hiring committee.

"Thank you, Dr. Cassidy. We've heard enough," the committee head said. "We are very impressed with your answers and efforts thus far, but we also have other candidates to consider. You'll get our final decision in a few weeks. Till then, we'd like you to continue the contract for six months as our temporary attending."

Ryan was relieved. "Thank you for your time, and I look forward to your final decision."

He stood and shook everyone's hand, leaving the committee head for last. The older man, with salt-and-pepper hair and matching beard, gave Ryan's hand an exuberant shake.

"You'll know sooner rather than later, Dr. Cassidy." He smiled warmly at Ryan.

"I'll walk you out," Dr. Garrison said and was on his feet and by the door in seconds. Amused, Ryan stepped out into the corridor.

"That went great, Ryan." Dr. Garrison slapped him on the back, and Ryan winced. "I can tell you that you are at the top of a very short list."

"That's good to hear."

"If you can cut your traveling down to one sabbatical a year and only a few emergency cases, you have a lock on the job."

He and Dr. Garrison were at the end of the long hallway and began to walk through the glass breezeway that connected the hospital offices to the patient floors. Outside, the sun was shining brightly, and it looked like one of those days where you would rather be in a park or on a hiking trail than indoors.

They paused at the other end of the breezeway. "So can I tell them that you are willing to make these changes?" Dr. Garrison asked hopefully.

Doubt filled Ryan and he answered honestly. "I don't know if that would be ideal,

Noel. Sometimes they are low on doctors willing to travel…"

"Ryan," Dr. Garrison said on a sigh, "you need to start making some firm decisions. You fit perfectly with the hospital, your work is impeccable, and the kids adore you already. But—and this is a very big but— we can't have you rushing off somewhere whenever you'd like to."

"Noel, I—"

Dr. Garrison held up his hand. "No, let me finish. You're going to help, and I commend you so much on what you have done for the past ten years. But the patients here also deserve your best care, and what happens when you have a child trust you and then you disappear out of their lives? Even if it is only temporary in some cases. These kids become ours from the time they are admitted to this hospital and their need is just as urgent."

"You know that I give every patient my all," Ryan ground out. "I would make sure their care is a hundred percent assured before I left for anywhere else."

"For eight weeks at a time? Not all of these kids have two months to spare. I can also counter that with how parents look to us, the doctors, as much as the patients do. The committee's going to offer you the job, I am ninety-nine percent sure of that. It's for you to decide how much you are willing to give, and if it's less than what you would give Medicine Across the World, I can't have you on my staff. Think on it, Ryan."

Dr. Garrison turned and headed back the way they'd come, while Ryan went on to the pediatric floor and saw patients. The chief of staff was right: Ryan had a tough decision to make. How many children might be lost if he didn't travel when he was needed? And then he looked at the kids whose smiles met him at each door when he did rounds. They needed him, too. Then there was Mia, a woman he cared about—more than cared, actually. Ryan had strong feelings for her and could see her sweet, open face instantly. Where did she fit in all this?

He knew her opinion about travel, and there was no chance she would be okay with him jumping in and out of her life. Ryan had left Minnesota to make his life easier, and yet he'd discovered a whole other set of complications. He certainly didn't expect to be falling for someone before he was even offered the spot as attending. His original plan was to simply do his best, and if the committee decided to go another way, he could leave with no fuss, having spent a great time in a new place. Could he leave Mia now, if he couldn't give the hospital what they needed from him?

The thoughts plagued him all day. He drove back to Ballad Inn still steeped in the hard choices that needed to be made. His mood was darker than usual when he stepped through the polished mahogany and frosted glass door.

"Whoa, if *it was a dark and stormy night* was a face, it could be yours," Mia teased. She was coming downstairs as he closed the door. Mia stood at the bottom step wearing her casual jeans and a green sweatshirt. Her glasses were perched on her face, and she opened her arms to him. "Do you need a hug?"

"Please."

Ryan's voice was gruff as he embraced her and inhaled the scent of her perfume like it was a balm that would ease his mind. Mia rubbed his back comfortingly, and he tightened his arms around her. She pressed a soft kiss into his mop of hair, and it was his undoing: she cared so freely and without question. There was no doubt she deserved better than him. Maybe he was selfish, holding on to her while he tried to figure out what he wanted.

"Bad day at work?" she asked softly.

"Kinda," he admitted.

She took his hand and led him toward the kitchen. "Come on, you can tell me about it in the kitchen. I think this deserves our special tradition of having dessert for dinner, which we do for particularly sucky days."

"Who came up with this idea?" Ryan asked.

"Me. I found I could get my sisters to talk to me over ice cream and not hold things in, and it stuck after that." Mia went to the freezer and pulled out two tubs of the sweet, creamy treat. "This might need to be a combo-type deal, or do you have a preference for Heavenly Hash or Rocky Road?"

"Let's go for the combo." Ryan smiled, feeling his spirit lighten just by being around her.

"Good man."

Mia winked at him and began scooping

them both some ice cream. She gave him a bowl and sat down beside him at the island. They ate a few spoonfuls in companionable silence before Mia spoke again.

"Want to talk about it?"

"I had my meeting with the hospital hiring committee today about my job being permanent."

"That bad?" Mia asked gently.

Ryan shook his head. "No. My chief of staff told me the position is basically mine."

"That's wonderful!" she exclaimed and then frowned when he didn't copy her exuberance. "Isn't it a good thing?"

"It could be," Ryan answered. "They want me to basically cut back or stop my work with MAW for the attending job. They don't feel my division of time would do the patients justice."

"And you think you can do both," Mia surmised.

"I don't," he confessed. "I know something has to give, but deciding where or which one is the problem."

Mia took a bite of her dessert, and he watched her face become thoughtful before she spoke again. "I thought that this job was something you wanted. You drove all the way here from Minnesota to give them six months. What did you think would happen then?"

He shrugged. "I don't know. I thought maybe they would give me more leeway with my travels."

"You've gone and got a position you like, sealed the deal and begun a great foundation for a life here in Charlotte." She was speaking frankly, he knew and appreciated that. "I would be jumping at the chance."

"But you're not me," Ryan told her firmly. "You are comfortable here, doing your thing. That might not be what I want."

"I didn't say you needed to be me. That was just my opinion." Mia's voice became stiff. "But it's selfish and a bit egotistical to think they would take only part of you and a disservice to other patients that will also need you."

Her words were hard to hear, but they were true.

"I have never given a patient anything but complete care and my utmost attention," Ryan replied. "Maybe you're pushing me to say yes so we can be together."

She straightened and the bronze flecks in her dark brown eyes seemed to become angry fire when she spoke to him. "First off, never say I'm pushing toward anything." Mia's voice was frosty. "Nor is a relationship being dangled in front of you like a carrot, Ryan. Do you think I'm that needy that I would want you to stay here if your heart wasn't in it, either for the job…or me? That's a big ol' ego you have there."

"I would think my saying yes makes things easier for us to see where this is going," Ryan said.

Mia took her bowl to the sink and washed the rest of the uneaten ice cream down the drain. "At this point, I can see it going into the large dumpster fire that you are building."

"It seems I can't make anyone happy with my decisions," Ryan muttered. "I wanted to protect you from this to find out what we have together. I thought we had more time."

"You have all the time in the world, Ryan. Don't make me a part of your decisions in the least." Mia moved to the door and turned to face him. "And protect me? That's where you went wrong, Ryan. Who asked you to do that? It wasn't me. They're your choices to make, so don't use me as an excuse."

"Mia…" Ryan looked helplessly at her, wondering what he could say.

"It's absolutely fine, Ryan." Her smile was stiff. "Please wash your bowl when you're done and place it in the rack."

He tried to smile. "I thought you were keeping me company?"

"You seem to have all the company you need… You are an island unto yourself," Mia answered, and without a backward glance she went through the kitchen door and left him staring at it.

"Well done, Doctor." Annoyed at his propensity for putting his foot in his mouth, Ryan shoved a spoonful of the melting dessert in with it and glowered into his bowl. There was a lot on his shoulders right now with one new addition. Buy flowers for Mia and apologize.

CHAPTER EIGHT

MIA WAS UPSET. She didn't like being mad. She hated how hot tears would spring to her eyes whenever she couldn't control or explain her emotions. Ryan was like a yo-yo, and she didn't want to be part of any game. It felt like her parents all over again, that tight sensation in her chest, that nervousness that made her want to scream each time they left. She tried to find ways to work off the negative energy.

As a kid, she did that by either skating up and down the neighborhood until she was too exhausted to care or sitting up in the branches of a tree with a book, sinking into the story and forgetting she was mad. She had learned to manage these emotions until now. Ryan brought them right back to the surface and Mia felt helpless. *I hate these feelings. I wish I could still go coasting on my longboard like a kid.*

Why not? Mia thought, suddenly brazen. She still had her sleek longboard she'd bought about two years back. A splurge purchase because it looked amazing. She'd had every intention of using it but then reality broke through and she'd put it in her closet.

Mia ran up the stairs to her room, quickly changed into an old baseball jersey and jeans before grabbing the longboard and heading out.

"Uh, where are you going?" Micki asked.

"Skateboarding in the neighborhood," Mia answered easily.

"Mia…not that you weren't good, but really?" Micki asked.

"Really." Mia made sure her laces were tight.

"I'm going to get Margo," Micki said quickly and ran off. "You might be coming down with something."

"I'm just fine, Michelle!"

Mia didn't wait. She went out the front door and dropped the board on the driveway and tried out a few stops. With a soft kick, the board was levered up into her palm. *I got this*, she thought and pushed off down the driveway to the sidewalk in front of Ballad Inn.

"Mia Ballad, aren't you too old to be on that thing?" Mr. Bolton called out.

"Age is just a number," Mia shouted back to him.

"So is 9-1-1," Mr. Marley hollered.

"Told you those Ballad girls were feral," Mr. Bolton said to his friend and pulled out his phone.

While she skateboarded, more people started to come out onto their porches, watching her, drinking iced tea and calling to her occasionally.

"You still got it, Mia girl!" Mrs. Stoll waved.

"I have ten on you wiping out," Stanley Myers yelled.

"Mia Janine Ballad, you stop right this instant or I'm getting Enid!" Margo hollered at her.

Micki stood beside Margo and grinned. "Don't listen to her! Do your thang, boo! I countered Stanley with a twenty!"

Mia rolled her eyes. *Of course they're betting*, and she had no doubt that Mr. Bolton had started it.

She remembered her old tricks, the jump,

the board flip. It was like muscle memory. So much so Mia got daring, looking at the narrow railing she used to grind on. If she built up enough speed, she could jump and glide along it, land easily and be able to kick-stop the board.

"Mia, don't you dare do it!" Margo yelled.

"Oh, she's gonna try it!" Micki's voice was filled with excitement.

By now it seemed like the entire street was outside to watch her make the jump or land face-first on the pavement. *They weren't that interested in my skateboarding when I was a kid*, Mia thought, and increased her speed. Maybe it was because she was more of a nuisance in other ways then. She angled her longboard to align with the metal rail and Mia made the jump, her heart racing. Everything was golden. It was the landing that was the issue because her plan to stop failed, and the board shot out from under her feet. Her legs went up and when she came down it was on her rear. The connection of pavement to bone reverberated through her.

"Ballad girl down!" Mr. Marley called with a practiced ease.

When did that become a catchphrase?
Mia wondered.

"You owe me thirty dollars, Stanley!" she heard her sister say.

"She crashed!"

"At the end, so you still owe me!"

Her sisters ran to her, Micki collecting the board and Margo helping her to her feet.

"I hope you didn't bruise your coccyx!" Mrs. Stoll called out worriedly.

"Language!" Mia gasped.

"The coccyx is your tailbone," Margo said, amused.

"Did she break her coccyx?" Mr. Marley yelled.

"Nothing worse than a broken coccyx," Mr. Bolton added.

"Everyone stop saying that word!" Mia demanded. "I'm fine!"

"Uh-huh, sure you are," Micki said under her breath and fell into step beside them. Mia leaned on her as well. "If you did break or bruise your...tailbone, I'm going to the hospital with you to see everyone's reaction to how it happened."

The neighbors started to file back into their homes, chitchatting happily with the short break in the quiet monotony of Sardis Woods, even if it was at her expense.

"Next time I have hurt feelings, remind me to go do a spreadsheet or something." Mia winced as they walked inside the inn and headed straight to her office. "They are not as painful as what I did just now."

"It was nice to see the old you." Margo smiled. "Until you wiped out."

"The old me is firmly back in her box," she murmured. "Do we still have that cooling donut to sit on?"

Margo laughed. "I'll get it."

In a matter of minutes, she was sitting on a plastic cushion that could be filled with ice to soothe her sore backside. Her work helped to calm her mood even more, but still, Mia kept her door closed so as to deter anyone from entering. That was the rule when she was busy. However, someone didn't follow her directions, and the persistent knocking annoyed her fast.

"You guys know the rules," Mia said as she got up, moping. "I know my butt is bruised, but I'm okay. So someone better be in a worse state than I'm in if..." She opened the door. "What in the nightmares-are-made-of-this am I looking at?"

Mia was staring at a grown adult in a head-to-toe brown-and-black dog costume. If that wasn't creepy enough, its bright eyes blinked, reminding her of why she hated animatronics.

"I'm sorry I'm in the doghouse…" a low muffled voice said.

"Ryan?"

The dog pulled his hand from behind his back, and Mia jumped with a small scream, thinking it could be something bad. Instead, a bouquet of gorgeous flowers was in its paw…hand—so confusing.

"Forgive me for being *ruff* around the edges."

That word was barked, and Mia couldn't get past the weird blinking eye thing going on. The front door opened, and the honeymooners came to a halt when they saw Ryan. Their time at Ballad Inn was soon coming to an end. They both had saved up all their vacation time to take an entire month off from work. In another week they would be checking out to go home.

"Whoa!" John moved closer with a grin.

"Should we ask what's going on, or pretend we didn't see anything and go to our room?"

"It's Ryan under there, I think." Mia glanced at the dog worriedly. "At least, I hope so."

"What's happening?" It was Micki coming from the kitchen to join them in the foyer. "As if the skateboarding wasn't enough entertainment for the day."

"It's Ryan, apologizing." Mia put her hands on her hips.

"Who was skateboarding?" the dog asked, falling out of character for a moment.

"Mia, and she fell and hurt her tailbone. So the apology is being done in a dog costume?" Micki asked with a grin. "All right, then. Weird, but I can dig it. Hey, Enid, wanna see something you've never seen before?"

"Don't call her." But Mia was too late.

"Oh my, my, my," Enid tutted, leaving the kitchen to now stand alongside Micki.

It only got more confusing when Margo came downstairs. After staring for a few seconds, she started singing the theme song from a TV show they watched as kids, which featured a big orange dog.

"Mia, forgive me. It's so hot in this thing!" Ryan blurted out.

"What did you do? Don't forgive him until he answers first," Micki said, folding her arms.

"This is the best bed-and-breakfast ever!" Heather clapped with enthusiasm and bounced on her toes.

John agreed. "Our review is going to be phenomenal."

"Mia, I have a serious case of insert-foot-into-mouth-itis," Ryan tried to continue. "Shoot, hold on."

They all watched while he struggled to get the dog head off. He managed it and dropped it on the reception desk.

"Are the eyes supposed to move even if you aren't wearing it?" Mia asked, staring at the head that was staring back at her. "Aren't you controlling that thing?"

He looked at it just as curiously as they all did. "Nope, didn't even know the eyes blinked."

Everyone took a step back at his words, and Enid lifted her head in a small prayer. Ryan seemed to ignore Mia's concern over what appeared to be a possessed costume and focused on her.

"I said dumb things and spoke out of turn," Ryan pleaded. "I was worrying about everything, especially the choices I've got to make. You are not one of the negatives but the biggest positive in my life since I drove into Charlotte and walked through that door. So, forgive me?"

"I guess I will if you take that thing out of this house," Mia said, pointing warily at the head with the blinking eyes. "I mean, seriously, is that scary or what?"

"Now I'm seriously wondering how it works," Micki said.

"You won't when it eats your face," Margo murmured.

Finally, at the end of one of the strangest conversations of her entire life, she walked with Ryan as he left the inn, with the head tucked under his arm.

"They got you, too, I see," Mr. Bolton called out to Ryan and laughed.

"Those Ballad girls do pull people into their unique life over there." Mr. Marley chuckled and snapped a photo of her and

Ryan with his phone, no doubt for future reference.

"I have something special for us to do if you're game," Ryan said, his eagerness clear. "It just came to town and it'll be an awesome time."

"Okay," she said skeptically. "What do I need to wear?"

"Dress comfortably and definitely put on sneakers," Ryan said. "So, not to scare you further, but Doodle has been sitting on the fence looking at me ever since we came out here."

"Did he see you in full costume?" she asked.

"Yeah." Ryan eyed the cat warily. "His tail is swishing, like he's planning something."

"He probably sees you as a threat that will keep him away from Monty." Mia patted Ryan's shoulder affectionately. "If it keeps him out of our house and stops his assassin ways, well, then yay for us."

"Huh, maybe. In any case, I'll meet you back here in five." Ryan turned but then hesitated. "Can you help unzip me?"

"Who helped you zip up in the first place?" Mia grinned.

"I was wearing it at the hospital to cheer up the kids. Did it impulsively," Ryan answered. "Matt helped me get into the thing."

"You're not naked under this, are you?" Mia asked, her brow raised.

"Uh no, but still, I'm pretty gross," Ryan said, his expression aghast.

"Not to mention you also had that demonic head on," Mia murmured.

He glanced at her. "You're right, I'll shower. See you in ten."

Mia watched him clumsily try to go up the stairs with the dog costume on. He almost stumbled a few times and a smile twitched at her lips.

She noticed that he'd left the dog head part of the costume on one of the patio tables. At least the thing was only staring at her. She sighed in relief, until the eyes slowly blinked.

"Nope, nope, nope." She hurried inside, looking back once. "Nope!"

Mia went upstairs to change. Ten minutes became fifteen with his full costume stowed firmly away in a box in the shed until he could take it back to the rental shop.

The new place that Ryan had heard of

turned out to be a massive indoor arcade slash amusement park in Huntersville. It had everything from virtual-reality games to go-carts and an actual roller coaster.

"When did all this spring up?" Mia asked, looking around in awe. "The last time I was here, this was a huge tech business!"

"No clue, sorry, but when Matt told me about it, I thought we should give it a whirl," Ryan said. "Margo told me how much of an arcade fan you were."

"The ones without mascots." Mia shuddered.

"Hey, Mr. Ruff was awesome," Ryan defended.

"Uh-huh." Mia twirled in a wide circle. "Okay, where do we start? I think we should go with the *Halo* game, knock that out and then move on to the motorcycles. Then we head for that basketball dunk game where I can win at least a thousand tickets for us."

Ryan looked at her, shocked. "Who are you?"

"My competitive button has been pushed," she announced.

"Well, there is one thing we have to try first."

Ryan steered her in the direction of a large glass tube where people were floating in midair. It looked like indoor skydiving, and her heart lurched.

"Um, no." Mia shook her head but Ryan extended his arms as if presenting her with a great opportunity.

"Activate your adventurous side," he said gently. "What could go wrong?"

"Everything can go wrong," she answered. "They are floating on air. If no air, then plop."

"There's a bouncy house floor underneath us, and we don't go in alone. Two trained professionals are there to help," Ryan said. "Remember the Gravitron ride that stuck you to the wall by spinning so fast? Well, if you did that, you can do this."

"If you must know I—"

"Margo already told me you went on it multiple times till the guy you were with puked." Ryan grinned.

"Well, well," she muttered. "Margo is a nark."

"Language! You get in an arcade and it's like you're a different person." Ryan pulled her close and gave her a quick hug.

"Okay, if I'm doing this, we are so playing *Halo* next." Mia took a step back and held out her hand. "Deal?"

"What is with you and that game?" Ryan asked, shaking her hand. "Do you have a console in your room?"

Mia looked away in embarrassment. He quickly threw his arms around her again and laughed out loud, a rich sound that Mia loved hearing.

"You do—you're a secret gamer!" Ryan exclaimed. "How is it you surprise me each and every day?"

Mia didn't answer; instead, she grabbed his hand and tugged him toward the line for the Skyfall Drop Zone. "Let's go float."

That was how she ended up, dressed like an astronaut, inside a tube and looking warily around at the whole concept. It did not seem like a good idea: the entire day was weird.

"I'm going to hold on to your hands and when the air starts, my partner will get you in position to float," the trainer said. "We'll do that to your friend as well, and you guys will be indoor skydiving."

"What about when it's time to stop?" Ryan asked.

"At the ten-minute mark, the air decreases slowly, giving Brad down there a chance to grab your legs and bring you safely to the ground," he explained. "Unless you want to drop? Then we turn the air off and you fall to the soft floor below."

"I'm for option two," Ryan said with a grin.

Mia looked at him, confused. "Why would you go for option two?"

"Sounds fun?" He shrugged. "Come on, be daring with me."

"I already had my quota of falling today." To the trainer, Mia said, "We want option one."

Hesitancy within Mia built when the turbines started and the only sound she could hear was the wind. But soon she and Ryan were floating with the air rushing past, their arms outstretched. Ryan reached out and together they performed small tricks like the instructors inside the tube with them were doing. But mostly they just held hands. When their ten minutes were up, she slowly felt the air pressure change so they would descend slowly. Someone gripped her feet, bringing her to the floor securely. Safely back outside the Skyfall tube, she and Ryan looked at each other, and a slow smile spread across her face.

"That was awesome," Mia said, releasing a burst of laughter so loud that others noticed and turned.

"Right!" Ryan agreed. "All the fun of skydiving but safely and no risk."

Mia rubbed her hands together, feeling a little mischievous. "Now, I seem to remember you promised that after this we would play the games I want, Dr. Cassidy."

"I am in your hands," Ryan said.

A slow smile spread across her face. "You may regret that."

For the rest of the afternoon and well into the evening, they tried their luck at numerous games and ate everything from cotton candy to chicken bites and Coke floats. Every time she sat down, Mia was reminded of her skateboard incident and when she told Ryan the story, he laughed until his eyes teared up.

At the end of their jaunt into arcade life, back at the car, they shared a kiss where Mia could still taste the cotton candy on his lips. Why did this have to be so hard? Why couldn't they fall in love seamlessly, without all the issues they had together and apart? She wanted to give him her love and to make a home in her heart for his. *Just believe for once in your life*, the little voice in her head begged, *just believe*.

EACH NEW DAY brought a revelation for Ryan.

One afternoon, Margo was at the front desk with Monty the lizard, who was wearing a bow tie and sitting beside the sign-in book. The day before, he'd yelled out at seeing a body go by his window, only to discover it was Micki descending and then unharnessing herself from climbing gear. Most mornings, he met Enid in the kitchen, who insisted on making him lunch to take to work because she assumed every meal from the cafeteria was awful.

Ryan loved living with a large family in Ballad Inn and all the chaos that ensued. Compared to his childhood of quiet rooms and empty hallways, this was great.

Still, there was a heaviness on his chest. He felt something soft and smiled, thinking maybe Mia had come into his room to give him a morning kiss. But when he slowly opened his eyes, it wasn't Mia's soft brown gaze that he saw but green eyes set into bright orange fur. The cat licked his lips and hissed. Ryan was instantly awake, and as he jumped off the bed, Doodle dashed for a corner.

"How did you get in here!" Ryan yelled. He made a move to block him, but in the process ended up being scratched on the neck by his claws, making Ryan yelp in pain.

His door opened, and Mia stood there. "What's going on?"

Doodle seized on the new escape route and sprinted out of the bedroom.

Ryan pointed to the orange streak. "That cat must have come in through the open window. He was sitting on my chest, possibly contemplating murdering me! I knew the dog costume bothered him. He's a feline assassin!"

"Doodle, get back here!" Mia left to chase the furry assailant with Ryan on her heels. "Micki, I thought you fixed the intrusion problem!" she called to her sister as she ran down the stairs.

"I did! It was a torn screen in the sunroom that I fixed, for free," Micki yelled.

"Just open the front door and let him outside!" Mia cried out. "Before he breaks or ruins anything."

Micki opened the door wide, and Doodle rushed out. The three of them watched the cat climb a tree near the fence, then use an overhanging branch to get back into Mr. Webber's yard.

"Micki, cut that branch down and keep him out of our yard!" Mia said, clearly exasperated.

"Mmm-hmm, I sure will." She sounded amused, which caught Mia's attention.

Mia then turned toward Ryan, and she, too, stopped talking.

"What are you both looking at?" Ryan asked and then glanced down at himself. He was in his neon-green moose-and-candy-cane pajama bottoms with matching top.

"Where did you buy the visual nightmare, Ryan?" Micki drawled.

Mia fanned her face, trying not to laugh or at least, to look away. "Do they need to locate you from the International Space Station? Are you their Earth beacon?"

She and Micki doubled over in laughter.

"I'm going to get dressed." Ryan huffed and felt his face turn red.

It got worse when Margo arrived at the open door. Her steps halted. "Why, hello! Aren't you a little early for the holiday season?"

The laughter tripled.

"So this is what it's like to have siblings," Ryan mused, feeling suddenly like he was under a microscope. "Doodle got into my room, tried to kill me and escaped."

"He tried to kill you?" Margo didn't sound convinced. "He's moved on to humans?"

"He was sitting on my chest contemplating it," he explained. "He's becoming a menace."

"How about you go upstairs, and I'll bring a first aid kit for those scratches," Mia suggested.

"Please do go upstairs. We want to give our pupils a chance to normalize," Micki teased.

"Micki!" Mia tried hard not to laugh and failed.

"See you in a few," Ryan said and turned to jog up the stairs.

He chuckled, hearing Mia trying to keep her sisters from teasing him any more than they just had. Doodle was annoying, for sure, but if it meant Mia acting as nurse to Ryan's wounds, maybe he would buy the little fuzz ball a can of tuna.

Soon there was a light knock on his open door, and Mia stepped inside. Ryan thought it best not to tell her he had a suture kit in his bag. He, of course, had changed into jeans and a T-shirt so no more fun could be made of his sleepwear. He sat on the recliner near the open window in question.

"I'm so sorry about Doodle," Mia said and sat on the corner of the bed close to the chair.

"Only Doodle, huh?" Ryan asked. "Not the unmerciful teasing that has probably given me a complex?"

"Uh-uh, no pity, buddy. You chose to buy that outfit and thought it was okay."

She poured a little peroxide onto a cotton ball to dab at the scratches. Ryan watched her as she worked and rambled on about the unpredictable tendencies of the neighbor's cat that only seemed to bother those at Ballad Inn. He could smell Mia's light perfume and the coconut shampoo she used on her hair. Even the cocoa-butter scent of her skin seemed to filter through and overcome his senses, raising his awareness of her. Mia had wrapped her way around his heart and she didn't even know it.

"Ryan, am I hurting you?" Mia covered the bottle of antiseptic before looking at him with wide brown eyes.

"Not in the way you think," he replied.

"Then how—"

Ryan leaned forward and took her lips in a kiss. She smiled when it ended.

"That was nice. But why did you do that?" Mia asked gently.

"Because you do something to me, Mia. I've never felt like this before. You're so incredible," Ryan said huskily. He kissed her briefly once more before taking the antiseptic from her. "I can finish this, go on back to work. I'll see you in a little bit. It's my day off."

"Ah, so that we can spend the afternoon together." Mia smiled again at him. "I'll wrap up work early."

"Sounds like a plan."

Ryan was sorry to see her go. He pushed

the recliner back with a sigh of happiness. He ached to tell her more about how he felt. But he knew he would have to be patient because he saw the skittish fear in her eyes sometimes, and he didn't want to hurt her. Who was he kidding? If he chose not to change his life or take the job, they both would be hurt. He didn't want to promise her something that couldn't be given, which was why he hesitated.

There was unspoken trauma in Mia and it would be something they would have to overcome to grow closer. Especially if he had to leave for medical missions in foreign countries. Ryan preferred to try to keep it safe between them because at the end of this journey he hoped that his choices meant Mia stayed in his life. Could she see past her fears to what he wanted to accomplish and share in the journey with him? Regardless, he would always come home to her. He knew that in his heart.

The wind, the soft birdcalls and maybe the whole atmosphere that surrounded him made him relax. Ryan didn't know when he fell asleep, but the nightmare began in the usual way with him standing in the field hospital with a gun pointed at him. The cries of children and the screams of adults could be heard while the facility was ransacked.

"Take anything you want," Ryan told the gunmen. "We're just trying to help," he raged.

His words got him beaten, but he didn't care. It took their focus off the doctors, the nurses, the terrified people who were in beds, waiting for care, or hiding in tents. *Yeah, something definitely broken in there*, he thought when the next kick to his ribs took his breath away.

"Ryan… Ryan…"

A soft voice called to him, one that hadn't been in his dreams before. His name was called again. This time he felt a caress on his cheek and a kiss pressed on his forehead.

"Ryan, it's just a dream. Come on back now. Come back to me."

He opened his eyes, and Mia stood over him, eyes filled with concern as she pushed his hair away from his face.

"Mia?"

"You were having a nightmare. I was going by when I heard you call out. Are they always that bad?"

He moved the recliner to a sitting position. "This one was tamer by far. What we deal with when we're overseas sometimes can leave a wound deep down in the soul."

Mia squeezed his hand. "I hope being here will at least start to heal that wound."

Ryan twisted their joined hands to drop a quick kiss on the smooth skin of her wrist. "I think it's already begun."

"I'll see you later," she said and offered a warm smile. "Take some time to rest. We can hang out later when you're up for it."

Mia exited his room, and he stared at the closed door for a long while. Leaving Minneapolis, he knew that it was a search for something, and it seemed that he had found it in Charlotte and Mia. Ryan felt the breeze come through the open window and rubbed the scratches on his neck.

Not willing to give up his love of the fresh air, he lowered just the window screen to protect himself from the feline menace. Ryan replayed the earlier scene with them chasing the little fuzz ball and smiled, his eyes closed. If he'd thought this new experience was going to be boring, life at Ballad Inn so far had shown him it certainly was not.

CHAPTER NINE

"OKAY, SO WHAT are we doing?" Mia, unsure, looked down at her outfit. "And why am I dressed like I'm about to catch a trapeze?"

"It's a magician's-assistant outfit, and you will please do rounds with me to entertain some kids who really need a smile," Ryan answered.

"How come you get to be dressed normally and even wear your white coat, while I have to look like this? I'm not usually in sequins and feathers," she countered.

"Hey, I do have the magician's hat and cape." Ryan smiled as he drove.

Mia made a face. "That can't compete with this costume."

He laughed. "It will, trust me. Drink your coffee and get perky."

"*Perky* is something that I've never been accused of being," she murmured.

Ryan knew exactly what she meant. Mia

was a woman of logic, facts and figures, and liked things just so. This was his way to shake up her life a little and hopefully show her that the unexpected didn't have to cause her anxiety. Stepping out of the norm could be good. He'd learned that when he had finally left behind the rigid world his parents had set for him.

Also, being in the hospital at any age was hard enough. For children, it was particularly challenging for them to understand why they couldn't run and play, why their bodies hurt or why they were so sick. Ryan fully believed that laughter could be truly helpful. He encouraged parents to bring in items from their kids' bedrooms to make the children feel more comfortable and at home. His antics were designed to make the kids smile as much as possible. He would give everything he had to see them all healed and happy, but of course, life didn't work that way.

He parked his Land Rover before he helped Mia out of the passenger seat and then grabbed his box of tricks from the trunk. Mia tried desperately to tuck the plume of feathers at her back underneath her cape. He appreciated what a good friend she was and that she didn't make a run for it.

Once indoors, they took the elevator to his patient floor.

"Good morning, Dr. Cassidy," the head nurse said as they stopped at the station. "Who do we have here?"

"My lovely assistant and girlfriend, Mia," Ryan answered smoothly.

"Am I your girlfriend?" Mia questioned.

"Uh, it just slipped out?" Ryan said, scrambling for an explanation.

"We didn't give it a designation." Mia fiddled with the cape.

The nurse's smile stretched wide now. "Do you want to discuss this in private?"

Ryan took Mia's hand and gave it a quick squeeze. "Mia, this is Nicole, the best nurse a patient could ever hope for. I'd be lost without her expert scheduling."

"Nice to meet you, Mia." Nicole reached over the desk to shake her hand. "I see the good doctor has pulled you into his idea of entertainment. I was a clown last week… That didn't go over so well. Kids don't like clowns much anymore."

"I kinda get where they're coming from,"

said Mia, who smiled along with the older woman with friendly hazel eyes.

"Any problems I need to know about?" Ryan asked the nurse.

"Sean's feeding port got blocked, but we managed to clear it with minimal fuss," Nicole replied. "Chrissy's pulse and oxygen dropped last night though, and that was a bit concerning. The medication you ordered in case that happens worked, but I don't like it."

"Schedule her another echo, and we'll see if we need to move up surgery," Ryan said grimly. "I'll start with her first."

"What's wrong with Chrissy?" Mia asked as she followed him along the corridor.

"She has a heart-valve defect that we are hoping to close when she is a bit stronger. We also need the graft to fit perfectly, and we need…well, time. It seems we're running out of it."

"Oh no," she said softly. "Will she be okay?"

Ryan smiled at her. "I am going to do my best to make sure she is."

"You're a good doctor." Mia squeezed his hand before they stepped into Chrissy's room.

Ryan watched Mia bloom that afternoon

with the children. She feigned wonder at his tricks, waved her arms and said "Ta-da!" like a pro. She even pulled flowers from her coat and performed the trick where she sneezed, and when pulling out a colorful hanky, there were more than a few tied together.

"Wait, I only needed one hanky," Mia said with a shocked expression on her face while the young girl in the bed laughed. "Where did all of these come from? Oh my goodness, this is just too much!"

She played her role so well that Ryan's heart ached a painful, sweet ache that he'd never felt before. It was love. While the thought filled him with wonderment, it also sent a sliver of fear through him. He'd fallen hard for Mia, designations or not.

By the time it was early afternoon, Mia was laughing and talking with everyone like they were old friends, including Matt, who revealed himself as the source of the reservation at the restaurant for their first date.

"Did Dr. Cassidy mention that there's another highly suitable, eligible bachelor doctor who would be available to date one of your sisters?" Matt cleared his throat and smartly flipped up the collar of his white coat. "I mean, I heard you had at least two."

"Oh, you heard, did you?" Mia gave Ryan a knowing glance.

Ryan shrugged. "You Ballads are great. I couldn't help but talk about you all."

"Uh-huh. Wait until I tell them you gave Matt their résumés," she said teasingly. "No extra desserts for you."

"Whoa, you get extra desserts?" Matt said. "I mean, when can I come over for dinner? You know how doctors' lodging is. It's a fraternity house, and I don't cook."

"I'll think about it," Ryan said, amused. "Right now, Mia and I are going to the park for lunch, and guess what, they packed a cooler full of food for us."

"I kinda hate you," Matt said with a grin.

Mia patted Matt's shoulder. "I'll pack a plate for Ryan to bring back for you. How's that?"

Matt kissed her hand. "Get rid of this chump and be mine."

Ryan deftly turned Mia toward himself. "Hey, no poaching."

Laughing, Mia followed him to the elevator, and they went to the main floor and out into the sunshine. It never ceased to amaze Ryan that no matter how nice they made the inside of a hospital, it could never match the feeling of the sun on your face or taking a deep breath of air outdoors.

By car, Freedom Park was a mere five to ten minutes away. And just as quickly, they were spreading a blanket under a red maple tree lush with leaves in front of the amphitheater.

"They hold concerts in the park in the evenings once a week in the summer," Mia said as she unpacked the food. "If you ever want to come, I could put a wine-and-cheese platter together, and we can sit and listen to the orchestra close to the pond."

"Why, are you trying to charm me, Miss Ballad?" Ryan said, pretending to be coy.

Her smile was wide before she asked, "Is it working?"

"Oh, honey, without a doubt," he answered. "Everything about you has seduced me completely."

"Isn't that too much power to give away?" Mia sat beside him. "It might go to my head."

Ryan leaned over to kiss her. "I hope so."

Lunch was fried chicken and street corn

salad, along with the fresh rolls he loved so much. They were one of Enid's specialties. There was also a variety of fruit as well as cream whipped to perfection. Ryan tempted Mia to taste the sweet treat.

"I think feeding you this might be my new favorite hobby," Ryan pointed out.

"I'm a peaches-and-cream type of small-town girl," Mia answered. "It's the simple things that make us happy."

Ryan took a strawberry for himself. "I feel the same way."

Mia teased him. "The unspoken promises make whatever we're building more powerful."

Ryan cupped her cheek and whispered as sweetly as the strawberry tasted, "I do promise, with everything I have."

She rubbed her cheek against his hand. "What are you promising?"

"Me," he vowed. "All of me to you."

"You can't promise that until you're sure," Mia told him.

"I'm sure of you. Everything else will work itself out," he insisted.

"I wish I had that type of faith. I just don't ever want to be hurt again, Ryan."

Mia stared at him, hard. "With my family, friends, I've had to walk through the fires and crumble enough times that I can't rebuild myself anymore."

"All I can promise is that I will never intentionally hurt you, Mia," he offered gently. "But in life, there's hurt, so it's who you share the load with that matters. Someone who won't let you break. Just give me a chance and take the plunge like we did at the Skyfall."

Mia nodded. "Okay… I have to try or I'll always regret not seeing where this goes."

Ryan squeezed her hand. "I got you, babe."

She gave a throaty laugh. "If you break out in the Sonny and Cher song, I may rethink my decision."

"I feel a song coming on," he announced.

Ryan took a deep breath, and she covered his mouth with her hand as people walked by. "Don't you dare."

He sighed and lay back on the blanket, his face tilted up to the sun and the Carolina blue skies. "I could stay here forever, but alas, work calls."

"I can take a rideshare home from the hospital," Mia suggested. "It's not a problem."

"No, take the car home. I'll get a ride." Ryan sat up with a groan. "Now I'm full and lazy. I think I feel like Doodle."

"No one feels like Doodle unless they are up to no good," she said dryly.

After making Matt's plate and wrapping it in leftover plastic, which Ryan assured her he didn't deserve, they packed the cooler into the trunk of his SUV. The ride back took only minutes on the roads that were light on traffic that time of day. After their goodbye, he stood outside the hospital, until she turned onto the street and the green Land Rover went out of sight. He returned to his office, but not before giving Matt the plate of lunch that Mia had made for him.

"There, you mooch," Ryan said teasingly. "Giving Mia big pity eyes for a free meal."

"You live at a great place where they feed you like a prince," Matt reminded him. "Friends share."

"I did. I paid off your student loans," Ryan said.

Matt choked on the bite of chicken he'd taken. "You what?"

"I couldn't see my friend paying off a debt

like that for the next twentysomething years. You're a great doctor. You deserve a break. Now maybe you can move out of the doctors' frat house."

"But how?" Matt asked incredulously.

"The means were there, and for a friend I wouldn't think twice," he told him. "I have a lot saved up, and I can do with it as I please. Helping a doctor out of debt is another part of giving back. I've been lucky in lots of ways."

"I literally don't know what to say." Matt cleared what sounded like emotion in his throat. "That kind of weight off my shoulders, brother... Thank you."

He held out his hand. Ryan grinned. "You're welcome, but I'm not shaking your chicken-covered hand."

"You're right." Matt wiped his fingers and jumped up to give him a huge hug. "No one, and I mean not even family, has ever done anything like this for me, let alone put a dime toward what I wanted to accomplish. Yet here you are, big as life... Man, I... Thank you."

"If you keep thanking me, neither of us is going to get any work done," Ryan said, appreciating his friend's reaction and touched by his words.

Matt laughed and slumped down in his chair. "I'd call you a jerk, but I'm all emotional right now."

"Well, hurry up and finish your meal and get back on the job." Ryan made to leave the lounge. "Let's go help some kids."

"You got it," Matt said with a smile.

Ryan resumed his rounds, feeling good about everything, especially the new level that he and Mia had gained in their relationship. Rough times would come, he knew that. Every relationship had them. But somehow, he knew they would be okay.

MIA SAT IN her office, tapping her pen against the notepad in front of her. Her mind had been on anything but accounts since her return from lunch in the park with Ryan. She was falling in love, maybe for the first time in her life, and it was downright terrifying. The thought shook her to her core because she usually kept herself distanced so she didn't have to get hurt. Yet, here she was at the beginning of a new romance that had bloomed so quickly she hadn't even seen it happen.

Mia's mind was on what would happen next, and this wasn't something she could share with her sisters. She wanted to build on her new relationship with Ryan. This time she didn't want it to be him that came to her. Mia knew this step had to be hers. She was invested as much as he. Mia decided that Ryan would find a surprise invitation that night.

"Why are you smiling like the Cheshire cat?" Micki asked, standing at the office doorway frowning.

"I am allowed to smile. I do it all the time," she answered her sister.

"Where? Alone in your room?" Micki leaned a hip against the wall. "I thought your face was breaking."

Mia rolled her eyes. "What do you want?"

"The deliveries for the gazebo are coming in today," Micki said. "I wanted you to know when the trucks will arrive. The contractor is coming to dig out the foundation today, too."

"This won't bother John and Heather, will

it? We can't have their honeymoon ruined with loud machinery."

"Nope." Micki smiled. "They're in Asheville for a lovely romantic night courtesy of me. That includes the hot springs, and by the time they return tomorrow, the foundation will be poured. I plan to work around when they aren't here and are out sightseeing."

Mia nodded. "Good plan. Thanks for thinking that up."

"I'm more than a pretty face," Micki pointed out. "I'll let you get back to thinking about seeing your doctor."

"I was not!" she declared hotly. "But tonight, will you and Margo stay away from the gazebo?"

"Oooh, what's going on out there tonight?" her sister asked. "A little love nest for the lovebirds?"

"Ryan spends so much time romancing me, I want to plan something nice for him." Then Mia carefully wrote on one of the guest postcards for Ballad Inn. "When Ryan comes home he'll find this, and there's also a dress bag on his bed."

"I can't get over you being all romantic and stuff." Micki's tone then became serious. "I like this new side of you, Mia. You've hidden yourself away for so long, made sure Margo and I shined. Now it's time for you to feel that warmth and light. I hope you're feeling the love and embracing all of it."

"I think I am." Mia felt tears threaten to fall. "I'm so scared, Micki, but I don't want to run away from it."

"Part of love is feeling the fall but you gotta jump anyway." Micki came around the desk and gave her a hug. "And if you do hurt, we will always have your back, and I'll run him out of town."

"That escalated quickly." Mia smiled and gave a watery laugh.

"It's my gift, it's my curse." Micki laughed along with her. "You should wear the black dress I loaned you."

"No!" Mia wiped at her wet cheeks. "Instead, I think we should talk about your clothing choices."

"Hey, not everyone can pull off a dress like that," Micki said mildly and headed off. "It's not my fault you're so much taller than me."

"You were such a nice baby and little

girl," Mia called out to her, "but from age twelve, you became a nightmare!"

Micki's laughter was all that wafted back.

Mia finished her last tasks as soon as possible so she could have time to prepare. First, she set up the gazebo the way she wanted it to look for a romantic prom night. She turned on the twinkle lights and added tea candles at certain places along the white carved railing. Arranging two chairs facing each other, she put the small table with a red satin cloth between them and added plates of finger food, plus punch to be authentic as possible.

After a long bath to calm her nerves, Mia added a small spray of her favorite scent to her neck before she stepped into her version of a prom dress. It was long, yellow and strapless, and one of the prettiest things she'd ever seen. Luckily it was warm enough that her bare shoulders would not be chilled in the least. Charlotte had two seasons: winter because sometimes fall started out with chillier temperatures, and then spring often skipped straight into summer. With her hair and makeup flawless, Mia made sure her dress was perfect, and the nervous butterflies in her stomach quelled when she went downstairs.

Luckily her neighbors had all gone in for the night and Mia thanked the heavens that her family was scarce as well. She kept everything dark until she saw Ryan get dropped off and go inside the inn. She switched all the lights on again in the gazebo and lit the tea candles before starting the boom box, which played her '80s and '90s mix CD to set the mood. It felt like forever waiting on Ryan to come out and join her. Maybe those butterflies weren't so quelled.

Mia had never planned anything like this in her life and she hoped that it would make Ryan happy and see that she, too, was trying to make this work between them. Suddenly, there he was. He looked so handsome in his tux, he'd even managed to tame his wild curls when in fact she liked them a little tousled.

"I got this invitation, but I don't know if I'm at the right place," Ryan said in a deep-timbred voice.

"Are you Dr. Ryan Cassidy?" Mia asked, calling the roll and taking the invitation from his hand to check it.

His tone clearly revealed how pleased he was. "Yes, I am."

"Then welcome to Mia and Ryan's prom of 2024," Mia said exuberantly. "I got here early to make sure everything was ready."

"You look amazing to start with," Ryan said, reaching for her hand. "And no one has ever given me a prom before. I love this."

"I'm glad you like it." She led him to the table. "Punch? It may or may not be spiked with sparkling cider."

He laughed. "I'll make sure to take it easy."

"I'm hoping it will loosen you up to dance with me," Mia told him. "No one really wants to dance, and you're my date so…"

"Of course I will dance. I'm not here to hang out with the boys," Ryan said with surety and followed her lead. "They can glower in the corner all they want. They're just jealous."

Mia almost choked on her glass of punch, laughing. "That's great. Your boys in the corner?"

"Too much?" Ryan asked.

"No, go with it." She shot him a smile.

A song began to play, and Ryan pulled her

into the center of the gazebo. "Let's dance the night away."

Ryan's fast movements to the quick, pulsing beat had to be experienced in person because she couldn't quite explain what he was doing. Except for the robot, she couldn't distinguish the rest of his chaotic steps. She was impressed that he had no reservations though about showing her that side of himself.

Between sampling the finger foods and dancing to one '90s classic tune after another, Mia felt the bond between them become more solid. He jumped into everything feetfirst, not caring about the outcome. He had such a vibrant spirit, it was easy to get caught up and embrace life like he did. He was like the yin to her yang, and around him she didn't feel like boring old Mia. The next song spoke of a couple facing the world together, and Ryan swept her into his arms.

"You and me." He whispered the words and placed a soft kiss on her lips.

"I like the sound of that," Mia admitted and caressed his cheek. "You fit in here so well. It feels like you always belonged under this roof with me."

"Hey, I may never let you go."

Mia bit her lip. "Don't say that. I'm not expecting more from you than you're willing to give. I'm living in the moment right now."

Ryan looked to the stars and then back at her. "Believe in us. I do."

Their prom ended with them on a large blanket, both staring up at the night sky filled with stars. Mia moved her hand to the grass and felt the dampness of the dew on the blades and sighed in contentment.

A star shot across the sky and Mia gasped. "Did you see that?"

"Make a wish," Ryan said in a soft voice.

Mia closed her eyes and wished for this night to never end. "What about you? Did you make a wish?" Mia turned her head to look at Ryan and realized he was watching her.

"I think my wish has already come true," he said, never breaking their gaze. "If you could have one thing right now, what would it be?"

Mia smiled and stared up at the sky once more. "World peace."

He chuckled. "Something just for you."

"To break the boundaries I set for myself," Mia replied. "To not be the logical one, the problem-fixer and all the usual parts or roles I have played in my life."

"Why don't you?"

"Because in a way it soothes me," she confessed. "I feel safe in my world because nothing can hurt me there. I had to build those walls high but now I have to wonder if I'd had a more typical childhood whether I'd be different, more like Margo and Micki. The responsibilities fell to me, and I embraced them like a security blanket."

"It's not too late, Mia, to find anything you seek in life," Ryan murmured.

"This is my plunge right now, with you." Mia gave a small laugh. "Maybe if I can traverse falling in love, I can be brave in other ways."

"You said...you're falling in love." Ryan levered himself up to lean on his elbow. "With me?"

Mia smiled wide. "I don't see anyone else here having a fake prom with me. I'm falling for you, Ryan—hard—and I don't know what to do about it."

"How about nothing and just let it grow because I'm falling for you."

"Aren't we a pair?" Mia said. "One wanting to stay on the foundation she grew up with and one who travels because he never had someone to ask him to stay."

Ryan nodded. "We'll figure it out."

It shook her, the power of their connection, and seemed to touch her heart and her soul. Being in his arms felt more wonderful than she thought possible. They returned to the gazebo and stayed there until well after midnight, talking quietly, sharing thoughts and dreams.

Eventually, Ryan helped her clean up the remnants of their prom before stealing a kiss at the bottom of the steps and saying goodnight. Mia made a mental note to have the tux he wore dry-cleaned before she took it back to the rental shop tomorrow.

After locking up and heading upstairs, she came across a sleepy Margo, who looked at her through bleary eyes, holding a glass of orange juice. "Hussy," Margo said sleepily and went back to bed.

Mia smiled, moved on to her room and closed the door with a soft click. She missed Ryan's presence. As she snuggled under the covers, she could still feel his good-night kiss on her lips.

CHAPTER TEN

THE KNOCK ON his office door was light, and for a moment Ryan thought it might be Mia surprising him with a late lunch at work. He would be on call overnight, and he already knew he'd gotten spoiled with the meals he ate at Ballad Inn. Not only that, but he and Mia were getting closer, spending even more time together. What he had with Mia made him think, evaluate his life choices and wonder what the future would hold.

"Come on in," Ryan said warmly, expecting to see Mia.

Instead, it was Dr. Garrison, his smile wide. "Guess what?"

"You won that big ol' lottery and you're chucking it all in to move to Key West," Ryan joked.

"I wouldn't have even told you goodbye." Dr. Garrison stepped inside. His white lab coat always seemed extra long, and he managed to swish the fabric like he was Sherlock Holmes running off to investigate a case.

"That's cold, but I can forgive. So what's your news, Noel?" Ryan sat back.

"You got it. The attending job is yours," he said. "Dr. Ryan Cassidy, you can sign the paperwork as soon as the contract is drawn up. It'll take about two weeks to get all the hospital's ducks in a row for you to become Armstrong Medical's new head cardiothoracic pediatric surgeon."

The words stunned Ryan because he'd half expected not to get it. This was a permanent job, one that meant he had something solid in his life, and he liked Charlotte more than any place he'd grown up in or lived in since.

"What are you thinking?" Dr. Garrison asked. "Are you happy with the news?"

"I am. I guess they're going to accommodate my traveling with MAW?" Ryan asked.

"Along the lines I mentioned," his colleague told him. "The two weeks should give you a chance to discuss with your people at Medicine Across the World about how to cut down your volunteer work to at least two or three times a year—two, hopefully."

"And if I don't want to do that?" Ryan asked.

Dr. Garrison met his gaze. "Then you have two weeks to turn down the offer and finish out the current six-month contract until we find someone else. I do hope you choose to stay, Ryan. You'd be an asset here, and your patients are taken with you. You fit in here like it was made for you. Not everyone is that lucky to find their perfect fit on the first try."

"I know. Thanks, Noel." Ryan watched his friend step out the door with a mock salute.

He had some major thinking to do that would change the course of his life forever. Everything within him screamed for him to stay, but the familiarity of how he lived his life pulled at him and filled him with uncertainty. The what-ifs, the unknown, it all played a part, and he had two weeks to get his act together. He would say yes—a grin spread across his face, regardless of the doubts—he would say yes, but for now he would keep that to himself.

Ryan went back to seeing his patients. In the back of his mind, he considered how his life would change and how Mia might fit into it, if she agreed. There were so many logistics to sort out but he needed time before revealing his plan. Yet Ryan felt lighter as he worked that night shift, a sense of tiredness didn't even ebb into his bones. This was the dawn breaking on his new life, and he felt more reassured than he thought he would.

EVER SINCE HE'D ARRIVED, Ryan had fallen into a routine that he had come to love. The air in Charlotte was becoming warmer, and from what he was told, by the end of May it would be full-on summerlike temperatures with the humidity to boot. This was one of the few weekdays he had off, and Ballad Inn was surprisingly empty when he woke up.

Even Mia was gone until early evening per the note she'd left for him. He'd dreamed of her kisses while he slept.

There was no doubt about it.

He'd fallen hard for the beautiful Mia Ballad. Ryan took the day to wander around the house. He walked in the landscaped gardens. Happily enjoyed one of the sandwiches Enid had left in the fridge. There was also a plate of frosted cupcakes, and while his mouth watered to grab one and sink his teeth into it, Ryan thought better of it. He closed the fridge door with one last longing look at the covered dish and moved on before he gave in to temptation.

He found his way over to the neighbors as they played chess. Mr. Marley and Mr. Bolton were two characters, for sure. Their houses were right next to each other, and somehow they were always on Mr. Marley's porch, involved in their board game.

"I see you getting a little close there with Mia Ballad," Mr. Marley said. His hair was gray and cut close against his scalp. Dark weathered skin showed his age, but when he brought out a glass of tea for Ryan, his gait was strong and his back straight.

"What kind of doctor are you, anyway?" Mr. Bolton asked. "Can you help me with my arthritis?" He was shorter than his friend, and his gray hair was in a ponytail at the nape of his neck. The two elderly gents were obviously the best of friends, yet they couldn't look more different.

"I'm a pediatric doctor, but I did my rotation in general medicine until I picked my specialty. I can probably take a look at you and refer you to a great doctor friend of mine," he answered. "And yes, Mia and I are kinda seeing each other…well, more than kinda."

Mr. Marley nodded. "That's good. That young lady needs to get out more."

"So much on her shoulders even from a young age," Mr. Bolton added. "She practically raised her sisters because her parents were always jetting off somewhere."

"I didn't know they were that well-off to do that," Ryan commented.

"Her father sold some valuable property he had uptown for a pretty penny, and he was good with investing, had a small fortune built there. Then they sold the house for a song to the girls when they were old enough," Mr. Marley explained. "That didn't stop them from traipsing off and leaving those girls with no one but Enid. Mia got them to school. In fact, she once made Ralph the neighbor boy regret his words for picking on Margo. They were nine or ten at the time."

Ryan chuckled. "Sounds like Mia. She is very protective of her sisters, Enid and the house."

"They're the only stable things she's had in her life." Mr. Bolton sucked his teeth, a sound of disapproval. "Prom night, every young lady is getting pretty and taking pictures. Mia...she stayed home because Margo and Micki were sick, and no matter how much Enid told her to go, she refused. Enid told me she returned the dress and never gave it a second look."

"I think when she made us a prom in the backyard that we both got something amazing to remember." Ryan warmed at the thought of their special night. Even though she'd warned him about never dancing in public again. He smiled to himself.

"Oh, that was what she was doing," Mr. Marley said to his friend. "I told you she must have had a purpose. She must really care if she did that, son."

"I think she does, and I do for her," Ryan murmured.

"That girl needed to be shook up, leave that house and be carefree for a while," Mr. Bolton added. "I don't think she's been past South Carolina. Always at home, no relationships, no fun, no nothing."

"Until you came around," Mr. Marley

stated and gave him a look. "You planning on staying in these parts?"

Ryan tried to hold back his grin at the question that sounded very old-fashioned. "Yes, sir, I am. I think I've decided this is home for me."

"Good." Mr. Marley nodded. "She's sweet and deserves your good intentions. And I ain't no preacher, so don't make me have to lay hands on you, son."

"Like you could lay hands on anyone," Mr. Bolton snorted.

"I was a pretty good boxer in my day, Larry," Mr. Marley retorted. "Just because you have Enid under your spell doesn't mean you're the top dog in Sardis Woods."

"Oh…oh! You and Enid?" Ryan was surprised.

Mr. Bolton turned bright pink. "Don't ask a grown man his business."

Ryan grinned widely as the two men picked at each other while playing their game without missing a beat. Soon he drained his glass and wished them a good day before he went back over to the Ballad house. Their memories of Mia had given him a deeper insight into her personality.

It was quiet on the main floor, so he went upstairs to check on Monty in the sunroom, where the windows were locked against Doodle's attacks.

"Hey, dude." Ryan reached into the glass terrarium that was Monty's home and stroked the bearded dragon's back. "No incursions of the feline menace today. For now, you're safe."

Ryan impulsively looked out the window, and it almost scared him when he saw Doodle in the neighbor's window directly opposite, staring intently at Monty.

"Dude, he is really out to get you," Ryan said incredulously. "I'll talk to his owner and see if we can't come to some accord, I promise."

Monty didn't seem to give a hoot one way or the other. *Maybe he has some plan of attack of his own*, Ryan mused.

Looking at his phone, the picture he'd snapped of Mia one afternoon as she stared musingly out the window was in the notifications as a missed call. He'd made it her profile picture, which made him feel like some goofy adolescent, but then again, he really didn't have many of those experiences to draw on. He was about to call her back when the landline rang downstairs. He bounded down the two flights of stairs to answer the front-desk phone.

"Ballad Inn, where the honeysuckle grows wild and free," Ryan said politely into the receiver.

Mia laughed. "Well, that's new. I didn't know you could handle the front-desk duties. I may need to hire you full-time."

A laugh escaped him. "I was just about to call you back. I woke up to an empty house."

"Enid has gone to see her sister in Winston-Salem. She'll be back tomorrow in time for breakfast. Margo pulled a double shift to help her friend out. Micki is off to some mountain to rock climb with her new friend, Craig, and then camping out for the night," Mia explained, listing the whereabouts of all the residents. "The honeymooners have gone to Greensboro to explore, and I'm at my new client's house in Ballantyne. Two years of not filing taxes, so there's a lot to go through."

"Your day sounds not so fun. That's from a person who hates the thought of numbers and spreadsheets," Ryan replied, loving the sound of her full voice.

"Yet you are a doctor who has to use said numbers and equations for medication and treatments," Mia pointed out.

"Completely different circumstances."

"I'll take your word for it," she said dryly. "In any case, there is a ton of food in the fridge, and it will only be us for dinner tonight."

"Instead of staying in, how about I plan something?" Ryan suggested.

"You already took me to Heat Wave. I'm okay with staying in. We could have an old-movie marathon in the living room on the big screen."

Ryan's smile faltered just a bit. Lately he'd been seeing more of her willingness to stay home, and while he had no problem with the comfortableness of it, there were still parts of Charlotte he wanted to see and things he wanted to do, with Mia.

"Compromise," he suggested. "Old-movie night tonight, and next weekend it's my turn to find an outing, something great."

"Fine, if I can get the time off," she agreed hesitantly. "I've got a few clients with tax issues who haven't filed yet and we have to get them figured out before the June deadline. There's a penalty for being late, remember?"

"Right. Okay. We'll work around your schedule. No problem," Ryan said.

"You really should know about your money. Any CPA could be embezzling from you, your 401K or other income and investments," Mia pointed out gently.

"Then you're hired," Ryan said resolutely.

"What? No! That's a huge undertaking, and I would never work for someone I'm so close to, like you. Stay with whatever company or financial firm that handles it now. I know my strengths, and that would make me break out in hives."

"I could kiss them better?" he said in an endearing drawl.

"And on that note, I'm getting off the phone with you, sir."

"Oh, I like that formality."

"See you later, Doctor."

"Calling me *Doctor*, you're just trying to charm me even more," Ryan said teasingly.

Mia laughed. "I'm going now, before my client asks why my face looks red."

Ryan said softly, "You're so genuine, Mia. How could I not fall for you?"

"Oh, Ryan."

Her whisper was filled with longing and went straight to his heart.

"Go work. See you tonight," he said and heard the rasp of emotion in his own voice.

"Till tonight. Bye."

Would he ever get used to how whole, how good, how relaxed she made him feel? Would it all abate into something routine? *Maybe, like, when we're seventy,* he thought with a smile but still doubted very much that would be the case. It was so unexpected how he'd come to this new state and town searching for something and not even knowing what it was, and he'd found it in Mia. She didn't care about his laurels, his status, what he drove or what he could give her. Her smile in his direction or the look in her eyes after they kissed was the real deal and left him reeling.

It showed him how jaded he had become and how every situation in his life had just added another brick of cynicism. If he hadn't come here, he would've lost himself, become a person he didn't recognize. Fate, destiny, whatever you wanted to call it had other plans in store for him, and Mia was at the center of them all.

Ryan walked into the kitchen and opened the fridge to see what exactly was inside that he could warm up for dinner. Mia wanted a night in, so he would make it special.

IT WAS AFTER eight before she made it home. For a moment, Ryan had begun to worry as he watched from the porch for Mia's light blue car to come up the drive and park in its usual spot under the cherry tree. There were at least three blueberry bushes by the fence, with their first blossoms. He knew she checked them daily and also looked up at the cherry tree before coming inside. It was easy to tell they were important to her, and he hoped to be around long enough to see them bear fruit.

Actually, he could've moved into his own place by now, but the thought of looking didn't even cross his mind. Ballad Inn and Mia felt like home. Even so, he knew at some point he would have to begin the arduous task of house-hunting. The thought made him grimace.

"Why do you look like you sucked on a piece of lemon?"

Mia's soft voice pulled him from his thoughts. Despite all his watching, he'd been lost in his thoughts and hadn't heard her approach. She was dressed for business, in white cotton slacks and a satin shirt of the same color under a red blazer jacket. Her shoes were red as well. Her hair, which he loved to see wild and free, was pinned back into a high bun. Mia also carried a thick leather satchel in one hand and one of those large gray pocket folders under her arm.

Ryan kissed her lightly. "It's nothing. I was thinking about the need to house hunt."

"You got the job?" she asked, looking at him with wide, excited eyes. "You got the job!"

Ryan nodded, a grin spreading across his face. Any thought he had of keeping this under wraps went out the window given her excitement.

"So maybe I can find a house in this area and you can move in with me?" Ryan hinted.

"Or you could live here permanently?" Mia said. "Maybe not right away, but we've got time to plan, don't we?"

"I do like it here." He pulled her into his arms and used a light touch to turn her face to his. "I wouldn't want to be anywhere that doesn't have you in it."

"I love it here. I can't leave my home," Mia said.

"I can understand that." Ryan had heard the conviction in her tone. "I love your family, but we would need some privacy, yes?"

"I assume so." Mia chewed the corner of her lip. "This is why I wanted to buy Crawford's pasture behind Ballad Inn, so we could spread out and build... I don't know."

"We don't have to decide this now," Ryan said, seeing that she was already ten steps ahead, and he hadn't even signed the contract yet. "Tonight is bad B movie horror night, just you and me together."

She smiled warmly at him. "Sounds good, and I have a surprise for you, too."

"Now, that's not fair, hinting at a surprise. I'll be curious all night."

Mia winked and said in a teasing voice, "I think you'll manage."

"Mia."

She turned at the door. "Mmm-hmm?"

"Leave your hair down?" he asked softly. "I like it when it's wild and free."

She nodded and went inside.

Love. The word was filled with so many promises of what might be. Ryan hoped the hospital and all of it was the right decision. His instincts screamed this was the woman he wanted for the rest of his life, so he had to take the chance, right?

Ryan followed her into the inn and got dinner ready while she got changed. The coffee table was moved away, and on the floor he'd placed two thick quilts he'd found in the box chest that sat in the bay window. Warmed chicken potpies sat in deep bowls, accompanied by a bottle of chilled wine and caramel-covered popcorn he'd made himself.

Every thought left his head when Mia stepped into the room, her hair free from the pins that had held it in place. This time she wore long pink pajama bottoms and a matching T-shirt that featured a tiny rainbow over her heart. She was also barefoot with bright pink toenails. Ryan hadn't seen anyone this appealing in his whole life. She was so fresh-faced and beautiful, he was awestruck.

Mia folded her long legs beneath her to sit next to him on the quilt and fixed her crooked glasses. Settling against the plush cushions arranged on the floor, she looked up as a sudden swath of lightning cut through the sky outside. Thunder rumbled in the distance.

"This is all so very comfy," Mia said, "especially with a storm coming."

"It was clear when we were on the porch earlier. Do storms always move in so quickly around here?" Ryan asked incredulously.

"There is a saying in the Carolinas," she said. "*Don't like the weather? Give it a minute. It will change.* It's coming up to the end of springtime pretty soon, even though we already have summer temperatures. With warmer weather, it tends to bring in unexpected storms. But it's nice for snuggling while watching scary movies."

"In that case…" He moved closer and handed her dinner, before turning off the main lights, leaving the room bathed in a soft amber from the accent lamps on the side tables. He pulled the second quilt over them both. "Let's eat."

While they enjoyed the buttery, flaky pastry that surrounded chunks of creamy chicken, potatoes, carrots, peas and celery, the black-and-white movie caused shadows to cross the walls. After dinner, Mia nestled in the crook of his arm while they shared the popcorn.

"I cannot believe you made this." She tossed a small handful of the treat into her mouth. "It's so good!"

Her compliment pleased him. "You tend to learn a few things when you are at home with only a housekeeper to teach you some of their tricks. Ours was an older guy named Jesse, and he taught me some easy recipes. He said a man should never be in the world without knowing how to at least make pasta to impress a date. Then he taught me that popcorn like this could nab me a wife."

"So I'll be down on one knee before the night is over?" Mia teased, leaning into his joke. "And here I forgot to go ring shopping on the way home."

"Oh, I don't need anything fancy," Ryan

replied. "Just a simple diamond that can be seen from space."

"That's the type of money that I don't have." She snuggled closer. "I can find a ring in the attic, maybe."

"I'd treasure it forever." He kissed her temple. "But promise me a honeymoon somewhere I'll never forget, so it can be our place anytime we visit."

"So sentimental," she sputtered and laughed. "I'll have to wrangle something in North Carolina. I have never taken a flight in my life to anywhere."

"Why?"

Mia shrugged. "Not my cup of tea. Watching my parents jet-set pretty much cured me of ever wanting to do the exact same thing."

"You're missing out on a beautiful world." Ryan played with a tendril of her thick black hair. "The smell of warm bread in Italy or swimming in the Mediterranean Sea or eating lobster in Monaco."

"Sounds expensive." Mia's lips became a tight line.

"We don't always have to go somewhere fancy. There are lots of great places that don't cost a lot," he said. "Then, we'd get to see the world together. Or you could come with me when—"

"That's not happening," she said firmly. "In the case of my parents, they weren't rich, just well-off enough from selling the land they had uptown and good investment sense. Charlotte was becoming a mecca for banks and people moving from the cities, so they made a fair amount. And spent most of it on traveling."

"Mia, did you ever ask their reason for the lifestyle they chose?" Ryan asked gently.

"Nothing they say could validate a reason to leave their young daughters so often," she retorted.

"I can see your point, but that doesn't mean you have to stay in one place to spite them or to make your point." He smiled as he cupped her cheek. "What if I wanted to take you away for a vacation so we could get out of our own heads? To enjoy cherry blossoms in Japan or listen to the singing steps by the sea in Croatia?"

"Sounds like a guy with no roots, who can do whatever he wants, whenever he pleases, and is as stable as a house of cards." Mia's voice was stiff. "Then it makes me wonder what we're doing here, what's going on between us?"

"Mia…"

The lights went out suddenly, plunging the house into darkness. Silence reigned, apart from the sound of the rain and a loud boom of thunder. Mia was startled enough that a little scream escaped her. Ryan couldn't deny the relief he felt that Mother Nature interrupted what had quite possibly been building into an argument.

"I guess movie night is over," she said with a nervous laugh. "I don't like storms much."

"Well, I'm happy to keep you safe," Ryan said. "But do you know where a flashlight is so we don't crash into anything trying to get around?"

"There is something even better." Mia moved and turned on the gas fireplace. "How's this?"

"Romantic." He laced his fingers with hers and kissed her hand. "Mia, this is home base for me. Charlotte, you, my job. What we're doing here is falling in love, and that's the strongest foundation that could ever be built."

"Ryan, I'm not sure," Mia whispered. "Like this storm, it's all so unpredictable."

"Be sure of me." He kissed her once, twice, before whispering, "Be sure of me."

"I'll try." She hugged him tight and repeated the words as if they were a promise to them both. "I'll try."

"You mentioned a surprise?"

"I almost forgot!" She pressed a kiss on his cheek before standing. "I'll be right back."

Ryan didn't know what to expect from Mia. When she returned, she had a plate with four cupcakes, and in each was a lit birthday candle, illuminating her face. She also had a large bag looped over her arm and a small blue one held by the crook of her finger.

"Happy birthday to you," Mia sang and Ryan laughed in delight. *"Happy birthday to you, happy birthday, Mr. President...* Wait, wrong person." She grinned and joined him in their cozy spot in front of the fireplace. *"Happy birthday to you."*

"That was great." Ryan couldn't help but chuckle.

"You have to blow out the candles and make a wish," Mia told him.

"What should I wish for?" Ryan closed his eyes and tapped his chin dramatically.

"Blow the candles out before we're eating wax," Mia said dryly.

There was no wish that Ryan could make: she was right there, and he was realizing that she was all he ever wanted. Still, it couldn't hurt to pad the deck in his favor; their relationship was important, and he wanted it to last for a lifetime. If that meant blowing out a few candles, so be it.

"What did you wish for?" Mia asked.

"I'm not too certain about the wishes thing, but I do know that if I tell you, it won't come true." Ryan kissed the tip of her nose. "How did you know it was my birthday?"

"The online reservation portal for Ballad Inn. When you booked the room you had to list your birthday to prove you were over eighteen," she explained. "I'm assuming you never did anything in the way of birthday parties."

"People did a little celebration in Somalia once when I was there. Does that count?" Ryan asked.

"It does." She licked the icing off her fingers after plucking the candles from the cupcakes. "But next year, I'll plan you a birthday bash and invite the whole neighborhood."

"The very same neighborhood that watched you bruise your tailbone?" Ryan raised a brow, he couldn't help the grin.

"Gee, rub it in, why don't you?" Mia said. "No presents or cupcakes for you, and I will let you know I made my special butterscotch ones for this occasion."

"Oh, come on. I'll be good," Ryan promised. "Give me a cupcake."

"Here." Mia pushed the dish toward him. "Cupcakes before gifts. What a sweet tooth you have."

"I know the real prize here." He took one of the desserts eagerly.

Ryan sank his teeth into his birthday cupcake. He closed his eyes when the taste of butterscotch filled his mouth and the tiny bits of crunchy toasted pecans gave the texture even more flavor.

"Oh, wow! Marry me?" Ryan closed his eyes, savoring the taste.

"Man, if I'd known these cupcakes would

garner me proposals, I would've baked long ago." She ate her own dessert while he devoured his cupcake, then another, with gusto.

"Nope, these are mine, and their maker is also mine," Ryan said. "At least, I hope she is. I'm not the sharing type."

"Me, either." Mia gave him a nod and passed him the larger of the two gifts. "Open this."

Ryan tossed the tissue aside exuberantly. In the bag was a remote control car that used Bluetooth. It was an expensive toy, all black, with the caduceus decal on the sides. It would be perfect to keep the kids entertained at the hospital.

"I figured you could get the hang of driving it, then share it with the kids on your floor," Mia said.

Ryan grinned and leaned forward to kiss her. "This is great. Thank you so much."

"This second one is all for you." Mia used her toes to snag the bag and hand it to him.

"Toe delivery," Ryan said, amused.

"Sticky hands."

From within the small blue bag with silver tissue paper, Ryan pulled out a shiny box.

Glancing at Mia curiously, he opened it to find a silver pendant on a thick silver chain.

"My family is originally from Barbados. We were brought here so young that I barely remember and Margo was a baby then. Micki wasn't even born yet," Mia explained while Ryan took the crafted piece out of the box.

"That is the coat of arms of Barbados, and usually if someone leaves the island, they buy or have one of these made. Whoever has the emblem on their person, no harm can come to them."

"That's a wonderful sentiment." Ryan held the piece up, watching it catch the light from the fire playing across the surface.

"You've traveled a lot, and I wanted to give you something that ties you to Charlotte and to me." She sat in front of him and took his hand. "It's a part of our home and heritage, and my sisters and I all have one, and now you do, too, because I consider you part of our home and family and my heart."

Ryan pressed his lips softly to hers. Nothing in his life had humbled him more than this gift, not only the pendant and chain, but the fact that she'd included him in those closest to her. This gave Ryan a sense of belonging that he couldn't describe.

"Thank you for this." Ryan cleared the emotion from his throat. "No one—no one has cared enough to make me feel like I should be with them."

Mia kissed him gently. "You are the sweetest man, and you aren't the temporary sort. You leave a mark everywhere you go, with healing hands, with your smile and the happiness you find in even the smallest things. I'm glad I got to share this birthday with you and let you know how much you are treasured."

He didn't know what to say. He was overwhelmed, not just by her kindness and generosity, but by her, period, full stop. In the end he just rested his forehead against hers and immersed himself in being with the woman who had his heart.

The electricity came back on and made them both smile, then the movie night continued with the lights dimmed and the plot playing out in black and white on the screen. At some point they both fell asleep, her head on his shoulder and his leaned back against the sofa. The rest of the uneaten popcorn was still between them.

When he woke up, she murmured but settled once again. Ryan smiled, restarted the movie and tucked the blanket around them. To him, he felt like they were so much closer than before. He had come to Charlotte for a new job and a new life, not knowing what he was searching for. He ended up finding Mia, and love as well, and Ryan knew his life would never be the same.

CHAPTER ELEVEN

A WEEK PASSED, and it was a known fact around the inn and the neighborhood that she and Ryan were seeing each other. More than once they were caught sneaking a secret kiss. So much for secrets. With a family that was everywhere and neighbors who were into each other's business, the kisses were never as secret as they'd like to think.

"There they go canoodling again in public," Mr. Webber grumbled loudly, holding his menacing cat.

"It's not public in my backyard, and you are staring over our fence!" Mia called out from where they sat on the swing, enjoying the afternoon.

"You were much nicer as a spinster," he said, turning away.

"No one calls me a spinster, Mr. Webber!" Mia said loudly.

Mr. Webber huffed, went indoors and slammed his screen door shut behind him.

"He's just mean," she muttered.

"Or lonely," Ryan replied.

Mia wanted to do something special for Ryan. He had recognized that she was a firmly rooted tree planted in Charlotte, and he hadn't run away as yet. He'd seen some of her quirks and the angst that came along with her parents' lack of availability while she was growing up, and he'd tried to reassure her about his intention to stay. Still, she wanted to show him that the area she loved and had grown up in was spectacular. Of course, the best way to do that was to enlist her sisters because, as always, three Ballad heads were better than one.

"Greensboro for the nightlife?" Margo suggested.

"We have a pretty good nightlife here," Micki pointed out. "Raleigh? There's a cool, niche restaurant there called Shakespeare's Quill, and the chef sears, like, a sixteen-ounce steak right in front of you, plus killer drinks, and the waitstaff dress up in period costumes."

"Explain the bridge that links a great writer with fine dining?" Mia asked, curious.

Micki shrugged. "I don't know. Poetry gives you a big appetite?"

Margo laughed as she rolled out pie dough. "She has you there, sis."

"The planetarium in Gastonia?" Enid suggested from the stove, where she was cooking the apple filling that would be in the pies for dessert that night. The scent was delicious.

"Is that still open?" Mia asked.

"I got it." Micki snapped her fingers. "I have a friend in Lake Norman with a sleek boat on the water, his own dock and everything. He's gone for a month to Cancún. He said I could use the boat or the house anytime. You remember how to take a boat out, right? Go enjoy the day on the lake."

Mia wrinkled her nose. "Not sure I'm up for that. Haven't been on the water for a long time. Might be squeamish."

Micki snorted. "Squeamish? You were a grown-up person skateboarding up and down the middle of our street."

"That's right, you did do that. People took photos," Margo chimed in.

Mia shook her head. "Maybe I should run off to see the world with Ryan after all."

"What! Are you going to travel?" Margo

asked. "Bring me like eight cookbooks from every stop you make."

"Calm down. He wanted to be spontaneous, but I nixed that idea," Mia said matter-of-factly. "We had a lovely time watching old black-and-white horror movies."

"But why would you nix that?" Micki asked. "You have a guy wanting to take you off to see the world, and you said no?"

"I'm good with being home. If I'm hoofing it all over the world, who will take care of the house, the business?" Mia asked.

"Pfffttt! Oh please, don't use that as an excuse. You're afraid of stepping out of your perfect little box," Micki said in irritation. "We are grown-up women, too. We can take care of the house and the business. We are not children anymore."

"No one said you were," Mia quickly agreed, hoping that it would end the subject.

It was Enid's turn. "Mia Ballad, your parents cannot be the be-all and end-all of your distrust. They traveled. I took care of you girls."

"Enid, I love you like a mother because half the time you were the only mother I knew," Mia said frankly. "Even when Mom and Dad were home, it was like eating dinner with strangers who were parents by default. I like being home. That's all there is to it."

"No, that's not it, Mia. You used to tell me about all the places in your books when we were growing up, and it dwindled away until your whole life revolved around this house and the neighborhood where we live," Margo said gently.

Mia looked at them, feeling hurt. "Is it Gang Up On Mia Day?"

"No, it's Mia Needs to Live Outside of Us and This Place Day," Micki said, still clearly frustrated. "I sometimes think it would've been better if we let the house go to another owner. Maybe then you wouldn't be so stuck."

"You guys are all I have." Mia felt tears threaten.

"Mia, you have Ryan now as well," Margo said.

Hurt filled her chest because this house, her sisters and Enid were all that had mattered before Ryan. It sounded like all the hard work she'd put into keeping them together didn't seem to matter at all.

"I'm sorry that me not taking an impromptu trip upsets you all." Mia slipped off the kitchen stool where she sat. "Or the fact that it seems so much more important than everything I ever did to make sure we stayed a family."

"Mia, no one is saying that. We love you!" Enid called to her retreating back.

Mia bypassed her office and went upstairs to her bedroom and closed the door. She lay on the bed and stared up at the ceiling angrily and hoped that the tears that pricked her eyes wouldn't fall. The door to her room opened, but she didn't look to see who entered. The wide bed sank on each side as her sisters climbed in with her.

"Just because you took the master bedroom doesn't mean we can't get in, weirdo. There's keys," Micki said, teasing. She laid her head on Mia's shoulder. "I'm sorry we hurt your feelings, sis."

"We only want what's best for you." Margo laid her head on Mia's other shoulder.

"I'm scared," Mia admitted, "of my feelings for Ryan, his work that takes him out of the country and the fact that he could just go, and if I didn't follow him, it wouldn't matter. Will I ever match up to that?"

"Ryan loves you. We all could see that even before you two did," Micki said with certainty. "I would love to see you send us pictures from any place in the world, happy and carefree. After all these years of being our protector, we want to protect you and give you a chance to live without worrying about us or this house."

"I know." Mia sighed. "I'll get there, but these hang-ups are mine to work out and on my own time."

Micki held up her hand, a set of keys dangling. "For the house and Paul's boat. Enid is going to make you a basket, and Paul has a great playlist. Go enjoy the day with your doctor and appreciate falling in love."

"We saw him in those garish pajamas that morning with Doodle," Margo teased. "He fits into all this zaniness, that's for sure."

"You both are too much." Mia laughed.

The moment ended with her being prodded in the ribs, which led to them tickling each other and laughing for a good long while. It was like being kids again, in the big bed with her twinkle lights on, making the space magical for them when they needed it most. Together they were all each other had then, and in the end, that was all that mattered. Now it was good for them to bring more people into their lives to love.

SATURDAY MORNING, instead of Ryan planning something for the two of them, it was Mia who drove. Ryan, she noticed, looked a little cramped.

Ryan shifted uncomfortably. He grimaced when his knee hit the dashboard.

"Button down by the seat. Press it and slide back." Mia chuckled. "It's called a compact car for a reason."

"Sardines are also kept in a compact space." He chuckled, too. "You may need to peel back the top for me like you do their cans."

"Shush, we are almost there." She glanced over at him and smiled.

He was as handsome as ever in his super-hero-graphic T-shirt and cargo shorts. The window was open instead of using the air-conditioning, and the light wind ruffled the hair that she had touched more than once.

It was a perfect day. The sunlight glistened on the lake's rippling waves, and it was breathtaking to stare out at the water as they drove by. "This is gorgeous," Ryan said. "That's it. I'm buying a boat for our summers on the lake."

"*Our*, huh? *On the lake*, that sounds nice," she said, giving herself permission to picture the future.

Mia felt like she had pulled off the gift of a lifetime when he reacted to the boat, named *The Promise*, at the dock. Ryan practically ran down the wooden walkway to the pristine white ten-foot yacht and turned as she came up beside him with the basket. One of the young men who worked at the marina waited patiently to help them take the boat out, just as Micki said he would. Mia was impressed with her sister's resourcefulness and connections.

Ryan pulled her into a hug that lifted her off her feet. "You did this for me?"

Mia nodded. "Yeah, Micki has a friend who is out of town, and we got permission to take the boat out for the day. That is, if you want to help me pilot one of these things."

"I do." He grinned as she slid to her feet.

"What would you have done if I couldn't be the captain?"

"Obviously, Doctor, I would have captained her. Please feel free to salute at will," she answered. "Permission to come aboard?"

"Oh, permission definitely granted." Ryan extended his hand with a flourish and returned her salute.

When they were on board, Ryan pulled in the temporary steps and laid them against the side of the boat, locking them into place, while the guy on the dock untied the thick rope that kept them moored. Mia was pretty impressed with how Ryan handled the boat, taking it out slowly and then making a gradual turn to direct them out to the middle of the lake.

It was early in the season yet, but there were already other people on the water, taking in the warm day, and a few more folks fishing from the banks, their lines bobbing in the water.

Mia took a minute to remove her shorts and white T-shirt to reveal the red bathing suit she wore. It had side cutouts covered with mesh, plus it fit perfectly. This had been an impulse buy that had stayed hidden in the back of her drawer for years, until today, when she felt daring enough to put it on. She looked at Ryan at the helm of the boat, and he shook his head.

"Definitely buying a boat or three!" he called to her, making Mia burst out with laughter before she went down into the galley.

Down below there was a cooler for the drinks she'd brought and other items that needed to stay chilled for the day. Back up top, the gorgeous sunshine reflected off the water, causing the ripples to look like diamonds. Ryan was dropping anchor and already shirtless.

"Today is perfect." He stretched his arms high above his head. "There is, like, zero humidity, and the breeze is great."

"It's Memorial Day weekend next week, the unofficial start of summer." Mia spread a beach blanket out on the deck and placed the cooler and food within arm's reach. "When we wake up on that Friday and Speed Street kicks off, it will not feel like this. The humidity will be so thick you'll be able to backstroke in it."

"What's Speed Street?" Ryan asked.

"Usually, an opportunity to rent out the whole inn, but since we have you and the honeymooners, we don't need to do that this year. It's basically an event to kick-start the car-racing season," Mia explained. "Uptown is blocked off, tons of tents, cars on display, live music and acres of food. Throngs of people pour into Charlotte for it."

Mia sat behind him and began to rub sunscreen on his back.

"Sounds busy." Ryan turned and took the cream from her. "Now you."

Mia turned so he could protect her skin with the sunblock that smelled like coconut.

"In Minneapolis, we had some strange seasons like winterfall, where kids have to celebrate Halloween in coats and hats, but then comes deep winter," he said and paused to shudder. "Brrr."

Mia chuckled. "Well, you will love winter here. We barely get any snow. Last year it was sixty-five degrees in December, and the snowstorm consisted of about five flurries and an occasional gust of wind."

Ryan laughed. "Your description sounds

lovely." He placed a kiss on her shoulder when he was done with the sunscreen.

The remote to the sound system was downstairs on the counter, she recalled. She went to the galley and picked it up to return to the deck. She pressed the power button, and the air filled with a mix of classic rock and oldies that only enhanced the atmosphere while they soaked up the sun. They sipped fresh fruit punch in the early afternoon and lunched on a lovely charcuterie platter that included her favorite pepper jam.

The lake was warm this time of the year. Taking a dip earlier, for instance in April, would have resulted in being frozen. Ryan dived into the water without hesitation, and his vibrant energy inspired Mia to do the same. She frolicked in the water with the man she had fallen in love with, sharing kisses and splashing each other. Back on the boat, they stretched out in the sun, side by side with sunglasses to protect against the glare.

"What are you thinking?" Ryan asked, turning his head to her.

"Nothing. My brain is pleasant white noise," Mia murmured. "Why—was I sup-

to remember, and I'm never going to let you go," Ryan said on a sweet note.

"Let's make these decisions slowly," Mia said. "We know what we want, and we don't have to rush."

"I trust my instincts, but I understand your need to not act impulsively. One day at a time, one foot in front of the other."

"Sometimes I wish I was more like Micki," Mia admitted suddenly. "I envy her ability to adapt to change so quickly and make the situation her own."

"And I'm sure she envies your ability to be stable and precise." Ryan's tone was gentle. "You are who you are meant to be. Your parents' lives affected you each differently, but your personalities are all wonderful."

Mia ducked her head shyly. "Thank you."

"I'm not done," Ryan said with a warm smile. "You are kind, funny, empathic to others' feelings, and you have a sense of home. I never felt anything like that until I stepped foot in Ballad Inn, so thank you, Mia, for giving me my first real sense of home."

His words got to her, and Mia felt tears threaten. Their lives were so different, yet they fit together like puzzle pieces, each looking for something and finding it in the other. More of her doubts faded away, and she let herself truly feel without the fear of the unknown. Ryan was who she wanted: she was in love.

"Okay, I'm thoroughly baked. I need another dip," Ryan said.

"I'll join you," Mia said.

They both dived into the water, and the rest of the day was spent in happy bliss being with each other. That was until they heard a scream and another cry from a boat close by.

"Get her, get her, Brandon!" a woman cried out.

"I can't see her!" A man dived down and soon popped up. "I can't see her!"

Without hesitation, Ryan struck out with long strokes, cutting his way through the water, with Mia right behind him. They reached the other boat in less than a minute.

"Our daughter fell in!" the man gasped.

Ryan and Mia dived instantly. Mia was the first to resurface for more air.

"She wanted to swim, I was getting her life jacket on and she wiggled out of my hands and ran." Tears streaked the young mother's frantic face. "She went off the edge like she saw her daddy do, before we could catch her!"

"We'll find her," Mia said, although her heart raced in fear when she went back down and came up again with no sign of the young girl.

"It's been too long!" the mom cried out.

Her husband came up out of the water, and with tortured eyes he shook his head. He took a deep breath, ready to go down again. But in a flash, Ryan appeared and he lifted the little girl over his head.

"Take her!" Ryan's voice was ragged as he struggled for breath.

The mother did exactly that and set her daughter down on the boat, laying her flat on her back. "She's not breathing," the woman sobbed, as the others reached the deck.

"He's a doctor," Mia said, and Ryan immediately started CPR.

Ryan did chest compressions and paused to check on the girl's breathing. He looked up at the worried parents. "Get us to the dock. Get on the radio, we need an ambulance waiting on the shore."

Together, he and Mia continued to try to help the little girl. Mia felt her own tears fall now. This was not something she ever wanted to see—

Suddenly the still child shuddered, coughed and brought up water. Ryan quickly turned her onto her side and patted her back with a firm but gentle hand, assisting her to bring up more water. A loud wail erupted from the girl, and they all looked at each other in relief. The mother fell to her knees and gathered her daughter up in her arms, rocking her. The father put his arms around them both. Mia and Ryan sat down away from the family to give them time and space.

The expression she shared with Ryan was one of elation. Ryan took her hand and squeezed it. That was how they stayed, hand in hand, until they made it to the shore where an ambulance waited. A boat from the marine unit of the local police came up moments after, just as the paramedics took over the care of the child.

Ryan became all business as he spoke to the EMTs. "Three or four years old, under the water for at least two minutes. We got her breathing, but she still needs to be taken to the ER."

"Are you a medic? Military?"

"I'm a pediatric doctor at the local children's hospital," Ryan told the young first responder.

"Thankfully you were out there, then," one of the marine officers said. "We'll sort out why she wasn't in a life jacket later."

"I think they'd appreciate that. They were trying to put it on her, but you know how jumpy and excited kids get," Mia said in defense of the parents.

She received a stiff nod in return, and after profuse thanks from the parents, she and Ryan were taken back to *The Promise* by the police cutter.

"That was a close call," Ryan said when they were alone.

It was then the whole event hit her, and Mia began to tremble, then cry. Ryan gathered her up against him.

"How do you do this?" she asked between her tears. "See lives in the balance and not be terrified?"

"Because they need my help more than

my fear, and I vowed to make sure they all have a chance," Ryan answered. "You did good, Mia. You jumped in and didn't lose your cool."

"I'm okay," she said, trying to sound strong.

"The adrenaline of the situation is gone, and now your body is reacting." Ryan squeezed her tight, the strength of his arms reassuring her. "She's okay, and you have every right to cry and feel like you do now. If we don't feel and are numb to a child being in danger or ill, then something is wrong somewhere."

"True." Mia wiped the tears away from her eyes. "In any case, I need a mimosa and something to eat to calm my nerves."

"Do we still have food? How much did you pack?" Ryan's tone was light, which she was grateful for. She headed for the basket.

"Plenty, since Enid prepared this," she said and winked at him.

Mia ate. Ryan also tucked into a full plate. After the nerve-fraying events of earlier, they now had a peaceful moment to watch the sun set. By eight, Ryan had maneuvered the boat back into place at the dock.

"I could stay out here all night," he said, standing on the deck while the moored boat bobbed merrily.

Mia sighed. "One day we will, when the summer gets warmer and fireworks light up the Fourth of July. You'll succumb to my charms for sure after grilled meat and an assortment of seasonal sides."

"That's rather specific." He laughed and folded his arms over his chest. "And here I was thinking I've been playing hard to get."

"Your hard-to-get game is pitiful." She shook her head. "I had you wrapped around my little finger from the time I let you kiss me in the tree."

Ryan gasped. "You're calling me a pushover!"

"Yes. Yes, I am."

Their joking continued and he pulled her into his arms and rocked her gently. "We're buying a lake house for days like this, maybe weekends and staycations."

"I like that idea." Mia nipped his chin before laying her head on his chest. "I'll keep my stock of bathing suits in the closet there…but first, I need to buy a stock of bathing suits."

His soft chuckle rumbled through him. "You are the best."

CHAPTER TWELVE

MIA'S EXPECTATION OF a wrench being thrown into the well-oiled machine of her life came in the form of her parents' arrival. She'd spent so much time building up her wall against being hurt, against the chaos they brought, yet when they showed up, she was hurtled back to being that girl, watching them come and go. Becoming an adult didn't take away the hurt of her past, and of course, Mia knew her choosing to hide from her feelings instead of dealing with them wasn't right, either.

None of it was made any easier as she sat happily smiling in her office, thinking about Ryan and the time they would spend together, only to have the fun images erased by the doorbell ringing and Enid's loud, delighted cry coming from the foyer.

"Mia, Margo, Micki, your parents are home!"

Mia heard the footsteps running down the stairs and coming from the kitchen, then the joyful laughing and enthusiastic greetings. Meanwhile, she got up slowly and just as slowly moved to the door. She wasn't one to hurry in excitement to see Brian and Rosie Ballad. Old feelings surfaced, no matter what her age, and resentment bubbled up.

All eyes turned toward her when she came from the office and walked over to where her family stood.

"Mom, Dad." She kissed a cheek of each parent dutifully. "How are you both?"

"We're good, Mia. We missed you."

She didn't respond to her mother. Rosie Ballad smiled, only a few wrinkles forming at the corners of her eyes. Sixty-seven was her mother's age, and seventy her father's, but looking at them, you'd think they were in their late fifties. Their lifestyle suited them.

"Well, where were you this time?" Micki grinned.

"A lovely little town in Spain for one." Her father pulled Micki close to him and put an arm around her shoulder. "And I of course got you a bell for your collection."

"Oh, the one from China she will love,"

their mother gushed. "We got all of you something nice from each stop."

"That will be great for after dinner," Enid said and smiled. "Our honeymooners are gone, but Ryan is still here."

"Ryan? Who is this Ryan?" their mother asked. "Whose beau has taken up residence in our house?"

"No, *our* house," Mia said briskly. "Dr. Ryan Cassidy is the attending doctor for Armstrong Medical."

"What Mia is failing to tell you is that she and the good doctor are in a relationship," Margo filled in the story.

"And the fact that he's so well-known, there's a hospital wing named after him in Minneapolis," Micki pointed out with a chuckle.

"Well, well, I guess we'll be hearing more about him, won't we?" Brian Ballad said.

"Not from me. It's my personal life and his," Mia answered. "If you wanted to know about your daughters' lives, you would actually stay around more often and not speak to us in the form of postcards or three-word texts from random places across the world."

"Baby girl," her father said warningly,

"we're still your parents. You'll respect us as such."

"And you will respect my personal business as such," Mia said simply. "This is my home. I won't be chastised in the place we work so hard to pay for."

Her father opened his mouth to speak, but her mother placed a hand on his arm to stop him. "You're absolutely right, Mia," she said, her smile a little sad. "We're here now if you want us to know anything about your life."

"It's not anything I can fit into a minute. A lot goes on while you're off on your adventures. I'm going back to my office. You guys know how to set yourselves up until you're ready to leave again." Mia turned on her heel. "I'll see everyone at dinner."

Mia closed her door, her hands slightly shaking. Back behind her desk, she looked at the computer monitor. The numbers and spreadsheets meaning nothing anymore as her eyes blurred with frustrated tears. Why had her parents shown up now, when she'd found a modicum of happiness in her life? To be snoops and pretend they're the perfect parents? Mia dreaded dinner as much as she did Ryan coming home to meet them. A defeated sigh escaped her. It couldn't be helped. She would have to deal with the whirlwind of her mother and father until they left again.

Mia chose to lose herself in her work. She didn't see the shadows begin to creep up as evening set in, and it wasn't until there was a quick knock on her door that she looked up in irritation, expecting to see one of her sisters or, worse, a parent. Instead, it was Ryan who stepped inside and closed the door behind him.

"Hey, sweetheart." He opened his arms, and without hesitation, she stood and walked right into the comforting embrace. "Margo called me about your mom and dad showing up. I just got home and came directly to you."

Mia rubbed her nose into the soft material of his shirt. "Thank you. They just pop up after months pass and like I'm supposed to do a dance of joy."

"You're entitled to your feelings." Ryan squeezed her tight. "But they're entitled to see their children as well and to live their lives. Maybe you all should sit down, talk and hash it out. I had my own issues with my parents for a completely different reason, but it didn't start getting better until I told them how I felt and put some boundaries in place."

"They didn't listen when we were kids. I doubt very much that will happen now." Mia took a deep breath and tried to calm her emotions.

"Enid said to tell you dinner is almost ready. Come on, let's go get cleaned up. I'll be right next to you, holding your hand the whole way."

A smile lifted the corners of her lips. "That sounds like it's more for you than me."

He dropped a brief kiss on her lips. "It's for us."

Ryan wouldn't let go of her hand even when they walked upstairs. No one was around to comment, and Mia counted that as a blessing.

Mia changed her clothes and freshened up before knocking on Ryan's door, and together they went to the dining room. Ryan was dressed in a dark red polo shirt and gray slacks, looking very much like a man who would be meeting parents for the first time.

She had chosen a pastel green romper with a white shirt and sandals, and when they stepped into the room, Ryan squeezed her hand encouragingly.

"There she is, my beautiful firstborn daughter." Her father smiled warmly and came over to embrace her. "And who's this holding my baby girl's hand?"

"Dr. Ryan Cassidy, sir." Ryan extended his hand. "It's so nice to finally meet you."

"Compared to what she's probably told you about us?" Brian Ballad said, amused. "It's nice to meet you, Ryan."

"I don't talk about you, so there's that," Mia muttered. She couldn't seem to stop herself.

"Ryan, this is my wife, Rosie, Mia's mother."

"Nice to meet you." Rosie shook his hand. "It seems you've brought our daughter a real happiness in her life."

"She brings me much more than anyone realizes." Ryan acknowledged the rest of the group.

"Let's sit down and eat before the food gets cold," Enid said warmly. "It does my heart good to see the family together for dinner. It's been too long."

"It all looks amazing, Enid," their mother said as they took seats around the table. "I completely missed your cooking. Not even the tres leches cake in Paris could compare to yours."

"You tell those Paris chefs to come to me, and I'll show them a trick or two." Enid beamed.

"Did you happen to go to Le Dessert Luxure?" Ryan asked conversationally while serving dishes were being passed.

"The exact same one!" Mia's mother gasped. "Do you know the place?"

"Of course he does, Mom. The man has been everywhere," Micki said dryly. "I bet any place you've been, he's visited at least three times."

"Not really," Ryan said, although he was grinning. "But to answer your question, I love their desserts. Enid is certainly big competition for them."

"It's on my bucket list, Paris, and trying all the lovely foods," said Margo, sounding wistful.

"Then you should go, darling girl. Why put it off?" their father said casually.

"Because our money goes into a mortgage, and she'd need to save. Also, she has people that depend on her," Mia answered, instead of her middle sister.

"I'd have to put in for time off from work. I'll get there eventually," Margo contributed.

Rosie shrugged. "Quit the job and then find a new one when you come home."

Margo frowned. "I can't be so cavalier about a job I love and seniors who depend on me. I put in a lot of time and effort to be where I'm at. I don't want to lose it for a spur-of-the-moment trip. I can be patient."

"Unlike others who packed up and left their daughters," Mia said under her breath. Ryan turned to her, offering a reassuring look.

"So, Ryan, where else have you been?" Brian asked. "The Red Sea?"

Ryan nodded. "Yep, twice. Did you ever make it to Sicily or Greece?"

"Greece. There is a lovely villa-type restaurant that looks over the water in Chania," Rosie said with excitement. "The owner's name is—"

"Papa Gelanis," Ryan finished her sentence with a smile. "He shows you how to stuff your own grape leaves, and the vanilla cream mousse he makes is to die for."

"Yes!" Brian laughed loudly. "His stories are legendary. Sitting after dinner with a sherry and the sun going down, listening to him talk, is one of my fondest memories."

Mia felt her irritation rise as the conversation continued. Plus, the way Margo, Enid and Micki hung on every word made her even more resentful. With all these memories, she didn't hear one from her parents about them growing up—an event they actually saw and not in a picture or letter sent in the mail or, later as technology bloomed, an email or video call.

"How do you find the time to travel being a pediatric doctor?" Rosie asked Ryan.

"I've spent a long time with Medicine Across the World," he explained. "A lot of places were layovers or stops where we waited for supply flights to be sorted out. Or I just took the time to be by myself and recover. I've been to Africa more often than any other place in my life. I saw the beauty as well as the dire need."

Brian nodded. "We got to Ghana and saw the same."

"There's a difference between staying on a resort versus bringing medical aid to those who need it." Mia cut a piece of her tender roast and chewed.

"Mia, not at the table," Enid said firmly.

"I want to take Mia to Morocco." Ryan deftly changed the subject. "We had so much fun on Lake Norman, I think a boat off the coast would be a fantastic vacation."

"That would be lovely!" Rosie clapped her hands. "It would be nice to get you out of Sardis Woods—well, North Carolina—Mia!"

"I like my home. Thank you so much for caring to fill out my travel schedule though," Mia said sweetly.

Her father cleared his throat. "I think your mother means it would be nice for you to see other parts of the world, open your mind a little bit to all there is out there to see."

"I think I see it enough through your eyes," Mia retorted. "Bells for Micki from each new stop, porcelain animals for Margo, notebooks for me. It's been a lifetime of trinkets, like pins in a globe to showcase your travels. But none from home."

"Mia, you girls were always cared for,"

Rosie said in a soft, but serious, voice. "Child-ishness does not become you."

"Uh-oh." Micki looked down at her plate and pretended to eat.

Margo's eyes filled with tears. "Can we please not fight at the dinner table?"

Brian sighed and put down his utensils. "If you have something to say, Mia, just say it."

Ryan's expression was concerned, but Mia was tired of pretending for her parents.

"It amazes me that one of your favorite memories is of a Greek man telling stories as opposed to your children." Mia's laugh was clipped. "How about Micki's fifth birth-day, or when Margo stopped the entire show and killed it with her solo for middle-school choir? Oh, or any of our graduations, from kindergarten to high school, college or nurs-ing school?"

"We were aware of each and every event of your lives," Rosie said calmly.

"But how often were you present? Two, maybe three times, because both of you were more often traveling to all these coun-tries instead." Mia was so angry she vis-ibly trembled. "It was Enid and I who held us together. I stayed with my sisters when they were sick. I planned parties and special events. I pulled loose teeth and was there for first kisses and first broken hearts. Instead of growing up, I was an adult from the time I figured out they needed me more than I needed to go skating or to a sleepover with friends. Who would be there when they had nightmares or thought monsters were under the bed? Not our parents because you were in Ghana or Greece or on the moon for all we knew."

"Mia!"

"No!" she cut off their beloved house-keeper and friend. "I love you, Enid, but now they call me childish? How would they ever know, they were never around." Mia stood and dropped her napkin on the table. "No, I can't sit here while they play Trade the Trip with Ryan and act like it's all okay."

Mia looked at an openly crying Margo, and her heart broke.

"She's crying because family dinner is her one, best way of keeping us close and find-ing some kind of normalcy where we had none. Micki can't settle down long enough to make a choice about school or a career because she has that same wanderlust as you, Mom and Dad, and she's terrified of her own potential." Mia shook her head sadly. "And me, I'm so messed up, I can't even think of stepping on a plane without being terrified I'll never see home again. I live in a gilded cage of my own making, content to look out at the world and never be in it. You broke all of us and then you call me out… I'm over it."

"Mia…" She left the table, but Ryan was on her heels. He stopped her at the stairs, and she saw the worry in his eyes. "Come back and finish this. Maybe it's time for all the cards to be on the table."

Mia rejected the idea. "They can keep their cards. I don't want to hear about it. I'm going to my room."

"Are you going to punish me for their failings?" Ryan asked in disbelief.

"No, but you seem to have more in common with them than me."

Mia pulled away and climbed the stairs, emotionally exhausted. It was all too much: her parents, Ryan and his diplomacy, the look of betrayal on Micki's face, the crestfallen and inconsolable Margo, and Enid, who would probably chew her out if she could.

Mia stepped into her room, closed the door and locked it. She knew this time her sisters wouldn't come in, and she wanted to keep everyone else out. It was the first moment in the last few months that she actually felt alone, and she missed Ryan's arms holding her and promising it would all be okay.

CHAPTER THIRTEEN

RYAN LEFT THE hospital room and took his tie-dyed scrubs cap off and shoved it in his pocket. The little guy was almost too weak but he had come through it in the end. The surgery was one of the most difficult times he'd ever had. Challenging, unexpected, it had taken every ounce of his skill and still he wasn't sure it would be enough. For now, it was, and for that he was grateful. But he didn't know where to go from here.

It was his goal to save lives, give a parent that one-in-a-million chance to watch their child grow up. But even he couldn't fight past a certain point. Sometimes things were beyond his control. Ryan thought of Amir and slid down onto the hallway floor. With his back to the wall, he brought his knees up to his chest.

His shift was over, there was no reason for him to be there still, but he couldn't move.

The gravity of grief kept him on the ground, arms and legs heavy, too tired to even stand.

"Hey."

Mia's voice made him look up. There she stood. His eyes went from the sneaker-clad feet to the blue-plaid capri pants and then the flowing navy blue shirt before he got to her face. She had her hair in a high pony-tail, and the look of genuine concern on her face was plainly evident. She had no prob-lem sitting next to him on the scuffed floor.

"I got worried when you didn't come home," Mia said gently.

Home. That one word stuck with Ryan, and it amazed him all over again how quickly Ballad Inn had become a place of comfort and peace. It was as if she instinc-tively knew he needed to feel that right now.

"Trying to escape your parents?" he asked on a soft laugh. "You haven't liked me much since dinner that night."

"It was two days ago," she pointed out. "You had work. I had work."

"You were avoiding me, and cold," Ryan said bluntly. "Putting me in the same cate-gory as your parents."

"Matt called me," Mia said, deftly switching the subject. "He said you had a tough surgery."

Ryan took a deep breath before he spoke. "A little boy, Claude… His heart almost couldn't take the surgery. In the end, he came through it…but for a moment there, it was touch and go."

"I'm so sorry, Ryan." Mia wrapped her arms around him. "That must have been scary."

He looked at his hands. "I have all this knowledge, talent… I worked so hard to… It made me think of Amir. I—I couldn't save him."

Mia turned his face toward her and kissed him tenderly.

"I know you feel each and every loss, Ryan, but it's not your fault." She cupped his cheeks. "Look at me. You did everything right. Sometimes…things… You can't stop the inevitable from happening."

"I just can't fathom the loss," Ryan admitted. "If it feels like this for me, how do the parents cope every day and survive it?"

"It takes strength. Courage. You have these traits, too, Ryan. That's how I'd describe you." Mia slipped her arm through his. Her tone lighter. "Come on. Let's go home, and I'll take care of you."

Ryan looked at her. "I've never had anyone say that to me before. I've been sitting here so long, and I'm so exhausted, I don't think I can stand."

"I'm here." She leaned her forehead against his. "You can always lean on me for whatever, until you can do it for yourself."

Her words felled him, and Ryan couldn't help but admit his true feelings. "I love you, Mia. I've been in relationships, but nothing like this, never like this. I can feel you in my heart, smell your scent like the honeysuckle in the air. You said I didn't come home and you worried. That's exactly what you are to me, home, a reason to step out of the dark and into the light, your arms. I love you, Mia. I would give you the world if you asked me to."

He watched the tears form in her eyes and slip down her cheeks.

"I love you, too," she said.

A shared kiss, and Ryan could taste her tears mingled on their lips. It was with her help that he finally got to his feet. He felt the stiffness in his joints. Together they walked down the hallway, out to his car, and she followed him home in her own.

Back at Ballad Inn, they bypassed the dining room, and she took him up to his bedroom and got him out of his shoes before starting the shower for him. By the time he stepped out from under the hot spray, there were sweats and a T-shirt on the dresser.

Downstairs, Mia had a meal waiting, and cold, refreshing sweet tea, which reminded him that he hadn't eaten all day. Ryan devoured his dinner, and it was then that exhaustion completely took over. He hardly remembered falling into his bed and her pulling the covers over him.

The one thing that stood out to him as he drifted off to sleep was Mia sitting beside him, stroking his hair. His body relaxed. She was being his protector, like the warrior she was, always putting others before herself, and Ryan loved her all the more. There were usually nightmares that tormented him after a surgery like this. It woke the PTSD from his journeys where his own life had been in jeopardy, as well as those of the people he was around. In comparison, this darkness was a relief.

The buzzing of his phone eventually woke him hours later. He looked at the number and frowned before tapping the button to connect the call.

"Hey, Ryan." His name was drawled with a familiar twang. "How's that simple life you're living there in the South?"

"It's *North* Carolina. So aren't I in the North?" Ryan said sleepily, turning over onto his back. He heard Mia's voice outside, through the open window, and he smiled, his eyes still closed.

"That's neither here nor there."

"Why are you calling me, Mac?" Ryan asked.

"Need your help."

"Equipment, right? There's still money from the grant. What do you need?" Ryan yawned. "I smell breakfast. You're keeping me from breakfast."

"I need *you*," Mac said. "We have a baby girl with a serious heart defect. She's six weeks old, and no one else has the experience. In fact, Ryan, we have several kids that could really use those mad skills of yours."

"Uh-huh." He sat up and leaned against the headboard. "How many children?"

"Two urgent, four non," Mac said. "I can't even tell you much more because we just set up three weeks ago…" Mac paused. "Dena's daughter—her name is Aiyla—is one of the urgents."

"Where are you?" Ryan pinched the bridge of his nose, and his heartbeat picked up speed. How would Dena feel putting her child into his care once more? Could he see past the death of Amir to do the job right? These questions plagued him, but he knew that he couldn't say no.

"Still Turkey, but a different compound closer to the border," his friend answered. "One of the better places, mind you. We have a fine building set up and two cardiologists on board but not someone like you."

"I have a good thing here, just starting my attending job," Ryan said hesitantly. "I don't think I can take the time off—"

"You know full well you have the means to jump on a plane if you need to. It has to be written into your contract," Mac said, cutting him off. "I need you, Ryan, for a few weeks. For sure, they'll hold your job."

"Mac, Mia isn't into me being a roving doctor."

posed to be thinking about something in particular?"

"Maybe moving in with each other?" Ryan hinted. "I can start the house search, and we can pick together."

"Or you can stay with us permanently," Mia repeated her offer from before. "I can reach out to Mr. Crawford's son again and propose buying the field out back, and between the two of us, we could build a house there."

"That sounds much better than having to search for a house," he mused.

"I do have some good ideas sometimes." Mia grinned. "When we get to that point in our relationship, we can talk about it more. Except the land. I want to buy that before someone else snags it."

"Aren't we at that point already?" Ryan rolled over onto his stomach and braced himself on his elbows.

"You've been here a matter of weeks, and we moved pretty fast," Mia told him.

"But we had this connection from the very beginning and is it fast if our hearts know what we want?" Ryan asked.

"A very good counterpoint," she said.

"How about three more months before we make any firm decisions? You may get tired of Charlotte and want to move on."

"I thought we'd established that wouldn't happen, since I took the job," Ryan said stiffly. "You keep lumping me in with people who I've never met that left you. I'm my own man, and if I didn't think I wanted to stay, I wouldn't have said yes to the hospital. It will be permanent when I sign the contract with them."

Mia took a breath, knowing that he was right, and she, too, flipped onto her stomach, mimicking his position.

"I'm sorry, you're right. It's my hang-up, and I shouldn't paint you with the same brush," Mia said. "You have a new job, and we are building these steps to a relationship we both want."

Ryan nudged her with his broad shoulder. "I wanted it from the first time I met you with your glasses all crooked on your face."

"Why would you remind me of that?" Mia groaned. "I almost fell to my doom because of that treacherous cat."

"You fell into my arms. That's all I want

"That makes this next part much harder, then," Mac said. "Have you signed the contract as yet?"

"In a couple days I will. Why?" Ryan asked.

"Our illustrious president is retiring, and I'm stepping into the role. I want you as vice, taking on my job."

"Don't do this to me, Mac," Ryan begged.

"The fact that you sound like that tells me the interest is there. You can do so much more than being just an attending at a hospital, Ry."

"But it's what I want." Ryan heard the doubt in his own voice.

"Is it, or did you convince yourself of that?"

"I don't want to lose Mia. She's incredible and won't be happy with this development."

"She'll forgive you, man, or even support it, but you won't be able to forgive yourself if these children don't get a fighting chance. You can think about my offer while you're here."

Mac was right. How could he look at himself in the mirror knowing that he didn't try to help? Last night he was broken and Mia helped him stand in more ways than one. When she heard this news, she would…

How would she react? Even with the doubt in his mind, Ryan knew he had to tell her he was going and hope she understood.

"How soon do you need me?"

"We have a supply flight leaving on Friday," Mac said. "They're based out of your neck of the woods."

"I'll be on it. Email me the details and my liaison's name and the files on the patients."

"On it!" Mac howled. "We're getting the band back together."

"We're not. It's just for—"

Mac had already hung up. Shaking his head, Ryan knew a couple of weeks could turn into double that amount of time. He'd have maybe a week to sort out his contract with the hospital, and then he would fly back and forth until the assignment was done. There was no other choice than to bite the bullet and find Mia and tell her.

He looked at the time and saw it was just a little past ten in the morning, so with her parents there, maybe breakfast was done early and he would be able to talk to her alone.

After a quick minute to brush his teeth and change his clothes, he went straight to the kitchen. Everyone was still there. Mia was actually smiling at the table, with her sisters, parents and Enid. She turned her head to smile at him. From the doorway where he stood, the sun steaking through the window formed a golden halo around her hair that she wore like a wild mane showing off her face. Her glasses were slightly askew, and her soft brown eyes radiated happiness.

"Good morning." She got up and wrapped her arms around his waist before pressing a quick kiss on his lips. An unusual public display of affection, but it warmed him nonetheless. "I thought you'd sleep awhile longer. I was going to make sure you had a breakfast plate warm and ready when you woke up."

"Look at her being all cutesy with her boo," Micki teased.

"Michelle, behave," Rosie admonished.

"Yeah, Michelle." Mia stuck out her tongue.

"Hey, we have to talk," Ryan whispered into Mia's ear.

She gave him a curious look. "Okay, sure. Sunroom or patio?"

"Outside is good. The breeze would feel

great right now," he admitted. "Oh, morning, guys."

"Don't mind us. Go canoodle with your
boyfriend," Micki said in an overly sweet
tone.

"Margo, please open our sister's bedroom
window and let Doodle the assassin get into
her room," Mia retorted.

Hand in hand, he and Mia walked outside. Ryan's heart was racing. Together they
sat down on the wide porch swing, and he
slowly moved it back and forth with his bare
foot touching the stained wood floor.

"So what do you want to talk about?" Mia
turned to face him.

"I have to make a trip, could be a few
weeks, possibly a month," Ryan began. "I
got a call from the coordinator I work with
at Medicine Across the World, and they need
me for some surgery. Lives depend on it."

Mia stayed silent for a moment. "Okay, I
understand. A month. I'll be here when you
get back."

He stopped the swing. "It might be longer.
Mac said there are urgent cases and some
non, but I couldn't leave until I've done all
I could."

"Why can't they send someone else?"

"I have to make sure it's done right… Remember Dena? I told you about her and her sick daughter. Well, she's one of the urgent cases." He hesitated a moment. "There's more. The coordinator I mentioned? He's taking over as leader of MAW and wants me for the vice role he's vacating."

"And you said…?"

"I haven't given him an answer yet."

"I think that's an answer in itself." Mia's gaze met his. "We had a plan. And now, you're just avoiding the inevitable. I'm not really sure you even know what you want."

"That's not true." Ryan took her hands. "I want this. We have so many plans. How could you think that?"

"Ryan, even if you stay here, what happens when another emergency comes up, and another? Will you be the one call they always make?"

"I'm the—"

"Best. I get that." She stood. "I also get, no matter what, you won't ever step back to let someone else take charge. You'll always feel you can do it better and take off, so why not take the vice-president role? It sounds like a great opportunity."

"It's not like that." Ryan got to his feet, joining her. "It seems like the exact same condition of the boy that I operated on at Armstrong, and as vice I could get so much more to those who need it."

"That's fine. That's what you will always do, should do, try to save everyone." Mia gave him a sad look. "No matter the cost to anyone else, even yourself or your relationships—they'll always come second. What happened to being burned out and putting down roots?"

"I want to do that, here with you," he implored and took her hand. "But I also know that I can—"

"As long as I'm willing to wait until you come back from one of your assignments from somewhere." She shook her head. "Sorry. I've spent my entire life doing that, waiting for people to come through that door, to put me first. I won't do that with love as well."

"Then, come with me," he begged. "We could do this together."

"And give up my career and home for this need of yours? I don't see how you and

Paula didn't get along. You have the same outlook."

"Low blow, Mia. I never asked for you to give up anything for me, just to meet me halfway."

Mia's laugh was short. "That's not going to happen, Ryan. Your halfway is—"

"Why? Because you're so stuck here because of your parents that you won't even get on a flight?"

His words were like an arrow that hit its target dead center. Ryan regretted them as soon as they left his lips because he saw the hurt bloom across her face. Mia quickly put up her wall of reserve, but the disappointment was still reflected in her eyes. Her barriers had come down slowly for him, and here he'd managed to get them back up in an instant.

"Yes, that's me," Mia said simply. "I also seem to believe in pipe dreams that are spoon-fed to me, a naive habit I will be sure to cure myself of."

"Mia, I didn't mean—"

"I expect you to pay your bill and vacate the Ballad Inn premises tonight. I'm sure with your connections you will find adequate living accommodations elsewhere," she said formally. "Thank you for staying at our little slice of heaven. I hope you had a wonderful experience. In your case, I know you did."

"Mia…"

She didn't respond but turned and walked through the front door with Ryan following her.

"Please, Mia!"

She turned, and the cold look she gave him stopped him in his tracks. The rest of her family had come out of the kitchen, and he saw the dark cloud of anger that crossed everyone's face.

Brian stepped forward. "I don't know what's going on, son, but if she wants to go, you don't try to stop her."

Ryan nodded. "My apologies."

"Margo, Dr. Cassidy will be checking out immediately. Please prepare his bill," said Mia politely. "He doesn't need the standard take-home basket. He's taken enough."

"Nothing that you didn't want to give me, Mia," he said, feeling his heart break even more.

"And all of it I wish I could take back." Her breath caught, and Mia swiped angrily at her cheeks. "Margo, please handle this, will you?"

"Sure thing, sis," she replied.

Ryan watched Mia run up the stairs and out of sight before he sat heavily on the bottom step of the old house with his head in his hands.

"You don't have to go…" Margo began.

He looked up with a sad smile. "Yeah, I do, and that's the problem."

"Where?" Micki sat next to him.

"Back to Turkey, surgery. They really need my help," Ryan answered. "It could take weeks or months."

"One-time thing?" Margo asked.

He sighed. "I don't know. Sometimes they need me, and… I got offered another job I have to think about."

"You have a problem with saying no," Margo stated. "Then, it is best you leave."

"Margo!" Rosie gasped.

"No," she snapped. "He knew that when he told her he wanted to settle down. Dropping this nugget about maybe traveling back and forth is on him. She would never have given him a chance in that case, and I don't blame her. No one wants to be at home waiting on someone coming in and out of their lives at a moment's notice."

"You're not seeing the big picture," Ryan protested.

Margo frowned at him. "In your case, yes, I am. Ryan, the places you go may mean you get hurt. And yes, Mom and Dad, that is how we learned to live and love with you as parents. It hurt Mia more because she was the oldest. Ryan, I'm not saying what you do isn't admirable and incredibly heroic, but it's not a life every person would want to live. You took away that option from her."

"But don't you see? I would stay here if I could," Ryan pleaded.

"I know," Margo said sadly. "Though, you can't expect her to say yes to a life, one she isn't capable of, even because of love. Mia can't go through that again."

Micki stood. "Gotta side with my sisters on this. You acted like you were done and said as much, she said you talked about building a house on the Crawford land if she could buy it. Mia isn't going to be sitting here, manning the home front and pining away for anyone. I won't let her. And while you didn't lie, you didn't give her the whole truth.

"It was Mia who kept it all normal for me when our parents were gone. I didn't even realize how much she did until I really sat down to think about it. It's hard for someone to love, when all she's ever seen are people walking in the opposite direction, away from her. Right now, I need to go hug my big sister tight."

"I'll get your bill ready. It's best you leave, to save her more heartbreak," Margo said and moved toward the main reception desk.

Ryan noted the despondent look that passed between Rosie and Brian Ballad. Maybe they were finally seeing how their life on the go had affected their daughters. As for him, his words had torn through Mia. These people were right—she needed to know everything about his life and from the very beginning and that he could leave without much notice, even though it wasn't his intention to.

With a heavy heart, he went upstairs to pack his things. Finally, with his paid bill in his hand and his suitcases at the front door, Ryan looked back up the stairs helplessly, feeling like someone was chasing him away from the only love and home he'd ever known. He wasn't ready to give up on Mia or what they shared. He stepped forward, hoping his voice would echo enough so that she could hear him.

"We're going to figure this out, Mia Janine Ballad! And yes, I know your middle name!" Ryan called out. "I'm coming back for you, and if you'll allow me, I'm going to love you for the rest of your life. You just watch!" He felt everyone's eyes on him, but he didn't care. It was good to say the words out loud.

With that promise, Ryan picked up his duffel and walked out the front door to his Land Rover. He looked up to the windows of the Ballad Inn, particularly to Mia's room that was at the front of the house. But the only thing that moved the white lace curtains was the warm Carolina breeze.

Ryan turned away, tossed his bag in the car and slid into the driver's seat. One last look before he drove slowly down the path, away from the woman he loved. One last crack in an already broken heart that had caused it to shatter completely. And still, he felt as if someone was watching him, until the road curved and he lost sight of the Ballad Inn.

How could a week feel like a lifetime? And with what he wanted so close, yet so very far away? The time went by with such speed it reminded Ryan that when it needed to, the organization that helped people across the world without the benefit of safe health care could move at breakneck speed. It was late Friday night—well, you could call it Saturday morning—and he sat outside a plane on a tarmac in Haiti.

While he was still very far from his destination, the urge to help had gotten him on his feet as soon as the plane landed.

"It's okay, Ryan, we've got this." One of the other doctors he knew well grinned at him. "Melissa and I are ready to start. Get yourself back on that plane."

"You need more than what's on that plane, and you know it, Anna." Ryan spoke more harshly than he'd intended. He was tired, hurt and heartbroken. "If it starts to rain soon, there is literally no shelter for half the people beyond those gates."

"We'll get them inside the airport," she countered.

"How? They're terrified to be inside in case of another aftershock."

Anna's dark brown eyes fired angry daggers at him. "These are my people, Ryan. I was born and raised here till I was ten. Don't you think I know they're scared? I am, too, but we'll make it work."

"I know," he said, his heart full of regret. "I'm sorry for…everything. There'll be another plane here within three days with tents, portable AC units, whatever is needed." He handed her a card. "Text everything you require to that number."

"I always heard you had a good heart and even better means to help out." She pushed the card into the pocket of her shirt. "You know the list of stuff is going to be long? You're only one man, Ryan. You can't save the world."

"But I can try," Ryan joked and smiled. "Take care of yourself here, Anna."

"You know it. Thanks, Ryan," she said and went back to her patients.

And now, two days later, he was sitting in the sweltering heat that didn't seem to abate at night. Each free second was spent recalling the day he'd left the woman he loved and a place that felt like home. He tried to be honest with himself and admitted he hadn't slept well since the argument, barely catching a few hours in an on-call room and living out of his bags.

He would be on the move again in a few days, and even in a plush bed in some nice hotel suite he wouldn't sleep, not without the feel of the warmth Mia gave him every time he stepped into Ballad Inn. It was all torment—her touch or the scent of her hair when he kissed her neck…

His mind turned to the hospital in Charlotte and his leaving there with not one but two of their residents in tow. Ryan would sign the hospital's contract when he returned, and if he had to make Charlotte one of the hubs for MAW, then so be it; he would work it out. The hospital board had loved Ryan's decision to go, actually. There was a news broadcast about the mission to save multiple children with delicate heart surgery. Even though he didn't want to be in the limelight, he gave in this one time.

All the good press for the hospital was

expected to generate many donations before he was scheduled to head back, so his temporary absence was not only approved but encouraged. He didn't tell them about the job offer from Mac, not yet, because he was still trying to formulate what to do. Could he do both jobs and stay in a place where the woman he loved was rooted so passionately? But what if Mia never gave him another chance?

The thought reminded him of his last conversation with Matt. His colleague's words were as blunt as a hammer. "What does Mia say about this trip?"

"She broke up with me." It hurt to say the words even then. "She was fine at first, but not when I told her it could be longer and I could be called to go again. It's not something she wants to sign up for. She wants to stay settled."

"But I thought you wanted the same thing?" Matt pinned him with a gaze. "Did that adventure bug bite you again?"

"No, but this is just my lot in life, to help, and I can't say no," Ryan answered, already knowing he was lost.

Matt's laugh was quick and short. "Oh

please, you're looking for redemption after the loss you suffered. People say we don't feel anything. That to us, it's only a job. It may or may not be true but we do replay the surgeries in our heads on a loop, and we remember those patients always for the rest of our lives. I know your intentions are good," Matt continued. "But that doesn't change the fact that you're doing something another surgeon can do. And do you want to know why?"

Ryan raised a brow. "I somehow think you're going to tell me, Matt."

"I sure am. You're scared of falling for a woman like Mia, who actually has roots put down in an area special to her. Who is going to make you her number one, willing to come pick you up from work, or listen to you, or take you to the park for some of the best food anyone could ask for—with those delicious little dessert cream things."

"You're food-spiraling. Reel it back in, buddy," Ryan said dryly.

Matt pointed at him. "The fact being you have it good, and it terrifies you, so why not derail it with a quest for valor when someone else could go in your place?"

"This isn't me trying to run away from anything, but to help a kid in trouble," Ryan said in frustration. "More than one if I can."

Matt put a hand on his shoulder. "That's true but there's more to it for you, and you know it. Have a safe trip, and I'll hold down the fort until you get back."

"That's all I ask. Thank you very much."

"I may go over to the inn and see if they will give me the desserts you left behind." Matt threw the teasing comment behind him as he sauntered away.

Ryan realized that it bothered him that Matt spoke more truth than he wanted to acknowledge. But he'd made the commitment. There was no backing out now.

"Wheels up!" someone called, and Ryan got up from the hard tarmac. He had a job to do, one that he'd given up everything for. Before the plane took off, he fired off a quick text, one that he sent daily, without fail, and would continue to, even if he had to climb a mountain, then a radio tower, to get a signal for it to go to its recipient.

He tried to get comfortable in his seat. Most of his colleagues were still asleep. The packed plane shuddered as it turned around and was soon speeding down the asphalt to take him farther away from Charlotte and Mia. The thought made him ache, and his groan of despair was drowned out by the engines. Was there any hope for him to come back to Ballad Inn and rebuild what he'd destroyed? Ryan had promised Mia he would, and he vowed to himself now, he would pull out all the stops. Mia was the love of his life.

CHAPTER FOURTEEN

NOTHING SEEMED TO make Mia smile. The usual pattern of her life just didn't make her happy anymore. Everything and everywhere carried a memory of him. The gazebo, her car, her clothes, especially the costume she wore to the hospital when they'd cheered up the kids.

She thought of that afternoon fondly, recalling how he showed her the fake bottom in his top hat and taught her the handkerchief trick. And of the day they'd watched reruns of an old spy series and taken turns pointing out how it was inaccurate, then described how they would do it instead. Mia inhaled the soft spiced musk of his cologne that must have gotten onto her costume, the scent was fading and soon it would be gone.

Her family kept looking at her with sorrow in their eyes, and of course, everything they did seemed to get on her nerves. The usual sisterly teasing made her irate, but she kept going to family dinner, even though she would rather stay in her room and lick her wounds. Micki's extension of the gazebo appeared to be taking forever. The landscaping and the barn were almost finished, yet her procrastination on the project had put them in a precarious position. The new guests would be arriving within a week, and there was no way Mia would allow wooden beams, sawdust and general chaos to greet them on the grounds of Ballad Inn.

Then there were her parents, who hadn't left for another one of their trips yet, and Mia wondered why. They were running into the end of week two for them being home—a record, actually—and one week since Ryan left, and they were still in Charlotte, strolling around the neighborhood, talking to old friends. It seemed like they were sticking around. Mia knew it wasn't the case but having them home meant she couldn't process in her own way—in silence, by herself. If one other person asked her how she was doing, she might burst into tears.

As Mia walked along the wraparound porch, she saw the gazebo was now an eyesore, with planks of wood leaning on it and other supplies left nearby, and yet no one working. Sighing, she used the back steps to go find Micki, which wasn't hard to do. Her sister's hideout was usually the shed with all the tools and her music blaring. Mia could see that she wasn't working on anything to do with the gazebo project.

"Micki... Micki!" Mia yelled over the music, and when her sister didn't answer, she pulled the radio plug from the socket, plunging them into silence.

"Hey, I was listening to that!" Micki cried out.

"Michelle, when will the gazebo be done? We have guests arriving in a matter of days and a bride and groom coming to see the grounds," Mia said as calmly as she could. "The very same gazebo that you said would be the crown jewel for any wedding we have here."

"Chill, Mia," Micki said with mock severity. "It's going to be done."

"How, when you're here, playing with magazines and making collages instead of doing what needs to be done?" Mia snapped.

Micki's eyes narrowed angrily. "Because I said it will get done."

"You said that five days ago," Mia pointed out. "You know what? Forget it. I'll get someone else to finish it and clean up your mess as usual."

"Excuse me?" Micki looked genuinely shocked. "When have you ever had to clean up my mess?"

"All the time. You have a tendency to start things and never finish, Micki, just like college."

Micki stopped and stared at her. "I get that you're hurting, Mia." Her sister took a deep breath, but it didn't stop the tears that sprang to her eyes. She swiped them away quickly. "But what you just said is unfair. I'll get the gazebo done so you can have that perfection you so seem to crave."

"I don't crave perfection," Mia protested.

"Yeah, you do, it has to be your way or no way, and when it doesn't happen, you end up alone," Micki shot back.

"Micki, I'm sorry…"

The words were wasted because Micki had already stalked away. Mia stood reeling before she went back to the house. Was that her problem, expecting everyone to fit into a world that she made and then reacting when they didn't?

In her office, Mia buried herself in work. She heard the front door open and close loudly and the conversation that ensued.

"Micki, why are you slamming the door?" she heard her mother ask.

"Sorry, Mom, just need to go grab some stuff and get the gazebo going." Micki's voice was rough. It was obvious she was still upset.

"What about our day out, the new Westinghouse outlet malls and lunch?" Rosie asked.

"Well, the gazebo has to get done. We have people coming in, and Mia wants it to happen today," Micki answered. "I don't finish things, evidently, so next time, Mom, okay?"

"Okay, sweet girl," their mother said consolingly. "You make things happen. You just march to the beat of your own drum. Mia didn't mean it. She's in a bad spot right now, and that type of pain isn't easy on anyone. Cut her a little slack, okay?"

"Yeah, I guess," Micki said.

It shocked her that their mother would defend her, especially since even Mia knew she had been a complete jerk to Micki. When did it start to feel better? she wondered. It was worse than just heartbreak. It was akin to a physical ache, and it never seemed to abate. She missed Ryan, and yet no matter how many times she picked up the phone to call him, she never did. So many questions swirled through her mind. Had she ruined the one true love that everyone searched for by being too rigid?

Even as Mia pondered the question, she recognized it wasn't that simple to answer. There was give-and-take in any relationship. Mia knew with his travels, his commitment to his work and the patients who needed him in places where care was lacking, well, it would be her giving more in their relationship, wouldn't it? She feared she'd end up resenting him, and that wasn't right. How could she make Ryan choose between her and a career? It wasn't fair for either of them. So each time she stared at his number, the entire debate came flooding back, and Mia placed the phone aside.

But there wasn't silence on his end. Each day, without fail, her phone lit up and vibrated, and when she hit the text to open it, it was from him. I love you. Don't ever forget that. Each and every time, her heart leaped, and she wanted to believe so much that when he came back, it would be okay between them.

Hours later, emotionally exhausted, Mia finally closed down her computer for the evening and poked her head out of the office. No one was around. There was a bit of time before dinner, and it was her intent to soak in the tub before heading back downstairs. While the water filled the tub, Mia put her hair up and sat on the edge. Her cell phone vibrated on the small granite vanity, and she picked it up, tapping the accept button without even thinking.

"Hello?"

"You answered. I didn't think you would." Ryan's voice was husky, a sweet timbre that was like a caress across her skin, and it made her heart ache anew.

"In my defense, I didn't look at the screen," Mia answered and cleared her throat. "How is the trip?"

"We just landed at the airport," he explained. "We do the customs thing before we head out via truck to the medical camp."

"How long will that be?"

"Pretty long, five or six hours. Some of these rural areas are hard to access. Roads aren't what they should be."

"Oh…well, be careful," Mia said.

"I will. I'm coming back home to you," Ryan pledged. "We're going to sort this out together."

"Please, don't say that," she whispered.

"It's the truth," he said, his voice as soft as hers. "Mia, there's no one else in this world that's going to love me like you do. And I can promise the same for you. Why wouldn't I come home to that?"

"Because you'll leave right after, again and again." Tears clogged her throat. "Ryan, I can never make you choose between your career and me. What you do is too important. Nor can I be the woman that travels with you or is at home while you come and go. We can't build anything with you in one part of the world and me in another… I just… Ryan, be safe. I have to go."

She ended the call and a sob escaped her lips. The bathwater was blissfully hot when she sank into the scented bubbles. The aromas of coconut and papaya surrounded her while tears leaked from her closed eyes. She would probably never stop loving him, and pushing him away would be the hardest thing she ever had to do. It was obvious Ryan needed that life, to be able to fly at a whim and save a life anywhere. And she loved him enough to let him go.

Long after the water had cooled and she was able to rein in her emotions, hiding them behind the facade she wore so well, Mia went downstairs to have dinner with her family. Sitting in her usual place, she noted that Micki sat on the opposite side of Margo, to be away from her. She was still hurt, and Mia couldn't blame her for that. Her father smiled at Mia when she sat down, and she returned the smile, even though the atmosphere in the dining room was tense and sullen.

"It always struck me that I'm the only male in this household and outmatched in beauty and wit," their father commented, smiling.

"Oh, Dad, you're just as beautiful as the rest of us," Margo teased.

"I see what you did there." He laughed.

"Pity everyone else gets chased away," Micki said under her breath.

"Don't see you bringing home any eligible bachelors, Michelle," Mia shot back. "Unless we count Rabbit, the biker. Was that his real name?"

"First off, Rabbit is his nickname, and he is a day trader," Micki retorted.

"Might I ask, if Rabbit is his nickname, what his real one might be?" Rosie smiled warmly.

"Peter Cage," Micki stated.

Their father's lips twitched. "So…um… Peter Cage, the day trader, is also known as Rabbit? Remove *Peter* and we have…*Rabbit Cage*."

Everyone was silent for a moment until uproarious laughter broke out. Enid leaned back in her chair, fanning her face with a napkin, and Margo held her sides. Her mother wiped away tears, and her father guffawed with glee. Mia couldn't breathe. Finally, the laughter faded away to sighs and giggles.

"Sorry, Cricket, I was mean just now, and today," Mia apologized.

Micki waved it away. "I know you're driving the bumpy road of heartbreak right now. The gazebo will be done, and Rabbit was just plain funny."

The shared laughter alleviated most of the tension while they ate, and Mia appreciated the feeling of normalcy that came with it. Over dessert and coffee, her mother spoke up.

"Girls, I think it's time you know why we travel so much, why it started and progressed. We've kept our secrets long enough." Their mother said it all so matter-of-factly it caught Mia off guard.

"Margo, give me my fifty bucks now on secret family overseas and that we're actually aristocrats." Micki held out her hand.

"Hey, spies are still on the table," Margo countered.

"Is that what you think?" their father asked.

Mia found her voice and spoke for her and her sisters. "In our defense, we were young. We didn't know what to think, so we would lie in bed and make up stories about why you guys were gone. It helped us not miss you so much."

"We were not spies, and there is no secret

family lineage, so keep your money," their father said. "Both of you."

"I have lupus," their mother said. "I was diagnosed at a very young age with it, and in those days, when Charlotte was brand-new, nothing like it is now, options were few and far between, and the treatment for me was expensive, even more expensive because we were Black, and…well, my life wasn't worth as much to some as I would like to think."

"Oh, Mom." Mia covered her mouth with her hand.

"Your mother's doctors were kind. She wouldn't be here now if we hadn't decided to take her away from the US." Their father held their mother's hand. "We went to Paris, and they started her treatment. We had to make a hard decision. To stay at home? Where she would be told she was being overdramatic about her pain? We knew it could lead to her dying sooner because of the possible effects like kidney disease or a heart attack. The second option was we could chuck everything in and live like no-mads, with the house as home base, so she had a longer, happier life."

"I know you don't remember it much,

Mia. And Margo and Micki were way too young. But there were days I couldn't get out of bed." Rosie gazed at her girls with deep sadness in her eyes. "Couldn't play in the sun with you because it hurt my skin. Flare-ups caused my joints to be painful and the rashes. I wouldn't be here now if we hadn't taken drastic steps."

"I remember it vaguely." Mia felt awful.

"We found out I had lupus after I had you," Rosie told Mia. "I had a hard pregnancy, I was really sick and doctors and nurses didn't listen when I said something was very wrong. There was one doctor though who heard me crying, and she was mad that no one listened to me."

Mia was riveted hearing the side of the story that had been kept from her and her sisters all their lives.

"She was white, adamant about patient advocacy, especially for Black women who had a higher mortality rate in childbirth then. Luckily she was adamant because you were in distress, the cord was around your neck and I was bleeding way too much. She saved us both, and when I kept getting sick,

I went to her to find out why. She helped me get a diagnosis beyond just being tired."

Margo asked, "Don't you think we should've known this sooner, since lupus is a hereditary disease and any of us could have it?"

"You don't. We had you all tested as children, and we were blessed that none of you carried the trait," Rosie answered. "My mother didn't have it, but my grandmother did, so it seems to skip generations in our family."

"So you traveled because you needed health care…but it became more?" Micki asked hesitantly.

Their father nodded. "We were adamant that none of you would ever worry or see her torn up with pain. This house, Enid and everything in it was how you all thrived even when we were gone. There is this closeness between you three, such a strong bond, and we never wanted to disrupt your lives," he explained. "Now you each have a personality that reflects what your mother and I did, and that's on us. I think we took away something from all of you girls, and for that I will be eternally sorry."

"Mia, people come back. And even if you

leave, this house, the love within it, your sisters, Enid, it will all be here when you return," her mother said. "Even planted roots spread. Trees pollinate. And honeysuckle grows away from the original vine. Baby, you have to get past this roadblock in your life, or you'll miss so much."

"Margo, baby girl, order a pizza and sit in your room and watch TV," their father said. "Your cooking skills are to die for, but, honey, stop making these elaborate meals. You need to stop cooking for everyone else and cook for yourself. Go to Paris. Enjoy the food and the life. Do something that inspires you."

"Micki, take your good self back to school." Their parents said the words simultaneously and everyone laughed.

"You are too darn smart to be building gazebos and hanging out with people called Rabbit," their mother said firmly. "Our wanderlust is not your own, and while we're not telling you not to travel and have adventures, you need a foundation, and education is the beginning. Try a school, do it away from Charlotte if you want, but do something to evolve yourself."

"Man, you guys came out with the gloves off," Mia said with a watery laugh.

"That's because Enid took them off with us," Rosie said. "She held nothing back."

Enid straightened and folded her arms. "All of you needed a wake-up call."

"We love you, too, Enid," Margo said dryly, and everyone laughed again.

The revelations at dinnertime opened Mia's eyes to so many things and gave her a new perspective on the relationship she had with her parents. That night, after the house was quiet and everyone had gone to their own rooms, Mia got ready for bed, still contemplating her life and the love she had for Ryan. A soft knock on her door caught her attention before her mother stepped inside.

"I thought you and Dad would be sleeping," Mia said gently.

"He's sleeping. You know peach cobbler and ice cream will knock him out." Her mother smiled as she sat on the side of the bed. "Come sit a minute, sweetheart."

Mia put down the clothes she was setting out for the next day and sat beside her mother. Rosie wrapped her arms around

Mia, and her mother's warmth and comfort filled her instantly.

"You've carried a big burden for so long." Her mother tucked some of Mia's hair behind her ear. "I know you're hurting."

"When does it stop, Mom?" she whispered.

"The question is does it have to? Ryan loves you, and you love him. There has to be middle ground. It doesn't have to be one way or the other, but meet in between."

"Where is the middle?"

Her mother laughed gently. "Well, that's for you and him to figure out, but it's there."

Mia lifted her head. "I held so much resentment toward you and Dad, I need to work through things, but I'm so sorry, Mom."

"You don't apologize for a thing. We could've—should've—handled it better," her mother said with certainty. "The whole 'the children don't need to know' thing went too far for too long, and we sure looked past how we affected you girls. But this is a new beginning for all of us, where middle ground can be found as well."

"I love you, Mom."

"I know you do. And I love you." She hugged her and stood. "And you love Ryan.

Now, fix that before you miss out on a great thing in your life. One of the best feelings in the world is to be loved like Ryan loves you."

"I know, Mom. I guess we will see when he gets back," Mia murmured.

Her mother kissed her forehead. "Or why wait? G'night, my sweetest girl."

"Night."

Mia watched her mom leave, then went back to preparing for the morning. After getting into bed and turning out the light, she stared up into the darkness, thinking about all that had gone on that day and how much her life had changed since Ryan had come to Charlotte. She smiled, remembering the magic show and the kiss in the tree. Impulsively she picked up the phone and responded to his text.

I love you.

The thunder rolled outside when she put the phone back on the bedside table. Maybe those three words would be the first step to that middle ground her mother seemed so sure about.

THE SURGERIES WOULD be long and involved for the conditions. When Ryan was able to assess the urgent cases, it was clear there was no way the operations could be done at the small clinic. He, of course, went into his version of fix-it mode, and in hours, there were Life Flights to take the sickest patients to Spain with their worried mothers. It became a sensational news piece when it was found out, and by the time they landed, there was more than one surgeon signed on and enough donations coming into the hospital to pay for the cost of care, housing and more while the kids healed.

It pleased Ryan more than anything to see strangers come together to save some of the most innocent. In the end, he would've found a way regardless. To start things off, he'd been the first contributor. *My banker hates me*, he thought, amused.

The facilities were state-of-the-art, giving the children a fighting chance. Everything fell into place more seamlessly than he expected.

Still, he had little time to think, but when he did, it was of Mia, wondering what she was doing at that exact moment. Did her heart ache just as much as his if his name crossed her mind? Did she long to hold him in her arms as he did her? He needed to focus and make sure all under his care came through the surgery. Dena was a hard case: she'd looked at him resentfully when he assessed Aiyla and he and Mac confirmed she needed to go to Spain.

"I don't want him touching Aiyla," she'd cried out. "Take me home. Take me and my daughter home."

Ryan had pulled up a chair to sit next to her. Her daughter lay in a small bed with an oxygen tube to help her breathe. He took Dena's hands, but she pulled them away. Ryan was not deterred and took them again, staring into her dark, angry eyes. The grief was still there for Amir, the son she'd lost. Ryan felt it, too.

"Dena, listen to me," Ryan began. "I would give my life to go back and bring Amir to you, but I can't. He was so weak. It was a risk, one I took and failed. For that, I am so sorry."

"Aiyla cannot die, my heart… I will die with her." Dena's tone was even thicker because of her worry and sorrow.

"I swear to you, I swear on everything I hold dear, if she has this surgery, she will be an active, healthy child," Ryan promised with all his heart. "She's sick but strong. And if you don't trust me, I will get someone else to perform her surgery. Please, don't take this chance from her."

Dena looked at him with pleading eyes filled with tears and took a deep breath. "You do it, Ryan." She grabbed his arm tight. "Give her this chance to live."

Ryan nodded, knowing that bestowing him with her trust was one of her biggest fears. It meant so much to him.

Surgeries started without a hitch, and Ryan spent the entire day moving from one suite to another making sure everything was running smoothly. Then it was his turn to operate on Aiyla, and he focused his attention solely on the child. It took almost seven hours, but Aiyla was, in fact, strong, and they were able to fix the defect in her heart. She'd come through the surgery perfectly. There was a moment of pure relief when Dena sat beside the child's bed, kissing her daughter's hand. She looked up as Ryan passed and mouthed the words *Thank you*, and that alone made this whole complicated journey worth it.

Ryan took his job seriously, he oversaw and was consumed with the health and well-being of these children. One after another, they were moved from an operating room to the neonatal unit stronger than they had been before. Ryan finally slid down the hospital wall to sit on the floor but didn't feel grief this time. Instead, a sense of satisfaction and relief filled him, along with pride. Three other doctors did the same as he did, all wearing happy, exhausted grins on their faces.

"We did it, guys." Ryan's words sounded sweet even to his own ears. There were celebratory smiles all round.

Pulling his phone from the pocket of his scrubs, he saw a message notification and expected it to be from Mac, needing an update. The other doctors would stay on to make sure the infants continued to thrive now, while he had to head back to Turkey and continue his mission there. While he played with the medallion around his neck, he checked his message. Instead of Mac's number, he saw the icon of Mia's face next to it.

Her message to him had been sent almost forty-eight hours earlier and had sat unopened in his phone, since the medical teams had been moving at such a hectic pace. His heart raced as he opened the message to reveal the three simple words… *I love you.* Hope sprang in his chest, and with a burst of energy, Ryan whooped and cheered.

"Another successful surgery?" one of the other doctors inquired.

Ryan waved the phone around. "She loves me!"

That generated a round of chuckles and pats on the back, and the reality dawned on Ryan. *She loves me,* he thought. Enough to text, even though she'd thought they wouldn't work out, even though he'd left and their lives were completely different and seemingly incompatible. The realization hit him that Matt was right. Ryan was running away. Running right back to what he knew—the security of his past life, as dangerous as it was, without any ties to speak of. What a fool he'd been.

The upheaval and challenges were his cloak of protection, one he needed to cast off. He had asked Mia to step out of her mold to try doing things differently, to travel with him, but he had chosen to say *yes* to Mac when it could have been an *I'll help you find someone else*. And that's what he intended to do now. Ryan scrolled through the numbers on his phone, found what he needed and pressed Connect.

"Hey, friend, saw you on the news, local and nationwide," Matt said. "Look at you, getting all famous."

"I was just trying to help some kids, and I needed a little international assistance. The best of the best."

"And yet, here I am, sitting in dull, old Charlotte, in my bachelor pad of nothing but—"

"Before you get on a roll," Ryan interjected, "how do you feel about packing a bag and taking my place?"

"You're kidding…" Matt's voice was full of enthusiasm.

"Nah, I want to come home, to Mia and the life I'm trying to build there," he said. "This isn't for me anymore, so if it's a yes, there will be a ticket waiting for you at the airport. My resources will be yours, and you will be in Mac's hands."

"Mac? Should I be worried?" Matt asked dubiously.

"You two will get along great. Are you in?"

"Am I in?" Matt seemed incredulous. "It'll be a huge challenge, but it's one I want. Definitely. Dr. Pascal can take over till you get here. The board will be thrilled you're returning to Charlotte. The ability to give back to people in these cases and to work alongside some of the top doctors in the world, this is the opportunity of a lifetime. When I'm done, I might even be as good as you."

"You are already as good as me and in this field you will surpass me. Let me get all this started for you. Meanwhile, my priority is to go home and make up with Mia," Ryan said. "I'll call the chief of staff about our plan and leave direct from Spain. Get in gear, my friend. You're on a red-eye tonight."

"I'm on it. Text me my flight info, and I'll be ready to go!" Matt sounded like a bolt of pure, raw energy; Ryan could hear him hustling around his apartment. "Ryan, buddy, thanks for this. I'll do you proud."

"Never a doubt," he replied. "I'll get everything set up. Later, buddy."

The last thing he heard was Matt, muffled, maybe rooting around a closet. Next he called Mac and filled him in on his idea.

"So...you're out, and this Matt is...in," Mac said slowly. "How good is he?"

"He has the potential of being even better than me," Ryan admitted easily. "You won't miss me in the least."

"Why didn't you send him from the start?" Mac said teasingly.

"That leads me to the next thing. The answer is no on the vice role, Mac, it's not in me to do this anymore," Ryan told him honestly. "You offered it and the automatic thrill of doing more good was there. But as soon as I got to that place, the heaviness was back, and I need to live and have a life beyond what I do now. I want children, sunshine, coming home to watch bad movies with my wife. I can't do that and travel on a moment's notice like I do now. There're better people than me out there. Give the job to one of them, someone whose heart is in it."

"I get it, man. We've seen and done a lot. Go live. Get married. Have babies. Do all of it."

"Thanks, Mac. What about you? When are you going to pass on the reins?"

A deep laugh escaped Mac. "When some woman sweeps me off my feet, I'll let you know. Live well. Be happy."

"Thanks. You're going to love Matt. And you know, ask for anything, and it will be yours. I'll always have you covered there with the grant from the Gallaghers," Ryan told him quickly.

Mac gave a cute, faux-dramatic sigh. "Being good friends with you is a pleasure and has its perks."

"Brothers, that's what we are. Come visit me in Charlotte sometime," Ryan suggested and hoped the guy took him up on his offer one day. "See you around."

Another call completed. Before he left Spain, there were many more he would have to make to be sure he wasn't leaving anything open-ended, and that all the kids were doing fine.

Ryan boarded the plane that would begin his journey back to the States, reminding himself that he would have to hurry across JFK, during his quick layover, to make his connecting flight to Charlotte. For the first time in his life, he was running toward something stable, pure and hopefully that would last for a lifetime. There was Mia and him, no one else mattered, and Ryan planned to spend the rest of his days showing how his love would grow just for her, like the honeysuckle around Ballad Inn.

CHAPTER FIFTEEN

THERE WAS NO word from Ryan, and Mia's heart broke just a little bit more because, in her mind, she knew she had pushed the love of her life away. Over the two days, she often checked her phone, heart jumping at any notification tone, only to leave it when it wasn't a message from him.

Along with that, one of the first big storms of the summer was coming in and they needed to prepare. Its path would bring some of the outer bands through Charlotte later that very afternoon. The forecast was bad enough that it meant bringing in the outdoor furniture from the yard and taking the porch swing down and setting it close to the house. Micki had finished the gazebo renovation but all the remnants of wood and extra supplies were being stacked and stored in the shed for safekeeping.

"We've got the battery-powered lanterns

out of the larder and one in each bedroom," Micki said as she joined her in the sunroom.

"We won't use the generator unless we lose power for more than twenty-four hours. We have to run the fridge to keep the food cool." Mia closed the shutters. "Glad we use gas instead of an electric stove. I do not want to be heating food over a camping burner."

"Margo and Enid are in the kitchen making those croissant things we like to have with tea tonight." Micki was practically bouncing up and down. "I love a good storm."

Mia laughed. "You always did, and it's pain au chocolat they're making."

Micki shrugged. "Don't care what they're called just as long as I can eat them."

Her phone dinged, and Mia took it out of her pocket to look at it quickly. Again her heart fell when there was no word from Ryan.

"Still nothing, huh?" Micki said, sympathy in her eyes.

"No, but after what we saw on the news, I'm sure he's busy." Mia tried to sound hopeful.

"Still, the man could answer a text." Micki made a sound of disgust. "I hope I don't need to go to the hospital and tell him what's what when he gets back to Charlotte."

"Thanks for having my back," Mia said and gave Micki a squeeze.

Together they left the room, Mia thinking about when they had seen Ryan on television. The medical emergency had become a worldwide feel-good story. She didn't know a thing about it until her sisters ran up the stairs to tell her, while she read in bed.

"Turn on your TV, quick! Your boo thang is on the news!" Margo had cried out, and Micki hurried to find the remote. Her parents then Enid were the next to arrive. Mia watched in awe as Ryan spoke about the children being brought to the hospital by a team of ambulances, and how the kind of surgeries they were dealing with were intended to save their lives.

She ached to reach out and touch his face, the curls of his hair still windswept and wild, his sea-blue eyes deep and penetrating as he somberly spoke about the importance of access to proper health care. She truly saw his passion, what he'd gotten on a flight to accomplish, and she felt so ashamed of her reaction when he'd come to her, the man she loved now thousands of miles away doing this.

"I feel like such a jerk." Mia fell back against the pillows with her hand over her eyes when the broadcast was over. "He's a hero, and those children are going to live because of him, and I broke up with him because he had to go."

"Honey, it's a little bit more than that." Her mother patted her leg. "People drift apart with distance between them, and looking at this, he'd be gone a lot."

"He asked me to go," Mia said. "I could've helped with making sure they kept up with timetables or supplies, comforting parents... I don't know, anything instead of being selfish and stuck here. We have so much, and... man, I feel like such a horrible person right now."

"Well, you stop it," Margo said firmly. "You know what you need to make you happy, and traveling on the fly isn't it. Some people are homebodies, and racing after him would've made him happy, but what about you? Mia, it has to be fifty-fifty, or it's not going to work."

"But each side has to take a step. He did

for me. I should've for him," she said miserably. "That's why he hasn't texted or called back after I messaged him. He saw the truth of the matter."

"I doubt that very much," her father tried to console her. "And if he did, he's not the man that I gave him credit for being. This is the time you go all in and fight for love. It's up to each of you to do what's needed. Fight. That's what has to happen from both of you."

"He did say he was coming back for you, that he wasn't giving up," Enid pointed out. "Hold on to that, sweet girl."

After the words of encouragement from her family, her room emptied out, and Mia went to sleep that night thinking about all the mistakes she had made.

Now, they were looking at bad weather, and while they'd made the house and property safe, she thought about Ryan. *Is he coming back so I can make it up to him?* Mia wondered, but in her soul, hope began to fade away.

That night, true to the forecast, the bottom fell out of the sky, and it opened up to a thunderous storm punctuated by lightning cutting through the clouds. On evenings like this, it was usually her guilty pleasure to read in bed with hot tea and the chocolate croissants made to comfort on such occasions. Instead, Mia's thermos sat unopened on the bedside table, and her nighttime treat was left uneaten while she stared into the darkness.

Suddenly, she sat up in bed just as the latest bolt of thunder cracked. She turned on the light. Scrambling, she went to her closet and, after digging deep, pulled out a suitcase, before throwing open the bedroom door and hurrying down the hall to bang on Margo's door, then Micki's.

"Mia?" Margo shuffled into the hallway. Her head bonnet had taken a chef's-hat tilt to one side.

Micki opened her door and asked sleepily, "Wh-what's going on?"

"Need your help, please, going to Spain and finding Ryan." Mia turned, talking over her shoulder. "I need one of you to find me a flight and the other to help me pack."

Their parents' bedroom door opened, and their mother stared out blearily. "Why are you girls up? You're going to wake Enid."

"She took her medication. Enid won't be up or hear a thing till tomorrow," Margo said, stretching her arms. "Mia's going to Spain, apparently."

"In a storm, honey?" Rosie asked, baffled.

"Of course not." Mia chuckled as people followed her to her bedroom. "But first thing in the morning I need to be at the airport when they give the all clear."

"We don't have the resources like Ryan does to just fly anywhere…" Margo began.

"We've got thousands of Air Miles racked up on credit cards," her father said. "Plus, I spoke to Leslie today. Our investments are doing well, and we can help you guys pay off the mortgage and make a bid for Crawford's land since we intend to spend more time at home with our girls…finally."

Mia and her sisters looked at their parents in shock.

"When were you planning on telling us this news?" Mia wanted to know.

"Once everything got sorted out," her mother said with a serene smile, "and it looks like it's beginning to do just that."

"Micki, get the laptop. I'll give you our

info," her father said. "I knew these flight miles would come in handy for something."

"I'll help you sort out what to take. I think it's hot there." Margo scrunched up her face. "Is it hot in Spain this time of year? It's a hot climate, right? Never mind, I'll check online."

"Pack a little bit of everything," Mia said. "And, guys, the earlier the flight, the better. I can drive out as soon as the rain eases up."

"Oh no. We'll drive you," Margo said. "I don't trust that little car of yours on wet roads. My truck will work just fine."

"It's, like, three in the morning. Makes no sense going back to bed. I'll get the coffee on." Rosie turned to leave.

From there it was all-out chaos trying to get Mia packed, on the right flight and waiting out the bad weather patiently with people yelling from each room. Mia made a mental note to ask Enid how much of her medication she was taking. All the noise and yet there wasn't a peep from her room. Mia showered and dressed. It was her intent that as soon as planes could take off, she would be on one.

"We got you a flight that leaves at eight."

Micki poked her head into the bedroom. "We figured he would still be in Barcelona because of the children, so I called and pretended to be a reporter, and they said all the doctors are there until the kids recover."

Mia flashed a grin at her sister. "I love you, you little con artist."

Micki winked. "It's a gift, really. Margo's got you packed."

The thunder rolled, and Mia frowned. "As long as the flight's not canceled. I need to be leaving at least by five."

"For TSA lines, yes," Micki agreed. "Check that bag, and only take your purse and laptop. Early in the morning, it should be a breeze."

"My first international flight." Mia breathed out nervously as she caught a glimpse of herself in the mirror. "It's all going to be okay," she reassured herself.

Mia was never more terrified in her life, but she also had never been more sure. This was a step she had to take, jump into the deep end feetfirst and show Ryan that what they had found together was worth fighting for. With a final twist to keep her thick, long hair up off her neck, Mia took another deep breath and left the bedroom, Micki and luggage in tow, to head downstairs where her family waited.

"Now, I don't know how long I'll be gone, so, Micki, you'll have to manage guest check-in for the wedding," she said. "You've seen me do it hundreds of times."

"We'll be around for a while." Her mother smiled warmly at her. "Me and Dad will help out as much as we're needed."

"Thanks for that." Mia was truly grateful they were here.

"We've got to see if our baby girl wins the guy," her father said and grinned. "Plus, it'll be good to really learn about our girls. We got lost a little bit in our own lives, and it's time we get lost in yours."

"Oh, Dad." Mia hugged him fiercely, then her mom. "You guys are always welcome, and while I'm gone, you can convince Mr. Crawford's son to sell us the back field."

"He'll sell it," her dad promised.

Mia dived into explaining her booking system to her family so any of them could take the reins. She had such a tight control on every facet of her life that she stunned herself with how easy it felt to just let go.

For the right reasons, she thought with a smile, *for love*. The doorbell rang and startled them all.

"It's not even six o'clock," Margo said worriedly. "The rain is stopping. Maybe one of the neighbors? The winds were gusting pretty good out there for a while."

"I hope it's not someone hurt." Mia took the lead and opened the door.

Ryan stood on the welcome mat, dripping water from his hair to his drowned sneakers. Mia stared at him in shock for just an instant, then threw herself into his arms, not caring how wet he was.

"What are you doing here?" Mia cupped his cheeks and kissed him. "I texted and called…"

Ryan moved them inside. "I wanted to surprise you, and then my phone suffered a horrible death on the way here. The storm canceled flights into Charlotte, so I drove here from my reroute to Atlanta." He looked at her, confusion on his face. "Why are you dressed and everyone else up?"

Mia beamed. "I was on my way to you. I have a flight at eight to Barcelona."

"Well, I'm not there."

Mia laughed. "I know!"

"I said no to the job." Ryan offered a weak, watery smile and drew her into his arms then lifted her off her feet. "I had to come home, Mia. I think I was running toward what I always knew, when I should have been running toward you. There might be some travel, but trips will be few and far between, I promise."

"And I will go with you sometimes when you do. I need to step out of my comfort zone and see more, live more," she said, matching his promise with one of her own. "I love you, Ryan, and if that means a few times a year I'll be looking at spreadsheets from somewhere else in the world, as long as I'm with you, it doesn't matter."

A warm, wide grin spread across his face now. "So we love each other."

Mia nodded. "We do."

"This is beautiful," her mother said in a teary voice. "How about you get him upstairs and out of those wet clothes before he ends up with the flu."

"I'm sure," Micki snickered.

"To bed with all of you and us." Their father gave his youngest daughter a gentle nudge toward the stairs. "Enid is going to be confused when she wakes up, with bags at the door and everyone sleeping in."

"I'll leave her a note in the kitchen," Margo said.

Mia held Ryan's hand as they went upstairs. Luckily, his duffel was waterproof, so he would at least have dry clothes to wear. He took a hot shower and got dressed while she changed into comfy clothes and waited with warm tea and a pain au chocolat in the kitchen. It wasn't long before Ryan joined her. After sipping the hot tea, Ryan happily munched on the croissants. Mia joined in.

"I missed Margo's baking, and I haven't eaten since yesterday, I think," he commented. "Pretzels and ginger ale don't count."

"You should be hungry then, not even a whole day to rest." Mia half joked, "You are the strangest person I've ever met."

"Thanks." His eyes were alight with happiness. "I was rushing to come home to you."

"I can't believe you're here," she said gently and leaned over to kiss his forehead. "But you kinda ruined my grand gesture to show up and profess my love."

Ryan looked positively devilish when he spoke again. "How about a grand gesture from both of us?"

"What are you thinking, Dr. Cassidy?" Mia looped her arms around his neck.

"We get everyone up and we get married."

Time stood still for a moment before she could answer. "Are you serious?"

"As a judge." Ryan moved back just enough so he could get down on one knee. "Marry me, Mia. I love you, and I've never been more sure of anything in my life."

The answer was easy. It rose to her lips as she followed his gesture and knelt on the floor.

"Yes!" Mia kissed him long and sweet and then smiled against his lips. "Once again, you ruined my grand gesture. I would've proposed in Spain."

His laughter was rich and deep when he held her close in his arms. "Hey, this isn't a competition."

"If we're doing this, we should wake them all up again around eight," she said and chuckled, thinking of them racing around earlier. "This time, Enid, too. We can eat breakfast, get to the courthouse and then go from there."

"Where can we get married?" Ryan asked.

"Asheville." Mia beamed. "The Biltmore estate has a small chapel, and as long as we have a marriage license, the preacher will marry us."

"Promise me one thing. We vacation in Paris in the fall?" Ryan rose, helped her to her feet and kissed her hand.

"Deal." Mia was practically bouncing.

Upstairs, outside her door, Ryan slipped his arm around her. "So, see you at eight o'clock?"

"At eight." Mia nodded.

He kissed her again quickly. "I can't wait for the moment I can call you my wife."

They parted, reminding Mia of their first date and how that was mere weeks ago, when spring had just opened the honey-suckle blooms outside the inn.

A FEW HOURS LATER, Mia woke ahead of her alarm thanks to her excitement. Ryan met her in the hallway of the family level of the inn and together they knocked on bedroom doors.

"Get up! We're on the move again! We're getting married!" they shouted.

Mia actually had to go into Enid's room to wake her. "Enid, how much medicine do you take? We're discussing this with your doctor as soon as possible." Enid blinked awake.

"Ma'am, we just got back to sleep," Margo murmured from the open doorway. "Married where?"

"We are heading to Asheville to the Biltmore," Mia announced. "We'll stay the night, and you guys can drive back in the evening."

"Wow, things sure do move fast around here when they start moving. Congratulations, sis. It's lucky today is my day off, almost-brother-in-law." Margo smiled and slung an arm over each of them. "Micki, we can double up in my truck, and, parents, you can take Mia's car."

"Marriage license?" Ryan reminded her.

"The courthouse opens at ten, so we can get a license and then head up the mountain," Mia said with a smile. "We'll have a great family dinner at the castle, it'll be beautiful, and we can stay there overnight or in one of the honeymoon guesthouses."

"Let's come back on Sunday—"

The rest of the family now gathered in Enid's room. "Why don't we all stay overnight and drive home the next morning, leaving the lovebirds to their bliss," her father suggested. "We will all come down from the adrenaline crash later." Everyone nodded. Her mother scooted over and gave her and Ryan a quick hug.

"Well, if we are doing an overnight trip, there's a place for dancing up there we can go, Margo. We're the single ladies." Micki rubbed her hands together as if she were ready to get started. "Let me pack my good party dress, the one I loaned Mia."

"No!" Mia and Margo cried out in unison.

"What dress?" Ryan asked curiously.

"Don't worry about it. It's not a dress," Mia said and rushed to end the discussion.

"Margo, help me get us a good breakfast before we go." Enid tightened the belt of her robe. "I'll meet you down in the kitchen in ten minutes. Mr. Bolton can feed the animals this evening."

"We know he's your sweetie," Mia said. "He told Ryan."

Enid pursed her lips. "I see I will need

to have a conversation with that man about privacy."

"I'm already packed." Ryan picked up his bag from the floor. "Got my ID and everything."

Mia hurried to grab her things. The flurry of activity continued on. Like Ryan, she would need to bring her identification and birth certificate for the marriage license and pack for the weekend. Not as big a trip as she'd planned but a much more exciting one, nonetheless. Mia smiled, switching her larger suitcase for a smaller one.

This would be a celebration of family. The word came easily because he was about to be one of them. Her updated bag and Ryan's duffel were soon by the door. By the time she and Ryan were home again, the bride and groom having their reception at the inn would have been there to decide the setup and menu for their big day. The first wedding on the property would be a grand event, although not hers, she would already be a married woman. The words thrilled her.

While Ryan spoke to his boss at the hospital, she impulsively wrapped her arms around his waist, pressing her face against his back as she squeezed. Ryan ended the call and turned to Mia, softly caressing her cheek before they shared a tender kiss. Hand in hand, they met everyone in the kitchen. Breakfast was loud, filled with laughter and excited chatter, because this togetherness was built and created with love.

"You ready to be a part of this chaos?" Mia asked after a chuckle over something Micki had said.

"More than ready because it's with you."

The Ballad family bundled out the door, onto the porch and into their cars. She sat in the passenger seat of Ryan's Land Rover. Once he got the bags in the back, he slid into the driver's seat. The sun was up, but the morning was slightly cooler than normal, at least, before the sweltering summer heat took hold. She and Ryan wanted to beat rush-hour traffic uptown and be the first for a marriage license, so they could be on their way to Asheville and the start of their new life together.

Mia watched Mr. Bolton standing at his door and speaking to Enid before he motioned for Mia to roll down the window.

"Congratulations, Mia Ballad. Embrace your happily-ever-after!" he yelled.

Mr. Webber was next, standing on his top step, in his bathrobe, holding Doodle. "You enjoy married life, Mia, you and Ryan. It was the best thing that ever happened to me."

And so it went as they drove down the street. Well-wishers at each house they passed. People she'd either grown up with or who had watched the Ballad sisters grow up were yelling congratulations to her and Ryan, as they and the family left the quaint neighborhood of Sardis Woods. They were a collection of mothers, fathers, aunts and uncles, kids of all ages and all of them good friends, and they came out early just to give their best wishes. This was her community and one of the oldest neighborhoods in Charlotte. Emotion made her eyes leak with happy tears, and she waved and gave a joyful laugh. Mia looked around. Love made her heart sing. These were all her people, in good times and bad.

"Thank you, guys!" Mia called out, waving wildly, and Ryan did the same.

"How do they know?" Ryan asked.

Mia chuckled more. "Enid probably activated the grapevine before she took our key to Mr. Bolton."

"You're going to have to tell me more about growing up like this later," he said, sounding amused.

Who knew that her falling into his arms one afternoon would change her life forever? Maybe destiny knew that when the bachelor came to Ballad Inn, her heart was never going to be the same.

EPILOGUE

Two Weeks Later

RYAN'S LIFE HAD become something new in a way that encompassed his past, embraced his future and made it whole.

The wedding in Asheville turned into a festive affair. Mia had chosen a simple white dress with a cinched waist and chiffon around the skirt that flowed down to her knees. He wore a smart blue suit and a classic white shirt. There was an arch leading into the chapel with tiny pink and purple flowers. He and Mia said the words that would unite them together forever, in a small vintage chapel, with the sun beaming through the stained glass windows. There were lots of pictures afterward. Everyone got in on the act.

BACK AT HOME, their family dinners post-wedding were just as interesting and entertaining as before. Like when Margo brought Monty to the table dressed in a tux and a hat. "He really needs a monocle," Ryan suggested, pointing at the distinguished-looking lizard. Everyone stared at him, their mouths agape at how smoothly he'd joked and offered the line. That was maybe the first sign his life was never going to be truly the same again.

The honeymoon was happening in the fall. It turned out to be a good idea because the family was in the midst of a busy season for weddings and other bookings. Thanks, he was told, to the improvements to the gazebo and amazing landscaping. Instead of feeling overwhelmed by the people and events, Ryan loved every minute of it. Still, he was looking forward to the trip to Paris with Mia and already had a lock made. At one of the lock bridges in Paris, he would present Mia with a lock engraved with their names to signify their hearts locked together forever. Until then, each night they sat outdoors on the porch swing.

Summer had finally settled over Charlotte. Fireflies danced between the trees. The air was thick with the smell of the magnolias blooming and lady-of-the-night, its petals open to the moon. The evenings were unforgettable. It was the first time he understood what sultry summer nights meant. They had iced tea and talked for hours on the porch swing, one of his and Mia's favorite spots.

"Ryan, together, you and me, we'll go wherever this life takes us."

Her admission made him realize they could go anywhere but that Mia would always be his home, and he was grateful to be the same for her.

"That sounds perfect to me," he replied. "Because you sure can't get rid of me now, Mia Ballad Cassidy. I climbed trees with you and gave you a ring, so you gotta keep me."

"You are so silly." She laughed and squeezed his hand. "I don't plan on pushing you away."

The memory of that conversation woke him up one afternoon after he'd done a full night shift at the hospital. He'd spoken with Matt during a break and was pleased to hear he was doing well taking his place overseas. Ryan knew the young physician was making a real difference in the lives of those who needed him. Meanwhile, Ryan felt completely settled at the hospital. Not once since he returned to Charlotte had he missed the travel that came with Medicine Across the World.

The mixture of sounds that he'd become accustomed to came through the window to him now. Being thoughtful, Mia always tried to close the windows when he worked late so the noise outside wouldn't wake him, but Ryan found he slept much better with the familiar noises of his new home.

The fence between the inn and Crawford's Field was coming down today. After finally negotiating an agreement with the owner, the land was purchased, and the first house—his and Mia's—would be going up. Their home would be right by the large magnolia tree where they'd first flown a kite. Enid's little cottage would be close by, and each of the sisters and their parents could have a home on the property if they chose to. Ballad Inn could then become a full-time bed-and-breakfast with a small staff when all was said and done.

Ryan got up out of bed, rather than doze some more, because he and Mia wanted to break ground on their new home before the big machines came in to dig the foundation. His stomach rumbled, reminding him that he'd grabbed only a quick sandwich when he got home before going to bed. Knowing Enid, she had made a full breakfast for all and left his in the warmer.

Ryan got washed and changed quickly. His heart told him he needed to see Mia. He didn't know love could fill a man like it had with him and was just as his father-in-law promised. *Wait until you have kids. They wrap you around their little fingers.* The words made him think about being a dad sometime in the future and he was terrified and excited all at once.

In the upstairs hall, a streak of orange made him take two steps back and follow it into a bedroom.

"Gotcha." He caught Doodle and settled the notorious cat in his arms. "Dude, I thought we discussed this. Eating Monty bad. And I'm sorry, buddy, but I bet Monty can take you. He may be quiet, but he is fast. Think ninja skills." He and the cat hopefully had now come to a tentative unspoken agreement. Doodle wouldn't try to eat

Monty, and Ryan would deposit him back over the fence without a further scolding. Ryan started to believe the cat's tactics weren't as much about getting at Monty as about being with Monty. Friendship could be weird at times, that was for sure.

Ryan stepped out into the sunshine and looked up and around, shielding his eyes. Walking over to the fence, he spotted Mr. Webber standing on his front steps, scratching his head.

"Found your runaway, Walter," Ryan called out and placed Doodle on top of the fence. The large cat scampered off—well, it was more of a mix of teetering and scampering.

"Thanks, Ryan," Mr. Webber said, coming off his porch. "I swear I don't know how that cat gets out."

"Don't you, Walt?" Ryan asked gently. "Just come over sometime and sit with us. You and Doodle are always welcome."

The older man's face turned red, which told Ryan his assessment of Mr. Webber as lonely was probably correct.

"I see you're breaking ground in the back pasture," Mr. Webber commented.

"For our first home," Ryan said with a smile. "You're welcome there, too."

"How do you think Mia and the sisters feel about homemade raspberry mint jelly?"

"I think it goes well with Margo's Chelsea buns and a good game of cards," Ryan replied. "See you this evening around seven?"

"You just might," Mr. Webber said gruffly, trying to hide his smile and straightening his black suspenders. "You just might."

Ryan turned from the fence just as Mia came around the house. She changed her direction from heading for the front door to crossing the lawn to meet him.

"Hey." She stood on tiptoe to press a kiss on his lips. "I thought you were still sleeping."

"No, I woke up and then caught Doodle and evicted him again." He smiled and slipped his hand in hers.

Mia smiled back and they began to walk. "How you get the little fuzz ball out of the place without complete war happening is still beyond me."

"Oh, and Mr. Webber will be stopping by for dessert on the porch later. He's bringing his raspberry mint jelly to go with Chelsea buns." Ryan's smile grew wider. "We should probably steep a little extra peach tea."

Her step stumbled. "Wait, what? He makes jelly, and is coming for dessert? Mr. Webber?"

"Yes. Our neighbor Walter is coming over for dessert and cards. I also think that maybe Doodle is in love with Monty. Or wants to be buddies, at least." He chuckled.

"Okay, I went to sleep in Sardis Woods, but you woke up in bizarro Sardis world," Mia said, partly laughing. "What magic do you have, Cassidy? And why didn't you use it sooner?"

Ryan laughed along with her and together they walked the long way around and on through the high grass to their magnolia tree. This wasn't a family affair or something they wanted everyone to see. It was an intimate few minutes for them with a small shovel at the spot indicating their home. Little red flags showed the perimeter of what would be their house, the breeze making them wave almost in greeting. Ryan could imagine him and Mia waking up next year in their place, windows open to the warm